"I talked to Daruwalla because I needed to talk to someone, and that's her job!" Willow snapped.

Buffy felt a tingling sensation in her shoulder, the voice of instinct telling her to start swinging.

Giles stepped between them abruptly. "We simply want you to be aware, Willow, of a possible relationship between Ms. Daruwalla and the problem at hand. Not likely, mind you . . . just possible."

Willow spun around and swept her books up off the table. She stalked to the front of the library. "I can't believe you'd think that about her," she said angrily through her tears. She stopped for a moment and looked back at them. "Did it ever occur to you maybe she's just, like . . . a nice person?" Willow looked directly at Buffy. "You don't know what I needed to talk to her about, and you don't care. Jeez, you . . . you've been chasing monsters so long, you're becoming one, Buffy."

Buffy the Vampire Slayer™

Buffy the Vampire Slayer (movie tie-in)
The Harvest
Halloween Rain
Coyote Moon
Night of the Living Rerun
The Angel Chronicles, Vol. 1
Blooded
The Angel Chronicles, Vol. 2
The Xander Years, Vol. 1
Visitors
Unnatural Selection
The Angel Chronicles, Vol. 3
The Power of Persuasion
The Willow Files, Vol. 1

Available from ARCHWAY Paperbacks and POCKET PULSE

Buffy the Vampire Slayer adult books

Child of the Hunt
Return to Chaos
The Gatekeeper Trilogy
    Book 1: Out of the Madhouse
    Book 2: Ghost Roads
    Book 3: Sons of Entropy
Obsidian Fate
Immortal
Sins of the Father
Resurrecting Ravana

The Watcher's Guide: The Official Companion to the Hit Show
The Postcards
The Essential Angel
The Sunnydale High Yearbook
Pop Quiz: Buffy the Vampire Slayer

Available from POCKET BOOKS

BUFFY THE VAMPIRE SLAYER™

RESURRECTING RAVANA

RAY GARTON

An original novel based on the hit TV series created by Joss Whedon

POCKET BOOKS

New York   London   Toronto   Sydney   Singapore

This book is a work of fiction. Names, characters, places and incidents are
products of the author's imagination or are used fictitiously. Any resemblance to actual events or locales or persons, living or dead, is entirely co-
incidental.

An *Original* Publication of POCKET BOOKS

Pocket Books, a division of Simon & Schuster Inc.
1230 Avenue of the Americas, New York, NY 10020

ISBN: 0-671-02636-4

First Pocket Books printing January 2000

10 9 8 7 6 5 4 3 2

POCKET and colophon are registered
trademarks of Simon & Schuster Inc.

Printed in the U.S.A.

This book is for
Buzz Burbank
My favorite swingin' newscaster

Acknowledgments

I had a lot of help and support while writing this book, and I'd like to thank the people who provided it. My wonderful wife, Dawn; Scott Sandin, Derek Sandin, Jack Barnes, Jane Naccarato, Cathy Bunting, Terry Kanago, Collier Mariano, Tim and Mary Kingsbury, Sandi Kessel and Wilma Kessel; all my friends in the Horrornet chat room; thanks to Scotty of the Tattooed Love Dogs; my parents, Ray and Pat Garton; my reps and friends, Ricia Mainhardt and A. J. Janschewitz; my editor, Lisa Clancy, and her assistant, Micol Ostow; and thanks to Don and Mike, who keep me from taking anything too seriously.

RESURRECTING RAVANA

Chapter 1

THE NIGHT SKY LOOKED LIKE AN ENDLESS EXPANSE OF black satin sprinkled with silvery glitter. An owl screeched from a tree branch overhead and a chilly breeze whispered an ominous secret warning through the pines and firs. At least, that was how it sounded to Buffy Summers. Secretive and ominous things made up a great deal of her life.

Buffy and her friends had moved silently since they'd left the van on Rockway Road. The only sound they made was the crisp crackle of pine needles being crushed beneath their shoes. As they crept through the patch of woods, two other noises grew steadily louder: the rushing of ocean waves against the rocky shore, and the muffled throbbing of raucous heavy metal music playing indoors somewhere nearby.

Buffy spotted light up ahead and slowed her pace. The others came to a stop behind her. The cabin came into view through a thicket of wild grapevines. Buffy raised her crossbow and loaded it with a wooden stake that came to a deadly point. This stake was different from those she typically used; it ended in a sharp and shiny silver tip.

"This is it," Buffy whispered over her shoulder to the others.

Willow Rosenberg, Xander Harris, and Cordelia Chase stood close together with Rupert Giles behind them. All four carried silver-tipped wooden stakes.

They were looking at a small, run-down cabin in the center of a clearing. It probably had looked very cozy and welcoming at one time, before years of neglect. A single bare bulb cast a dull yellow glow over the covered porch. Behind the cabin, the woods thinned considerably and a narrow path disappeared into the night toward the rocky beach. In front, an old barbecue grill leaned crookedly near a picnic table.

They faced the southern side of the building, where vines had nearly consumed a small rowboat that lay upside-down on the ground. Five large motorcycles were parked side by side in the front. The music coming from inside the cabin was like thunder, and somewhere in all the noise, Buffy heard high, hysterical laughter.

The Slayer looked up at the moon in the ink-black sky. While it indeed appeared fat and round, this was the night after the full moon, so it was no longer truly full. But it was enough to keep Willow's boyfriend Oz locked up for the night.

"The Blood Moon," Willow whispered.

Buffy turned to her. "The what?"

"According to the *Witch's Almanac,* this is the month of the Blood Moon."

"Oh." Buffy looked up again as a bat darted back and forth overhead. "Well, let's just make sure we don't spill any of ours tonight, okay?"

"Good plan," Xander said.

"Now, remember," Giles said quietly, "it's not necessary to hit the heart as it is with vampires. Getting the silver anywhere into the flesh is what counts. That should make this a little easier. They'll be moving very fast, so—"

"And they'll be hungry," Willow added quietly. When the others turned to her, she whispered, "Remember what the book said? About the hunger? That's what drives them. Even though they've already, um . . . you know . . . eaten."

"So when they look at us," Xander said, "they'll be seeing five double bacon cheeseburgers with a side of intestines."

"Speak for yourself," Cordelia hissed, slapping the back pocket of her Tommy Hilfiger khakis.

Buffy said in a firm whisper, "Hey, focus. The book also told us how well these things can hear, remember?"

They fell silent, but Cordy still threw an icy glare Xander's way.

Buffy said, "Giles and Willow, you stay on this side of the house. Xander and Cordelia, you go around back to the other side. Hang back until I kick that door open and get their attention. I'm gonna draw them outside, and then I wanna see some serious stakage. If they think I'm alone, they'll be less prepared for you guys."

"Approach from behind whenever possible," Giles whispered. "One bite, and . . ." He took a breath, cleared his throat softly. "Well, that's all it will take. To, uh . . . to become like . . . like them."

They moved into the clearing and spread out around the cabin. Willow and Giles stopped at the southern end of the rickety-looking covered porch while Buffy went to the three wooden steps in front of the house.

The music inside pounded on, reverberating like the stomping footsteps of a giant. The hysterical laughter continued, grew louder, and became higher in pitch. The laughs melted into a high keening wail, which became more rounded, throatier, until it was a cold, piercing howl.

Buffy went up the steps to the long porch, but before she could kick the cabin's door in, it was pulled open.

The open doorway framed a tall but slightly hunched figure wearing what was left of a white tank top. The tank top was covered with dark stains and hung from the figure in shreds. The broad, tall figure was backlit, and light shone through clumps of thick fur on the head, shoulders, and arms. It held something in its right hand, something that looked like a short club; unidentifiable threads dangled from the end of it. The figure stepped forward into the pool of yellow light.

The creature's snout glistened with blood, and as its black lips pulled back into a sneering grin, they revealed long, sharp, bloody fangs with bits of meat stuck between them. The deep, dark eyes absorbed every bit of light around them and reflected it back in piercing pinpoints of silver.

Although the light was poor, the thing in the creature's hand was obviously not a club, but a human arm torn off at the elbow; the black, furry paw held the arm's pale, dead hand. Chunks of flesh had been gnawed from the arm, like meat from a drumstick.

A thick growl began to rise from deep inside the creature as it spread its arms expansively. The sound was not remotely human, but it formed a word. "Company!" It tossed the arm aside and hunched down even farther, preparing to pounce. "And just in time for dinner."

When they first began the investigation, it had looked as if they might be dealing with cattle mutilations. Again. But this time the cattle had not exactly been mutilated. They had been . . . eaten. Right to the bone. Bones were all that had been left of the cows in a pasture just outside Sunnydale. All muscle and flesh had been eaten away, and parts of the remaining skeletons had been gnawed on with some very sharp teeth in some very powerful jaws. A local radio newscaster speculated that wild animals—perhaps coyotes or mountain lions—were responsible, but Giles disagreed.

"Not even the hungriest mountain lion would clean a skeleton of every last bit of flesh like that," the Watcher told Buffy. "This is something else, something . . . unnatural."

"A hellhound?" Buffy suggested.

"The fact that ten head of cattle had been reduced to skeletons on the night before the full moon makes that very likely," Giles replied. "But why cattle? Why would a werewolf—or even a pack of hellhound-like creatures—feed on *cattle* in an area so populated with *people?*"

"Maybe they don't want to hurt anyone," Willow suggested.

"Uh-uh," Oz said. "As far as werewolves go, once the change has taken place, you can't control yourself."

They all paid attention. When it came to werewolves, Oz knew what he was talking about. He'd been bitten by his cousin Jordy, who was a werewolf. As a result, Oz became a werewolf on the nights before and after the full moon, as well as the night of the full moon itself. Not wanting to harm anyone, with the help of his friends, Oz took precautions each month. He was securely locked up on those three nights so he was unable to do any damage to property or people.

"What do you mean?" Buffy asked.

"I mean, I'm a werewolf, right? And I don't wanna hurt anybody, right? Well . . . it's kinda like watching Jerry Springer. You know you shouldn't, but you just can't help yourself."

"Perhaps we're not dealing with werewolves at all," Giles said.

The next morning, a grisly, but unclear, story topped the local newscasts. Several people had been killed the night before in a biker bar called Hog Heaven on the southern edge of Sunnydale. Although there was no mention of gunfire, everyone assumed, at first, that it had been a shooting. Then more details came out as the day wore on: that no guns had been used . . . that the victims had been eaten.

According to three eyewitnesses, five men had come into the bar around dusk and rudely taken over the pool table, upsetting the regulars. A fight had broken out, which was not uncommon in Hog Heaven.

At that point in the story, the accounts of the eyewitnesses diverged.

One witness thought the strangers used knives, because blood was flying and the regulars involved in the brawl were wailing like animals caught in traps; then that eyewitness fled the bar. The second, who had not been far behind the first in fleeing, insisted that a wild animal of some sort had gotten into the bar and attacked the brawlers.

But the third, a young man who'd had more than a

few drinks that evening, claimed that the strangers who'd entered the bar had changed . . . that they'd grown hair and fangs and had stopped punching with fists and had started tearing with claws. He said they'd driven away on five Harley-Davidsons, their thick fur blowing in the wind, and the one in the lead had lifted his head and howled at the night sky as they sped away. It was noted by newscasters that the third eyewitness, who left the bar in hysterics, was arrested a bit later for possession of certain controlled substances, a fact which was used to explain away the young man's bizarre account.

Authorities thought one of the quintet was Waldo Becker, an ex-con from a small Maryland town who, along with his four friends, was believed to be responsible for murders in three other states.

"Right the first time, traveling hellhounds," Buffy said to Giles when she and the others gathered in the library to talk about the mystery. "Or devil dogs. Or whatever."

"Not werewolves," Giles agreed. "Werewolves either are or aren't. This . . . this in-between existence is another creature entirely."

"Traveling hellhounds," Willow muttered. "It's like a bad movie."

Cordelia said, "Oh, like bad movie territory is new to you people?"

"These are hellhounds who are not at all concerned about their condition or the welfare of others," Giles said. "By all accounts, they seem to enjoy their altered state."

"We've got to stop them," Oz said.

"And we're gonna have to do it tonight," Xander said.

They were silent for a moment, contemplating the body count of another night if these hounds were free.

"This is gonna take some massive patrolling," Buffy said.

Staring intensely at one of her fingernails, Cordelia said, "Does anybody have an emery board? My nail broke." She looked up at a wall of impassive faces. "What?"

Willow accessed regional newspapers on the Internet and tracked the movement of Waldo Becker and his companions across the country. It took a couple hours, and there were a number of gaps in their trek, but she found that they focused on seedy bars on the outskirts of small towns, where they slaughtered, dined, and moved on, and sometimes they got takeout and took dinner with them. They were never in any one town for more than one full moon cycle.

They agreed to take Oz's van out to find Waldo Becker and his friends. Giles presented them with the silver-tipped stakes he'd made for just such an occasion. "We can only assume the silver will work on these . . . hellhounds, for lack of a better name."

"Um, I don't know about everybody else," Xander said, "but I'd be a lot happier with some silver *bullets*. I mean, these guys don't exactly sound like the up close and personal type, you know?"

"You've had no training in the handling of firearms," Giles said. "And we don't know what sort of situation we'll find ourselves in. I can't have you inadvertently shooting innocent bystanders. Or each other."

"Giles is right," Buffy said. "Besides, you guys have gotten good at using stakes. You seemed to do a pretty good job of using them to save the world from evil while I was out of town." She looked around at them with a grin. "You'll do fine with them tonight."

Buffy phoned home to beg off dinner yet again, promising her mom she'd be home tomorrow night for sure. An hour before dusk—much earlier than usual—they locked Oz in the library's cage, where Giles kept his rare books and manuscripts.

"Sorry for doing this so early," Willow said, pressing both hands to the steel mesh cage. "But we need to get a head start on these guys."

"I understand," Oz said, bobbing his head and stuffing four fingers of each hand into the back pockets of his jeans. "Hey, it's not like I don't have anything to read." He leaned forward and kissed Willow through the bars. "Be careful."

She nodded and smiled. "See you in the morning."

Oz wished them luck as they left the library to pursue their quarry.

They took Oz's van and drove slowly through town, paying special attention to the Fish Tank and Willy's Alibi Room as they drove by. The Fish Tank was where the first attack had taken place; Willy's Alibi Room was three blocks away and just as unsavory.

In the hour before sunset, they saw four motorcycles: two parked side by side and two others, each solo.

As the sun slowly disappeared, the streets were very quiet. In Sunnydale, on the Hellmouth—an entryway for the undead and other supernatural creatures—that usually meant something very bad was going on. But on this particular evening, the town was not just quiet and still . . . it actually seemed safe.

"Is this our town?" Xander asked. "Or did we take a wrong turn somewhere?"

"Well, I like it," Cordelia said. "Hanging out with

you guys is never this quiet. It's kind of refreshing, if you ask me."

"Which, of course, no one did," Xander muttered.

"Okay, then," Cordelia said with a sigh, "even if you don't ask me, it's still refreshing."

Along with the Fish Tank and Willy's Alibi Room, they were surprised by how many run-down bars existed within the city limits of Sunnydale. They lurked on the edges of town, off the main roads, but they were there—dark, usually small, and inviting to those whose tastes ran to that sort of thing: not much light, bowls of peanuts and pretzels on the bar, condom dispensers in the restrooms, pool tables, dart boards, a jukebox with plenty of country and western weepers on the menu, sports on the television, a pinball or video game or two to take your quarters, and a lot of thick cigarette smoke that violated California law.

On the western edge of town near the beach was the Hidey Hole, next to a rickety-looking pier and with a red-and-white Styrofoam life preserver on the door. To the east lay the Red Rooster, a red barn affair with a huge, weather-beaten rooster standing on the roof. But it wasn't until they got to the northern end of town that Giles parked the van at the curb.

The Trap was a small bar with a gravel parking lot. There were no lights in the parking lot, and the bar itself was so dark, it would have looked abandoned were it not for the cars parked in the lot around it. It had two small windows with a glowing neon beer sign in each.

There were several cars and pickup trucks parked in the gravel lot . . . along with five Harley-Davidson motorcycles standing side by side beneath one of those two windows, metal gleaming in the glow of the flickering beer sign.

Giles let the van's engine idle as they all looked at the bar and the motorcycles parked in front of it.

"We aren't certain those are the ones we're looking for," he began quietly. There was a tense edge to his voice and he clutched the steering wheel tightly.

"Five parked in a row outside a bar that looks like some alcoholic's id?" Buffy asked. "I'd say chances are good these're the guys."

"Wait a second," Willow said. The others turned to her as her eyebrows curled downward over the bridge of her nose and her lips tightened and drew together without touching. She turned to Giles and said, "We've forgotten something. We're all too young to go in there."

Giles removed his glasses and nodded once, looking out at the bar again. "Yes, you're quite right."

"We can't wait out here," Xander said. "If our guys are in there, they could start making beer nuts and pretzels of everybody any minute now."

"Not to worry," Giles said, killing the engine. "I'm of age." He replaced his glasses and opened his door.

"You can't go in there alone."

"We don't seem to have much choice, Buffy."

"Reality check, Giles," she said. "You Watcher, me Slayer. There are five of those things in there. You could get killed."

"I'm quite capable of handling myself if need be, Buffy." He got out, then reached back inside and took two of the silver-tipped stakes from the middle of the seat. He tucked them beneath his belt, then closed his tweed sportscoat over them. "I'll stay near the door, and should anything happen, I'll signal you immediately. Once violence breaks out, I seriously doubt anyone will take the time to ask for your IDs. Pay attention and be prepared." He closed the door, walked around the van, and headed across the parking lot.

"I've got a bad feeling in my stomach," Buffy whispered as her eyes followed her Watcher.

"Let's hope it's something you ate," Xander quipped.

The sound of Giles's shoes crunching on the gravel faded as he neared the bar. He was less than three feet from the entrance when a guttural scream came from inside the bar.

Buffy's door was open in an instant and she jumped out of the van with her loaded crossbow in hand.

At the first noise Giles froze. Now as he looked back over his shoulder at the van, the door of the Trap burst outward and broke off its hinges beneath the force of a large, bloody man who shot through the air, a screaming human missile. Giles stumbled backward quickly enough to avoid being hit by the door, but the man slammed into him and both of them rolled over the gravel, coming to a halt about eight feet from where Giles had been standing.

Buffy ran across the gravel parking lot as more screams rose from inside the bar. Horrible, painful screams . . . wet screams. She glanced over her shoulder at the van and saw that no one was following her.

"Come on!" she cried. "What're you waiting for?"

She ran by Giles and shouted, "You okay?"

"Fine!" he said as he got to his feet, waving her on.

The closer Buffy got to the open doorway of the bar, the louder the screaming inside became. There were crashing sounds inside, as well. And something else, something beneath all the other sounds . . .

Low, animal growls, and sloppy, moist chewing.

Buffy entered the bar with her crossbow held ready to fire . . . and her feet went wild beneath her. She slipped on something wet and slick, and the floor slammed against her back, knocking the breath from her lungs.

She couldn't move for a moment as bodies rushed by her above, towering over her, shooting in and out of her field of vision with lightning speed. Behind her, she heard Willow cry, "No! No!" and Xander let fly a few choice curses as motorcycle engines roared to life.

Something howled as the engines revved . . . and then began to fade away.

Silence. It was deafening. The bar was completely silent . . . except for a gentle, thick dripping nearby. The coppery odor of blood slowly filled Buffy's nostrils . . . the blood in which she'd slipped and fallen.

She began to struggle to get to her feet, and hands gripped her arms, helping her up. Giles and Xander were with her, and Willow and Cordelia were standing just outside the door.

"C'mon," Buffy said urgently, dismissing the carnage inside the bar with a glance. "We've gotta follow them. Let's go!"

The five of them ran to the van and got inside.

"Which way did they go?" Giles asked as he started the engine.

"Straight ahead," Cordelia said. "I saw them."

"Do me a favor, Giles?" Buffy asked quietly.

"What's that?" he asked as he pulled away from the curb.

"Forget you're British and step on it."

He did, and the van shot forward. He turned his head and said over his shoulder, "Seatbelts, please? Everyone?"

Everyone in the van remained silent as Giles sped through the night, his foot pushing the accelerator to the floor, breaking the speed limit in a very non-Englishman sort of way.

The road was curvy, but with their windows rolled down, it wasn't long before they heard the roar of the motorcycles up ahead. The sound of the motorcycles led them west. The area around them became more and more wooded, until they were driving between tall pines and firs, beyond which lay thick woods on both sides of the road.

And then the sound of the motorcycles stopped.

It didn't stop instantly, it faded. But it faded very quickly . . . and was gone.

Giles let up on the accelerator and the van slowed.

"Where did they go?" Giles asked. "I can't hear them anymore."

"Neither can I," Buffy said, leaning her head out the window.

"Maybe they outran us?" Willow said uncertainly.

"No, no, they didn't do that," Buffy said. "It sounded more like they . . . like they . . ." Buffy suddenly spun around and clutched Giles's shoulder. "Stop the van. Stop it, now."

Giles slowed down, his mouth moving nervously, but silently.

"No, no, Giles, pull over and stop! Now!"

He did as she said, parking the van on the slanted gravel shoulder.

"What do you have in mind, Buffy?" he asked.

"They went into the woods," she said, looking out the side window into the dark woods on the western side of the road. "On those motorcycles, they could drive right in there . . . and they did, I know it. Somewhere along this road, maybe a little ways behind us, they went right into the woods."

"You think they're hiding in there?" Xander asked.

Cordelia let out an annoyed huff of breath and said, "No, Xander, they're collecting frogs for a class biology project."

"We've got to go in there after them," Buffy said, ignoring the exchange in the backseat.

Giles pushed his glasses up and rubbed his eyes with the heels of his hands as he let out a long sigh. "All right, then," he said. "We're hardly equipped for it, but . . . we'll go into the woods."

There was a long, tense silence in the van.

"Into the woods?" Cordelia asked. Her voice was a quiet whimper. "At night?"

"What are you afraid of?" Xander asked.

"Well, aren't there . . . you know . . . snakes and spiders and—"

"Cordy, we're going into the woods after hellhounds," Xander said with a chuckle. "Snakes and spiders should be the least of your worries."

Cordelia sighed and shook her head. "You people are so priority-impaired."

Buffy smiled faintly at Giles, then at the others in the backseat, then at Giles again. "So . . . what are we waiting for?"

Things on the porch went downhill almost immediately.

As the creature flung the severed arm over the porch railing, blood spattered in all directions. Buffy raised her crossbow, aimed, and fired. But the hellhound had already leapt from the porch and flew over her head with a loud growl. The stake sliced through empty air and disappeared into the open doorway.

Buffy reached beneath her jacket for another stake as

she spun around on the porch. Through the old wood slats beneath her boots, she could feel the stomping rush of the four other hellhounds hurrying toward her from inside the cabin, while loud rock music continued to rumble.

She had the second stake in the crossbow before she had turned all the way around, but she never had a chance to fire it. The hellhound in the tattered, bloody tank top rose up out of the darkness less than two feet in front of her. With a flick of his black, furry hand, he knocked the crossbow from Buffy's grip and sent it tumbling into the night.

Buffy's hand was already beneath her jacket, reaching for another stake—she had her fingers wrapped around it—when the snarling creature slapped a hand on her shoulder and another on her hip and closed his grip. She felt his claws pierce her clothing as he lifted her off the ground. With no apparent effort, the hellhound turned and threw Buffy away from the house. The cold night air hissed past her ears and her hair blew in her face as she flew through the air, the hellhound in furious pursuit.

Buffy slammed into the trunk of a tree. She was unconscious before she hit the ground.

From the time the front door of the cabin opened, only seconds had passed.

As Buffy flew from the porch, Xander and Giles hopped over the railing and moved in from each side. They stopped beside the open door, stakes raised, listening to the snarls rushing toward them.

As if expecting them, the next hellhound out the door swung his arms open wide, knocking Xander and Giles in opposite directions.

By that time, Willow had climbed onto the railing at

her end of the porch. She dove off the railing and over Giles, who had been knocked on his back, and onto the hellhound. Unprepared for the attack, the creature fell. Willow wasted no time.

She buried the stake in the hellhound's neck.

The creature immediately began to convulse and released a painful shriek that echoed through the woods around them. The hellhound's thrashing became so forceful, Willow was thrown down onto the porch. The creature stiffened after a moment and its back arched. It made a horrible gurgling sound in its throat as its dark, fanged muzzle began to shrink rapidly. Willow backed away on all fours, disgusted by the thick, wet sound of bones moving against bones, of muscle tissue shrinking, dissolving.

The body fell limp suddenly and released a harsh death rattle. It looked like nothing more than a vicious dog now. A dead one. His eyes were open and stared glassily up at the yellow porch light.

Willow released an explosive breath as she reached forward and pulled the stake from his neck.

While Willow had been diving for the unsuspecting hellhound, Xander and Giles had been getting to their feet. By then, three more hellhounds had rushed by them and off the porch. They were somewhere in the darkness, beyond the dull pool of yellow light cast by the bulb over the door.

"Where's Buffy?" Xander whispered.

"I-I-I don't . . . I don't know," Giles stammered.

In spite of the chilly air, perspiration glistened on their faces, and their hearts were trip-hammering in their chests.

Giles turned to see Willow backing away from the convulsing body on the porch.

Once she'd pulled the stake from the hellhound's neck, Giles leaned down, gripped her elbow, and helped her to her feet.

"Hey, somebody help me!" Cordelia cried. "I'm stuck!"

Xander, Giles, and Willow turned to the other end of the porch, where Cordelia was trying to climb over the railing. She had one leg over, stake in hand, but her khakis had gotten stuck on the end of a shard of splintered wood.

Xander rushed toward her.

A clawed, furry hand slapped the top of her head, closed on her hair, and jerked her off the railing. With a scream, Cordelia was swallowed by the darkness.

"Cordy!" Xander shouted.

She didn't hear him. The hellhound's snout was next to her ear and its hot, snarling breath, smelling coppery of blood, drowned out all other sounds. It still held her by the hair, pulling it hard, as it turned her around. Its black lips pulled back over its fangs, exposing its long black-mottled pink tongue.

Cordelia barely saw the thing's face. Her eyes were tearing from the pain of her hair being pulled so hard. All fear rushed out of her as anger welled up and made her clench her teeth.

"Don't . . . mess . . . with the hair!" she cried as she drove the stake into the creature's abdomen.

The hellhound released her hair and fell away, hitting the ground with a loud thud. It thrashed and kicked and made horrible choking sounds in the dark, but Cordelia turned away, and came face to face with Xander.

"Are you all right?" he asked, clutching her shoulders.

She winced as she patted her hair. "Yeah. I am now. No thanks to you."

Giles went down the front steps of the porch cautiously, with Willow a couple of steps behind him.

Although the moon was almost completely full and shone through the tall surrounding trees in needles of electric blue, the night was dark with black shadows that grew even blacker when they overlapped.

A low predatory growl came from the darkness and seemed to be everywhere . . . to the left and right, straight ahead, even above them.

"Buffy?" Giles called.

An instant after he called her name, Buffy regained consciousness. She had no idea how long she'd been out, but knew it couldn't have been long, because she was still alive. The stake was no longer in her hand. She sat up, leaned to her right, and began to grope for the stake on the ground. The tips of her fingers touched its smooth surface—

And she was knocked onto her back again as the hellhound suddenly straddled her waist and pressed her shoulders to the ground.

The creature's saliva dribbled onto Buffy's face, warm and thick and noxious.

Buffy reached out as far as she could with her right arm, her fingertips tickling the ground in search of the stake.

"A *Slayer*," the hellhound said. The words were nearly buried in the deep growl that came with them.

Her middle finger lightly brushed against the stake's silver tip. She reached farther, making her shoulder hurt. With the tip of her finger, she drew the stake a little closer to her . . . a little closer.

From the corner of her eye Buffy could see Xander and Cordelia join Willow and Giles, as the four of them moved away from the cabin, their eyes fanning out to look for trouble.

There was a low, quiet growl behind them.

All four of them spun around at once to see two sets of fangs and eyes glinting at them in the moonlight.

The hellhound on top of Buffy leaned forward until his cold, wet nose almost touched the tip of hers. Its lips pulled back and its long fangs dripped tepid saliva onto her chin. The creature's foul-smelling breath washed over her face, hot and rank with the smell of decaying meat.

Buffy placed a second fingertip on the stake . . . then a third. She curled her fingers, pulling it a little closer. Then a fourth finger . . . and her thumb . . . until she was able to close her fist around the stake.

The creature pulled back a few inches and opened its snout wide, ready to plunge forward and sink its fangs into her throat.

Through clenched teeth, Buffy snarled, "Eat this!" She slammed the stake into its throat. The hellhound sat up with a startled growl. The stake remained in Buffy's hand . . . with the silver pointed tip pointing at her. She'd stabbed the hellhound in the throat with the wrong end of the stake.

The hellhound grinned to reveal all its fangs as it grabbed Buffy's right wrist and began to squeeze, trying to get her to release the stake.

Closer to the cabin, Xander tackled a hellhound without hesitation. As the two of them rolled, Xander shoved the stake in without even knowing where.

Meantime, the other hellhound pounced at Giles, who dropped to his knees immediately and thrust his stake upward.

Buffy swung her left fist around and punched her

hellhound in the face once, twice, a third time. The second the creature was off balance, she rolled her body to the left and heaved it off of her.

The hellhound was on all fours in an instant, lunging for Buffy.

Buffy swung her right leg out and kicked the creature in the face. It tumbled away from her with a pained grunt, landing a few feet away. But it didn't stay there long.

She was up on her knees as the hellhound rushed toward her again. She flipped the stake in her hand, so the silver tip pointed outward, then stabbed it upward as the hellhound pounced on her.

The stake went in deep, and the creature landed heavily on Buffy, making a horrible gurgling sound in its throat. It was immediately still as it lay pinning Buffy to the ground.

"C'mon, c'mon," Buffy muttered as she rolled the dead weight off of her, "I don't know you well enough, big guy." She got up and brushed herself off, then looked down at the hellhound.

Blood was caked on his lips and chin, and his eyes stared flatly up at the moon.

Footsteps hurried toward her in the dark.

"Buffy!" Giles said with relief. "Are you all right?"

She nodded, but reached around and gingerly touched the back of her head. There was a large knot, but no blood. Her back hurt, and her legs felt stiff. She popped her shoulder back into joint. "I'll live . . . it just won't be fun. Not for a little while, anyway."

"We're going to have to leave quickly," Giles said, "or we'll have a great deal of explaining to do . . . and most likely to people who will laugh in our faces as they apply handcuffs to our wrists." He turned and looked grimly down at the hellhound on the ground.

Buffy turned to the group and asked, "We got 'em all?"

The others said yes, all at once.

"Unless, um, there are more in the cabin," Willow said.

"There are only five motorcycles," Xander said. "I doubt they'd ride double."

"Yeah, there's only five, let's go," Cordelia said with a hint of an impatient whine in her voice.

"No, Willow's right," Giles said. "We need to be sure."

Buffy leaned down and jerked the stake out of the dead creature on the ground. "I'll check the cabin," she said.

She limped a little at first, but recovered quickly, and covered the rest of the distance at a jog. Up the steps, across the porch . . . she stopped at the open door.

Inside, the cabin was a mess, and had a smell to go with it. Apparently, hellhounds had the same bathroom habits as regular hounds . . . none at all. They didn't use the refrigerator, either, because their leftovers were scattered all over the place. A foot here, a head there . . . it wasn't a pretty sight. She went through the entire cabin, careful not to step in anything. The place was empty.

Buffy got out of the cabin as quickly as possible, went down the steps, and joined her friends.

"It's empty," she said. "Let's motor."

Chapter 2

THE NEXT DAY WAS A BUSY ONE FOR GILES. EVER since learning of the cattle that had been eaten just outside Sunnydale, he had dropped everything to learn more about it, certain it was a sign of trouble. The week before had been spent with Buffy and the others ridding Sunnydale of a very ill-tempered voodoo priestess. In the meantime, his other work had gone mostly neglected.

Rupert Giles was Buffy Summers's Watcher . . . but he was also the librarian at Sunnydale High School. There were returned books that needed to go back in their proper places on the shelves, new books that needed to be processed and placed, overdue notices that needed to be filled out and sent, and a calendar and several notices on the walls that needed to be updated. He didn't use student volunteers to work in the library; too many of his volumes were a bit irregular. With the undead crawling out of the ground every night and all manner of evils popping up in Sunnydale, it was easy to forget the more mundane responsibilities that rested on one's shoulders. Life went on . . . even at the Hellmouth.

Xander and Oz were seated in a corner, talking quietly over open textbooks. Giles hadn't seen Buffy since early that morning, but she would probably be back soon with the others. Quarterly exams were coming up next week, and several students had come in throughout the day, looking for a quiet place to study. Usually the Slayerettes were press-ganged into service in the library, but Buffy and her friends had had little time to study for the tests lately, so he expected them to have their heads buried in books for the rest of the week. Unless, of course, something more urgent came up, something more ominous. At most high schools, one would be hard-pressed to think of something more ominous than quarterly exams, but not so at Sunnydale High.

Cordelia Chase waltzed into the library and stopped at the front desk.

"Hello, Giles," she said wearily.

"Good afternoon, Cordelia. How are you?"

"You kept me up until the wee hours last night and you can ask that question with a straight face?"

"Well, you realize, of course, that you didn't have to come with us."

She released a single abrupt, sharp laugh. "I'm the only sane person in your little traveling monster movie. I'm scared to think what you'd do without me."

"I should think we'd get by somehow," Giles said with a smirk. "But I must say I'm glad you were there last night, Cordelia." He gestured toward the corner where Xander and Oz were sitting. "If you're looking for—"

"I'm not. I'm looking for a book I was supposed to read last month. It's called *The Wedding Member,* or, um, *The Member* . . . um . . ."

"Carson McCullers," Giles said. *"The Member of the Wedding."*

"That's it! Do you have it?"

"As a matter of fact," he said as he stepped over to a few stacks of books, "it was just recently returned." He started running a finger down the spines of the stacked books, looking for the title.

"The Member of the Wedding?"

Giles looked up to see that Xander had joined Cordelia at the desk.

"But I told you, Cordelia," Xander said, "I'm just not ready to make that kind of commitment."

"Oh, you're ready for commitment, all right," she said. "But I doubt there are any mental institutions that would have you."

Giles handed the book to her. "Would you like to check it out?"

"Well, maybe," she said. "It's not very long. I'm gonna see how much of it I can read here." She headed for a table.

"If you need any help with the big words, let me know," Xander said, smiling.

"Xander," Oz called from the corner. "We doing this?"

Xander turned to Giles and said, "We're going to quiz each other."

Giles returned his smile. "Best of luck to you both."

It was not in a Watcher's job description to become friendly with the friends of his or her Slayer. That was due, in part, to the fact that Slayers typically had few, if any, friends.

But Buffy Summers was not a typical Slayer.

A Watcher's job is to alert the Slayer to her purpose, then focus the Slayer's attention and energy on that purpose so intensely that little time is left for a social life. A Slayer's responsibilities were formidable indeed, and preparation, training, and focus were all that stood between life and death, so normally there wasn't much time left for outside interests.

But Buffy had somehow managed to do something neither Giles nor the Watcher's Council expected. Instead of walking away from her normal life to bury herself in her training under his guidance, she had brought some of her life with her, and made him a part of it. It had not been intentional; her friends had stumbled onto the truth about Buffy accidentally. But their willingness to work with her to fight vampires, demons, and other evil creatures had been completely unexpected. Before he knew it, Giles was not just working with a single Slayer, but a Slayer and four . . . well, assistant Slayers. It was unprecedented, and he had no doubt the council disapproved.

Giles had been terribly worried about them at first, afraid they had no idea what they would be dealing with if they chose to help Buffy. Technically, his only responsibility was for his Slayer, but he felt responsible for her friends, too. He was surprised by how quickly they had accepted the nighttime world of evil that would come to make up so much of Buffy's life. He found their resiliency and good humor refreshing . . . even if that good humor did include some ribbing of Giles's very British mannerisms and personality. Although he sometimes found them frustrating, even exasperating, there had been times when their presence had been invaluable.

And he enjoyed their company, being a part of their lives; in a line of work made up of darkness and unpredictable sinister forces and the Dewey decimal system, they helped keep things rather light, and even made him feel young. *Well . . . at least younger.*

Giles picked up a stack of returned books and left the front desk to put them back on their proper shelves.

Willow stepped into the library, one thumb hooked under her book bag's shoulder strap, and was surprised by how quiet it was. Like any library, it was always quiet, but more so today than usual. There were no low voices, no stifled laughs, no shuffling chairs or sounds of movement. Even the front desk was abandoned. Farther inside, she heard quiet murmurings, followed the direction of the sound with her eyes, and saw Oz and Xander in the corner, heads down, a book open in front of Oz.

Willow stepped up behind Oz, leaned down, wrapped her arms around his neck, and kissed the top of his head. Oz jerked beneath her, startled.

"Hi, guys," she said, smiling.

Xander looked up at her, wincing slightly, as if annoyed. "Oh, uh . . . hi, Willow," he said. He straightened in the chair, stretched, reached back, and massaged his neck.

"We're quizzing now," Oz said.

She let go of him and moved around to the side of the table. "Oh. I'm interrupting something?"

"Kinda sorta," Xander said.

"Boy talk?" she asked with a smile.

Xander shook his head. "Oh, no. We're committing *Beowulf* to memory in Spanish."

Oz said. "Actually, studying."

"We're taking turns quizzing each other," Xander added. "And hard as it may be to believe, we've kinda gotten into it. So maybe we could, y'know . . . talk later?"

Willow's smile fell away. "Oh. Okay." She tried to put it back on, but it was crooked and a little stiff. "Okay, then, I'll . . . catch you later, I guess." As she started back through the library, walking slower than before, Willow was about to sigh when she noticed Cordelia sitting alone at a table, reading a book. "Hi, Cordy," she said as she passed.

"This sucks," Cordelia said.

Willow stopped walking. "What?"

"This book."

Willow looked over her shoulder at the open book and read the title at the top of the page. "Oh, I read that. It was good."

"It sucks. It takes place in the South, and all the people are so . . . Southern. Why are all books and movies about the South so depressing? Everyone's either drunk, insane, or sleeping with their parents, or something. It's like a soap opera, but without the charm."

"I'd suggest you see the movie, but—"

"There's a movie?" Cordelia asked excitedly. She pushed her chair back and turned to face Willow. "You mean, I could rent a tape instead of reading this whole thing?"

"Um, I was about to say . . . none of the video stores in town carry it. I checked once a couple weeks ago. I don't even know if it's available on tape. But maybe you could—"

"Great!" Cordelia huffed and turned back to her book and hunched forward. "I'm stuck reading this . . . this thing."

Willow let that sigh out as she walked away from Cordelia and took a seat at one of the computers. She put her bag under the table and logged on to the Internet, where she surfed through a few of her favorite sites, catching the updates.

I should be studying, she thought. *Getting ready for exams like everyone else.*

But at the moment, Willow did not have a studious bone in her body. Her mind was on other things. First, there was the matter of the motorcycle-riding hellhounds and the possibility that she was responsible for bringing them to Sunnydale. But more immediate was the chill that had fallen over her friends and herself.

Then there was the possibility that she inadvertently had created trouble for them.

A few weeks ago, using the Internet and some of Giles's books, Willow had pieced together an ancient spell that had once been used for multiple purposes. Among them: to reverse spells that turned one into certain animals, such as dogs, pigs, rodents, that sort of thing . . . and to reverse lycanthropy. Willow didn't know anyone who'd been turned into a rodent or dog, but lycanthropy—or the condition of transforming into a werewolf every full moon—was another story.

The spell was ancient and had fallen out of use. When she first stumbled onto it in one of Giles's books, only a fraction of the spell was given. But she kept looking, and looking, until she found the whole thing. She'd thought it was the whole thing, anyway. Looking back now, she wondered if she had used an incomplete version of the spell. It didn't matter either way at this point, though; she had done it, and it could not be undone.

Willow thought curing Oz of his werewolf condition—something that caused him a good deal of anxiety and depression once a month—would be a wonderful gift, and a gift that only she could give him. So just twenty-four hours from the first of three nights that would put Oz through his painful transformation, Willow cast the spell. She hoped the fact that the coming full moon would be the Blood Moon would enhance the spell's power.

Not only was the spell not enhanced, it did nothing. She locked Oz up in the book cage in the library the following night. He didn't like her to see him change, so she always left right away. On that night, though, she only pretended to leave. As she waited in the shadows, his grunts of pain, which sounded human at first, became deeper, throatier until there was nothing human left in the savage sound. Unable to listen any more, she rushed out of the school into the cold night, angry with herself. She'd done something wrong, misread the instructions, misquoted the words, something.

Then those five bloodthirsty hellhounds had come to Sunnydale. A lump of guilt quickly formed in the pit of Willow's stomach. Instead of curing Oz's lycanthropy, her spell had summoned a pack of hellhounds to town! She didn't want to tell Giles what she had done, but she had no choice. He was always trying to get her to slow down on the magic and wanted her to clear everything with him first, to practice it under his supervision. He wasn't going to like the fact that she'd performed such an ancient spell on her own, especially when she wasn't exactly sure if she was working with the whole spell. But every time she approached Giles, he was too busy to talk.

Willow felt a little better after they'd staked all five of the hellhounds. At least they wouldn't be moving on to other towns to wreak havoc. But she still felt angry that the spell had not cured Oz and felt the need to discuss it with Giles. After all, maybe she was wrong about the spell going awry. Maybe it just did nothing. Giles would most likely know. But she didn't want to risk being told, "Sorry, not now, Willow," or, "Can we talk later, please?" She'd been hearing that sort of thing a lot lately, and not just from Giles. That was the other thing that had been occupying her thoughts lately.

Normally, with exams just around the corner, she and Oz would be studying for them together. Buffy and Xander and Cordelia would be coming to her for help in preparing for the tests, too. Buffy—who usually panicked in the face of important tests—had gained some confidence after her high SAT scores, but she still was no ace student and normally would be asking Willow for study tips, or even asking to study with her. Instead, Oz was studying with Xander, Cordelia was preparing for the exams alone, and Willow had no idea what Buffy was doing.

It wasn't just the studying, though. It felt as though they hardly even talked to her anymore. The only time she seemed to have any interaction with her friends at all was when some evil raised its ugly head—like the hellhounds on wheels—and they needed her to dig something up on the Internet or work on a potion or spell. Outside of that, they seemed to be unaware she existed. Like Giles, they were always too busy or preoccupied to talk or do anything after school. Even Oz, her boyfriend, seemed distant when they were together, as if his mind were somewhere else, or there were other things he'd rather be doing.

It had happened gradually over the last week and seemed to get worse . . . a noticeable coldness among her and her friends, and an even chillier one between her and Buffy. Willow wanted to talk to them about it, but what good would that do if they didn't hear her, or didn't have time to listen? While she sensed no malice from most of her friends, Willow wasn't sure what she sensed from Buffy. Sometimes—and she hated even thinking about it—she felt afraid of Buffy. And she had no idea why.

On top of all that, she'd been immersing herself in learning as much as possible about magic. Wondering if perhaps things might go back to normal with her friends if she made herself useful, Willow had decided to speed up her education in the magic arts, all on her own, and see if it made a difference.

The recent distance that had grown between Willow and her friends had been bothering her so much, she'd been having recurring nightmares about it. She thought the nightmares were about that, anyway. She couldn't remember the details, but she awoke from each one with an odd mixture of feelings: she felt upset, as if she'd just seen something horrible and infuriating, and at the same time, she felt strangely satisfied, as if something, some outside force, had suddenly and seamlessly solved her problem. She'd had a difficult time getting back to sleep afterward, and she hoped the nightmare, whatever it was, didn't recur.

Willow pulled her eyes from the screen and slumped in her chair with her head down, releasing a long sigh when she heard light footsteps. She lifted her head to see Giles walking from the back of the library toward the front desk. She got up and hurried over to the desk. She reached it seconds before Giles and was smiling when he arrived.

"Hello, Giles," she said.

"Good afternoon, Willow." He went behind the desk and began sorting through a stack of books, making two more stacks as he separated them. Occasionally, he stopped to look at a spine and murmur to himself.

"Um, Giles . . . do you think we could, um . . . maybe talk?"

He said nothing for a moment, focused on the books. Then he started and turned to her. "I'm sorry, Willow. Did you say something?"

Before Willow could repeat the question, Buffy burst into the library and ran to the front desk, stumbling to a stop. Her blond hair was windblown and she carried about her some of the fresh air from outside. She was out of breath and her eyes were wide beneath a frown.

"You have a radio in here, right, Giles?" she asked, speaking so fast that it sounded almost like one big, long word.

"Is something wrong, Buffy?" Giles asked. He looked very concerned as he turned away from the books, his task forgotten.

"The radio, can you get it? It's important."

"Well . . ." Giles went into his office and returned a moment later with what looked like a battered old silver-and-black lunchbox with two knobs on the side and an antenna on top. It was a portable AM/FM radio of indeterminate, but considerable, age. Maybe Giles bought it as a kid and didn't even know radios had changed since then. For all Buffy knew, it was the first portable AM/FM radio ever made.

"Is it safe to use this thing?" Buffy asked as she stared at the old radio on the counter in front of her. Giles reached down and turned it on. "I heard a rumor," Buffy said, turning the dial quickly, "and I just want to see if it's true." She fumbled up and down the dial, passing music and talk shows. "C'mon, isn't there an all-news station around here?"

"Twelve-thirty AM," Willow supplied.

Buffy turned the dial back. "Local news, right?"

"Yeah," Willow said with a nod. "Every fifteen minutes. Or maybe it's every half hour, I'm not sure."

Buffy found the station and turned up the volume. A male voice was finishing up the local weather, giving the forecast for the next couple of days.

Xander and Oz joined them at the desk, curious.

"Buffy," Giles said, "why don't you tell us what's wrong?"

"Because I don't know if it's true or not."

"What difference does that make?" Xander said.

"I don't want to cause a panic and then find out it was over nothing," Buffy replied impatiently.

"Panic?" Oz asked. His eyebrows were raised high as he exchanged a look with Xander, then Willow.

"What are you guys doing?" Cordelia asked, approaching the desk. She stood beside Xander and looked at the radio with distaste. "You're listening to the news?"

Xander turned to her. "Hey, you never know what that Saddam Hussein is gonna do next. Or, more importantly, Madonna."

"Buffy, I'm really quite busy," Giles said. "Perhaps you could—"

"Ssshhh!" Buffy shushed, holding up a hand. "Listen!"

"More cattle have been killed at a farm just outside Sunnydale," the newsman said. "The cattle were eaten to the bone, leaving only skeletal remains. This is the second such incident in three days. The cattle were found this morning by farmer Leland Rhine, who then called the police. Police have speculated that mountain lions may be to blame, but local wildlife authorities say the remains bear no resemblance to the work of a mountain lion, although they had no suggestions as to what the cause might be." He paused for a moment, then moved on to a story about the apprehension of a telephone sales con artist who had been preying on old people.

"Oh, my God," Willow whispered. The others were staring silently at one another with expressions of dread, so her quiet remark was not out of place. But Willow's expression of dread was prompted by a reason known only to her.

Her magic may have brought those hellhounds to Sunnydale, and even though they'd been killed just last night—the last night of the full moon—her magic had brought them back again . . . and Willow had no idea if there was any way to stop it.

Chapter 3

"IT CAN'T BE THOSE HOUNDS," BUFFY SAID, SHAKING her head slowly. Her jaw was set firmly, her forehead lined with a frown, and her voice was solid with confidence, certainty.

"How do you know?" Cordelia asked.

Everyone turned to her, waited for her to continue.

"Well, you should know by now, all those things you people deal with . . . I mean, they're dead, they're not dead, they're undead. You never know what they'll do! Right? So, maybe they came back. Did you ever think of that?" She turned to Oz. "Can you guys do that?"

"What?" Oz asked, frowning.

"Come back from the dead."

He shrugged. "Don't know. Haven't been killed yet."

"The creatures we encountered last night," Giles said, "were most definitely hellhounds. And hellhounds most definitely do not come back from the dead."

"This is something else," Buffy said. "I don't know what, but it's not hellhounds, and it's not . . . well, it's definitely not something we're familiar with." She turned to Giles and leaned forward with her hands flat on the countertop. "Unless you're holding out on us."

Giles folded his arms across his chest and frowned as he lightly chewed his lower lip, thinking. He dropped his arms suddenly and turned to Buffy.

"Uh, ho-holding out? Me? No, no, of-of course not."

"You're not aware of anything that . . . eats cattle?" Buffy asked.

Xander cleared his throat. "Do hamburgers count?"

"Doubt it," Oz said quietly.

"I have never encountered anything quite like this before," Giles said as he reached down and turned off the radio. "I will consult my books, particularly the more obscure volumes, but . . . if this violence is confined to cattle, perhaps we need not worry about it."

"But what about the cows?" Willow asked, a touch of pain in her voice.

Cordelia rolled her eyes. "Cows? Oh, God . . . don't tell me you go around splashing blood on fur coats, too."

"No, it's just that . . ." Willow paused and looked around at the others. "We don't know exactly what's going on out there. The thing that's . . . or the things that're doing this might start eating those cows while they're still alive, if they're not already. I mean, if that's the case . . . well, it's horrible. Right?"

There was no response for a few ticks of the white-faced institutional-style clock on the wall.

"Cows feel pain," Oz said with an agreeable shrug.

Willow turned to him, the beginning of a smile playing at the corners of her mouth. She took his hand, curled her fingers between his, and said, "Thank you, Oz." To the others she said, "I mean, maybe they're just cows to us, but . . . well, to Bessie and the girls, they're, like, other cows! They're like company . . . friends, even. So how could we—"

"Whoa, wait, wait, scoot back a sec," Xander interrupted, holding up a hand. "I'm down with the pain thing, but . . . you don't really think cows are capable of socializing? Or having names for each other? I mean, what, you think they're out in the field playing Bingo when nobody's looking? I just wanna be clear about what I'm agreeing with, here."

Willow asked, "Well, shouldn't the whole being-eaten-alive possibility be enough to—"

"Yeah, that's what I agreed with," Xander said, nodding. "I don't buy cow barn dances or toga parties on the pasture, but yeah, we should do whatever we can to prevent the being-eaten-alive thing."

Cordelia said, "God, you've sure got a lotta sympathy for beef all of a sudden, Xander. It doesn't seem to keep you out of Burger Barn, though, does it?"

Xander sighed as he turned to Oz. "See? I *knew* hamburgers would come into this somehow."

Giles took off his glasses and walked slowly around the desk. "Why cattle?" he asked. "There's no apparent danger to human beings, and nothing indicates a supernatural element to any of this, but the similarity is enough—"

"Oh, I think there's something that indicates a supernatural element," Buffy said. "There's no meat left on those cows. The bones are cleaned, practically spotless. That's not natural. And there's not that much in the way of cattle around Sunnydale. What happens when it, or *they*, run out of their favorite food? Sunnydale would become a smorgasbord. Especially if there's a lot of them . . . and I'm guessing there's more than one . . . whatever they are."

"No doubt," Giles said. He put his glasses back on as he took in a deep breath and let it out slowly. He headed toward a shelf of books, his steps quicker now, more determined. Everyone turned, their eyes following him. "Well, no point in delaying any further. I shall see if I can find something with a habit of . . . well, eating cattle to the bone." He winced with disgust. "Willow, depending on my success, I may need you to—"

"Surf the 'Net?"

"Precisely." He climbed onto a stepladder, scanned a shelf, and carefully removed a thick, heavy volume with yellow-edged pages and aged leather binding. He came down off the ladder and turned to see the others watching him. His eyebrows popped up and he said, "I believe you were all otherwise occupied a few moments ago. Weren't you?"

The small group broke up as Xander and Oz returned to their table and Cordelia returned to hers.

"Like you said, Giles," Willow said, "no point in delaying any further. I'm online, anyway, so I think I'll just start looking now and see what I can find." She went back to the computer, typed a search engine into the address window and hit the Enter button.

Giles stood in front of Buffy and put the large book on the counter. "If you'd like, you could peruse another book while I'm looking through this one."

One side of her mouth curled up into a weary look of disinterest. It quickly disappeared when she put a hand over her mouth to cover a long yawn. "No . . . thanks, I should probably study. But I feel like taking a nap. I'm wasted."

"Drop in this evening, would you? Maybe we'll have something by then."

She lifted a hand and waved once as she turned and left the library.

Clouds were gathering in the blue sky, creating an early false twilight and taking the sun's warmth from what was already a chilly afternoon. The clouds were large and dark, big bullies ganging up on what remained of the day, and it was clear they intended to stay awhile.

As she went up the front steps of her house, Buffy wondered if it was getting cloudy and dark all over southern California . . . or if the clouds were just gathering over Sunnydale. Sometimes it felt that way, and given the fact that Sunnydale was a Hellmouth, it wasn't out of the question.

In the house, she went into the kitchen, dropped her books on the table, took off the black leather jacket she'd been wearing over a light-blue sleeveless shirt and gray pants, and draped it over the back of one of the chairs. Her mother wasn't home, as usual, and that was fine with Buffy, because she didn't feel up to any cheerful chatter at the moment. She found a container of raspberry yogurt in the refrigerator, got a spoon from the drawer, and sat at the table for a snack.

The wise thing to do would be to study until it was time to go on patrol. The quarterlies were getting closer and closer. *Like the giant tarantula in that old movie, closing in on the small desert town to eat everyone and crush anyone it might miss,* Buffy thought grimly. But she knew if she studied, there was no way she would absorb or retain anything, not as tired as she was.

There had been a lot of excess slayage lately, complete with late hours and little sleep, and she was feeling overworked. Unfortunately, the job of being the Slayer didn't come with vacation time, or even sick time. And the benefits were . . . well, there were no benefits. When she slept at all, it had been fitful sleep the last few nights. She'd had an odd nightmare that she couldn't quite remember. It made her wake up suddenly, feeling angry and a little scared, but at the same time, feeling as if everything was going to be fine because all of her problems had been solved . . . or at least taken away, abolished. She could never get back to sleep after waking from the nightmare, and each time, she'd gone back outside to patrol some more.

The very thought of taking a nice, restful nap made Buffy feel good all over. She threw away the empty yogurt cup, washed the spoon, and took her books and jacket to her bedroom, where she flopped onto her bed with a long, weary groan.

As tired as she was, all she could do was stare at the ceiling of her room. She couldn't stop thinking about those cows.

What would do such a thing? The kind of creatures typically found around a Hellmouth did not usually waste their time with something as boring as cattle. Their tastes usually went beyond the mundane . . . and straight for the jugular. Whatever it was, Buffy knew in her gut—and she trusted her gut—it was going to be trouble. The fact that it was something completely unfamiliar to Giles was a bad sign. There were many kinds of hellhounds with many kinds of talents, but this seemed to go beyond that. They didn't know what it was, what it wanted (besides cows), or how to stop it.

Buffy propped herself up on an elbow, reached over and turned on the radio on her nightstand, then dropped back down onto the mattress. Music helped, a little. She closed her eyes, took a few slow, deep breaths, and felt herself starting to relax.

What felt like a moment later, Buffy opened her eyes and found she was lying on her stomach. The gray light that had shone through the curtains over her window was gone and her room was dark except for the hall light shining under her door. She could hear her mother's voice somewhere in the house, words muffled.

Buffy sat up on the edge of the bed, turned on the bedside lamp, checked the clock. She'd gotten over two hours of sleep. Not bad. No nightmares, no dreams at all, very restful. Even better. She yawned and stretched, feeling like she could use a couple hours more. But she needed to go back to the library and check with Giles, and she was feeling a bit hungry, so she'd have to get some dinner before she started patrol. And at some point that night, she might even study.

Buffy found her mother moving around in the kitchen, preparing a salad as she talked on the cordless phone, which was held between the side of her face and her shoulder.

"Of course I told her no," Joyce Summers said. She waved and smiled at Buffy, who flopped into a chair at the kitchen table. "The pictures she showed me, well . . . you had to see them. I mean, the pieces were awful! And she was so . . . so . . . well, annoying. At first, I thought maybe she was, you know, challenged in some way. But I'm pretty sure she's just annoying."

Buffy smelled something cooking. While her mother made the salad, she went to the oven and took a peek. Tuna casserole. A boring dish to some, but her mom made the best. She closed the oven, hoping it would be done soon so she could have some before going back out.

In just a few minutes, Buffy and her mom were at the table, eating salad and tuna casserole, chatting about nothing in particular.

"Are you feeling okay?" Joyce asked.

"Yeah, I'm fine."

"You're sure? I usually don't come home to find you sound asleep."

"Oh, that. I just took a nap. I need to study for exams and I wanted to, you know, rest up for it. How about you? What was that phone call all about?"

"Oh, just some crazy woman who came to the gallery today and wanted us to exhibit her collection of . . . well, I don't know what to call it except ugly art."

"Crazy?" Buffy asked.

"Well, maybe not crazy. But she definitely has bad taste." Joyce took a bite of food, dabbed her mouth with a paper napkin with a border of embossed flowers, and asked, "So, you'll be studying for exams tonight?"

"Yep."

Joyce stared at her.

"Well, yeah, that and . . . you know, some other things."

"You're wearing yourself out, that's why you were asleep, isn't it?" Joyce asked. She shook her head and sighed. "I never see you, Buffy. This is the first time we've eaten dinner together since . . . well, since—"

"Friday, Mom," Buffy said. "Not that long, so don't go all Lifetime TV on me. And by the way, the casserole is delicious."

"Thanks," Joyce said with a brief smile. "There's nothing . . . well, nothing . . . wrong, is there?"

"There's always something wrong, Mom. But that's not necessarily bad." She took another bite of her casserole, chewed, and swallowed. "Right now, I'm just sitting here having a good dinner with you. Know what I mean?"

Joyce's worried frown slowly melted and she smiled a little. "Yes. I know what you mean. And I'm glad you're here."

"Me, too," Buffy said, just before she shoved another bite of the casserole into her mouth.

Chapter 4

THE NIGHT WAS DARK AND COLD AND WET, SO THE library, while not exactly warm, was a welcome shelter. It was also dark and quiet. Buffy heard the faint, erratic clicking of a mouse coming from the computer and the clock on the wall clicked the time away, but those were the only sounds. Apparently, Willow was still at work trying to find something on the Internet. Behind the front desk, the door of Giles's office was open a few inches and a shaft of light spilled out onto the floor. Buffy rounded the desk and entered the office.

Giles had two large books open on his desk, and another in his lap, all three of them old enough to have yellowed pages and spines that crackled when they were opened and closed. He was ignoring the book in his lap for the moment and leaning over one on the desk, the one to his left, running his finger slowly down the page, searching for something.

"Hello, Giles," Buffy said very quietly. He was swallowed up by what he was doing and she didn't want to startle him.

His finger continued to move down the page and he didn't respond for over half a minute. Then he sat back in his chair with a sigh and looked up at Buffy wearily. He straightened his glasses as half his mouth curled upward, as if he were too tired to greet her with a whole smile.

"Hello, Buffy."

"So . . . how's the huntin'?"

"Huntin' . . . you say? Well." He took off his glasses and rubbed his eyes hard with thumb and fingers, then put his glasses back on and looked up at Buffy again. "I'm afraid I've not been able to find anything that resembles our particular problem. I have spent nearly four hours going over book after book, and I have come up with absolutely nothing."

"Not that it matters," Willow said, "but I haven't come up with anything, either."

They turned to see her standing in the open doorway of the office, leaning on the doorjamb.

"Hi," Buffy said, smiling, her voice so tentative, as if she were talking to a stranger, that it surprised her.

Willow smiled back. "Hey, Buffy." But her body was tense as she smiled at her friend . . . and she had no idea why.

"If what we're dealing with is in any of the books I've checked," Giles said, "I shall need more information to find it. 'Eating cattle to the bone' is simply not enough."

"What does that mean?" Willow asked, taking a single step into the office.

"It means there has to be something else," Giles

replied. "Some other trait, some other factor . . . something besides eating cattle."

"And since we don't know of any other traits," Buffy said, "we'll have to wait for it, or them, to show us one, right?"

Giles nodded. "I'm afraid so."

"Ooooh," Willow said with a shiver in her voice, "You know, to be honest, I'm not too down with the sound of that."

"I'm not too down and I'm not very happy about it, either," he said, turning to her. "But we have no choice. All we can do now is wait for something else. Some other characteristic that will help us understand what we're dealing with, if we're dealing with anything at all."

"What do you mean, if we're dealing with anything at all?" Buffy asked as she leaned forward and placed both hands on his desktop.

"We have not yet ruled out the possibility that this is just the work of some kind of wildlife. If not mountain lions, then perhaps something else."

"Tell me you don't really believe that, Giles," she said, leaning closer to him. "Tell me you're just saying that to sound thorough, like you're covering all the options."

"The incident that took place today was, without a doubt, very strange," Giles said. "But there is no sign of it being supernatural."

"Waiting for these things to show other traits means *people* start getting eaten to the bone," Buffy reminded him.

He lifted the open book from his lap and placed it on top of the others on his desk, then wheeled his chair back from the desk and turned it toward Buffy.

"I've thought of that, and needless to say, I find that possibility . . . well, unpleasant at best," he said. "There is nothing we can do now, because we have absolutely no idea what this thing is. Or, of course . . . things."

Buffy pushed away from the desk and leaned heavily against the wall. "This isn't any local wildlife, Giles. It's something we're unfamiliar with, but it's not coyotes or a bear or a pack of ravenous possums."

"I'm inclined to agree with you, Buffy," Giles said. "But for now, our hands are tied."

"I could patrol cow pastures tonight," Buffy suggested.

Giles carefully closed the three books on his desk. "I suspect that would be a waste of time. So far, this has only happened twice, and in different locations. For all we know, it may not happen again, and if it does, we haven't a clue where it will be. I'd like you to confine your patrol to the usual locales, Buffy. Tomorrow, we'll see what happens."

Buffy said nothing, but she thought about how easy it would be to just go ahead and do it, anyway. She could call Oz, and he could pick her up in his van. They could find a pasture somewhere around Sunnydale, and she could wait . . . just wander and wait for something, or things, to show up.

That was what Buffy would do under different circumstances, but not these. Deep down, she knew Giles was right. They knew so little—nothing really—about what they were dealing with, it would be a waste of time. And any night Buffy spent not patrolling her usual route was an invitation to trouble.

Both girls stood silently in the office, their faces thoughtful and a little tense. Giles looked back and forth between them, waiting for one of them to do or say something. When neither of them did, he spoke:

"I believe you have a number of tests coming up, correct?"

They both flinched, as if slapped out of their own thoughts. "Yeah," Buffy and Willow said simultaneously.

"Then I suggest you go study for them while things are quiet and uneventful." He smiled a friendly but dismissive smile, letting them know it was time for them to go.

Outside the library, the hall was dark and their footsteps echoed in the empty silence.

Willow felt tense. She'd been up and down these halls a million times, even at night when they were kind of creepy, as they were now. It wasn't that. It was the way she'd been feeling lately, neglected by her friends, especially her best friend, and it was making her uncomfortable around Buffy. It was the knowledge that something was still out there eating whole cows, something she might have brought to Sunnydale with her uncertain magic, with that ancient, moldy old spell that might not even have been intact.

"So," Willow said hesitantly, glancing at Buffy, whose eyes were directed straight ahead, "are you really, um, going to go study now?"

"I'll probably patrol for a while. I'll study later."

Willow chewed her lower lip as she silently debated whether or not to ask the next question, then: "I could help if you'd like."

Without turning to look at Willow, Buffy said, "Nah. Slayer's hours. Some midnight oil-burning. That kinda thing. You'll be asleep."

That hasn't been a problem in the past, Willow

thought. Her feet felt very heavy as she took the remaining steps to the door. She stiffened as they turned to face one another.

"Then I guess I'll see you tomorrow," Willow said, forcing as much of a smile as she could muster.

"Yeah, tomorrow." Buffy nodded once, then pushed out the door. Outside, she opened her umbrella and went down the steps.

Willow hadn't brought an umbrella because it hadn't been raining when she came to the library earlier. She watched Buffy disappear into the night, then braced herself against the cold and hurried down the steps through the rain.

What was that all about? Buffy wondered as rain pattered loudly on her umbrella. She wasn't wondering about anything Willow did, or didn't, do . . . she was wondering about her own discomfort around Willow, her behavior toward her. *She's my best friend, and I felt like she was some kind of stranger . . . someone I didn't want to be around.*

It was bad enough that there was something going on around Sunnydale that neither she nor Giles understood, something she knew was going to be trouble, although she didn't know when or how. Behaving in ways she didn't understand and experiencing such negative feelings toward her best friend, however, was much worse. Vampires, hellhounds, demons . . . a disagreement with Willow over which they could make up, a misunderstanding that could be explained away— she understood all those things and could deal with them. But the idea of losing a hold on her own feelings was disturbing, and it seemed that was what had just happened.

Buffy tried to shove those thoughts into the back of her mind as she headed through the rain to the nearest cemetery. It was time to focus all her attention on the night, and the dangerous things that moved through it.

While Buffy patrolled, pausing on her stroll now and then to kick, punch, and stake fang-baring vampires that lunged hungrily from the dark, Willow lay on her bed trying to study. She had trouble concentrating as she reviewed material she would be expected to know next week, but she managed to absorb a few bits of information. The hard part was going to be hanging on to it until the tests.

By the time Buffy headed home to do some studying, Willow was sliding between the sheets of her bed. In spite of the sound of the falling rain outside, the nighttime silence of her bedroom was deafening, even smothering. She turned on her clock radio, set it to turn the music off in an hour, then settled back in bed.

When she closed her eyes, hoping to sleep, Willow saw the flesh-stripped carcasses of those cows in her mind's eye: blood-streaked ribs curving up from the spine, then back down again . . . empty eyesockets staring from a skull that narrowed to a snout, naked teeth lined up in flat rows.

Willow opened her eyes and turned on her side, looking at the green glow from the clock radio. But in her mind, she could hear the sounds that might have been made in those pastures when the cows were eaten: wet slicing sounds, the whispery tearing of warm flesh, teeth clacking against bone, loud, sloppy chewing, and worst of all, the deep, ragged, throaty wailing of the cows that might have gone on until whatever it was that was eating them began to consume their internal organs.

Shuddering from head to toe, Willow rolled over on her other side and stared into the dark corner of her room.

While Buffy studied, Willow finally—after twisting and turning in her bed—drifted off to sleep. During her restless sleep, Willow had the nightmare again, most of the details of which she could never quite remember upon waking.

When Buffy went to bed, she was so tired, she fell asleep immediately with ease. She had her nightmare again, too. It was the same nightmare Willow had.

Buffy and Willow both dreamed they were lying awake in their beds, their bedrooms dark and quiet . . . until voices began to whisper at them. The voices came from all around the room, and when they lifted their heads, both girls saw small, slanted, flaming red eyes glaring at them from the darkness. At first, the whispering made no sense, but the eyes moved closer and words formed, then sentences. Both girls tried to get out of their beds but found their bodies were paralyzed, numb. They had no choice but to lie there and listen to the sibilant chatter.

The eyes were low, and when they moved forward even more, both girls could see why; the visitors to their bedroom were very short. They could make out no details of the small figures because they were still in the dark, but they were close enough for the girls to see their stumpy outlines. Buffy and Willow didn't care about that, though, because by then, they were paying close attention to what the creatures were saying. They were so caught up in the whispered words, they hardly even noticed the glowing red eyes anymore.

In the dreams, the voices whispered horrible things that frightened both Buffy and Willow at first, but soon made them feel relieved. Because the voices told each of them what was causing all the problems in their lives . . . and how each of them could get rid of it.

Chapter 5

BY MORNING, THE RAIN HAD STOPPED. THE CLOUDS pulled back to reveal a clear and astonishingly blue sky, but stayed within sight, indecisive, as if debating a return engagement. Once it rose above the large wreath of clouds, the sun warmed the chilly air and dried up the tiny gems of moisture that clung to the leaves.

While the students of Sunnydale High were just arriving at school by bus, car, or on foot, two aging retirees stepped out onto their front porches in the well-kept residential neighborhood known as Clover Circle. It was one of the oldest neighborhoods in Sunnydale; many of the people who lived there had moved in when it was a new development, and had stayed there long enough to grow old with it.

Tom Niles and Delbert Kepley were two such residents. They had lived next door to each other for over forty years. In their younger days, they and their wives had gone dancing and to movies together, camping, hiking . . . they'd done everything together. As the years

54

wore on, they took up bridge; Tom and Delbert went fishing together several times a year, and their wives got together afternoons to crochet and watch their stories on television. When Tom's wife died, Delbert and his wife, Madge, had given him the support he needed to adjust to life alone. Tom and Fran had raised two children, who were now gone, grown and with children of their own. Madge was unable to have children, and she and Delbert had discussed adoption, but somehow they'd never quite gotten around to it.

Their yards were immaculate, cared for daily with loving hands. Short, perfectly trimmed shrubs grew along the white picket fences that went around each of their large front lawns, and in the years since Tom's wife died, Madge had tended the flowers that grew on both sides of the white picket fence that separated their yards.

The two men stood on their porches, surveying their yards. But they did not come down the steps and greet one another or chat over the fence, as they usually did. Nor had they done so the day before, or the day before that. A chill had developed between the two friends, suddenly and for no apparent reason.

Madge had questioned Delbert about it after Tom hadn't come over to watch "Wheel of Fortune" and "Jeopardy" two nights in a row, but he'd replied with no more than a frown, a shake of his head, and a growling mumble about being fed up with something or other. She assumed he would tell her about it when he was ready, providing it lasted that long; whatever tiff the two men were having would most likely disappear unacknowledged very soon, as it always did.

As Tom disappeared into his garage, Delbert went back into his house and returned with a portable radio and a steaming mug of coffee. There were two battered old chairs on the covered porch, and Delbert sat in the one that rocked. He put his coffee on the porch's bannister, found a sports talk show on the radio, and set it next to the mug. He sat back in his chair contentedly to rock gently, sip his coffee, and listen to the radio host discuss pro football with his callers.

From next door, a sound roared to life so suddenly and loudly that Delbert jerked in the creaky old rocker and spilled some coffee on his lap from the mug that was halfway to his mouth. He sat forward, put the cup back on the bannister, and cursed quietly as he brushed at the coffee on his pants. The sound continued: an obnoxious growl so loud and deep, Delbert could feel it in the porch beneath his feet when he stood. He went down the steps to the front walk and turned toward his friend's house.

Tom was on the riding lawnmower his son had given him last Christmas. It was small and compact, but sounded like a monster truck rally, as far as Delbert was concerned. Besides that, it was completely unnecessary, because Tom's yard wasn't big enough to need a riding lawnmower.

Although Tom's back was to him at the moment, Delbert shouted at him, told him it was too early in the morning for all that racket, sprinkling his diatribe with a few choice curse words. His words were swallowed up by the lawnmower's noise, but as Tom turned around and headed back in his direction, he saw Delbert's mouth working, saw his fist shaking angrily. Tom yelled back, waving an arm at Delbert several times. Neither one could hear the other, but each made his point.

Delbert went back up on the porch as Madge pushed

the screen door open and leaned out from inside the house. She wore a green-and-yellow flower-print dress and a white apron hung from around her neck; she tied it in back as she spoke.

"Did I hear you yelling something out here, Del?" she asked.

"Oh, it's that damned riding mower of Tom's," he muttered as he grabbed the coffee mug from the bannister. "Acts like he's tilling a field over there. Hell, we've got a bigger lawn than he does." He started back down the porch steps.

"What's wrong with you two?" Madge asked. "Are you having some kind of stupid fight?"

"Never mind," he called over his shoulder. "Go back inside."

"For goodness' sake, Del," she said, louder, "you've been friends for forty years!"

"Just go do the dishes!" he snapped.

Delbert went down the walkway a few steps, then onto the lawn, over to the fence that separated his lawn from Tom's. He started shouting again as he emptied the coffee mug onto the grass. Tom saw him and yelled back, gesturing obscenely. That stiff middle finger stabbing up in the air, knobby with arthritis, angered Delbert even more. He hefted the heavy ceramic mug in his hand a few times, then drew his arm back and threw it as hard as he could, aiming carefully. His throwing arm wasn't as sturdy or strong as it used to be, but his accuracy was still pretty good.

The mug hit the front of the mower and shattered. The thick, heavy pieces scattered in all directions, and some of them hit Tom, at least one right in the face. He jerked backward and swung his arms up to cover his face. He fell off the mower and hit the grass hard.

Something far in the back of Delbert's mind told him to go over the fence and check on his friend, see if he was hurt. But it was gone in a flash, like a flying insect suddenly zapped by a blue-glowing bug light. Instead, Delbert smiled and nodded once with satisfaction as he watched Tom get slowly to his feet.

The riding mower idled as Tom went to the front to check for damage. He turned and glared at Delbert, upper lip pulled back over his dentures. He got back on the mower and drove it forward, still glaring at his neighbor. The mower changed course slightly so it was headed directly for Delbert.

Delbert tilted his head back and laughed as he pointed a finger at Tom.

"Oh, yeah, come and get me with your big mower!" Delbert shouted before laughing some more.

Without hesitation, Tom drove the mower over the flowers, then through the white picket fence. The fence was there for looks only, wasn't very sturdy, and went down immediately, crunching and crackling as it splintered beneath the mower's wheels.

Delbert stopped laughing. He didn't think Tom would do it. But he was still coming straight for Delbert.

"Hey, Tom, hey, stop!" he shouted, holding up both hands.

The mower didn't even slow down.

Delbert tried to walk backward, stumbled, and went down. He tried to crawl backward on his elbows, screaming, "No, stop, Tom, stop, I'm sorry!" He rolled to the left, went over on his belly, and started to get up.

The mower hit his right side and knocked him to the ground, knocked him on his back again. One wheel rolled up over Delbert's hip.

Madge came out of the house and hurried down the porch steps. She was about to shout at Tom when something heavy and wet slapped onto the front of her body. She looked down at her white apron. It had turned a dark, dripping red.

Madge began to scream, but Delbert never heard her.

Chapter 6

WILLOW FELT AS IF THE DAY WERE STRETCHING ON forever. Each class had seemed longer than the last, and every teacher seemed to speak with a slow deliberation that bordered on the absurd. Willow was sure it didn't seem that way to anyone else, because all the students around her seemed to be having a good enough day, walking in small groups, talking, laughing, eating lunch with their friends. The day was dragging along slowly for Willow alone, it seemed, and she supposed it was her own fault for letting herself sink so low. But she couldn't help it.

She'd seen Buffy a few times throughout the day, always in a hurry to somewhere, always preoccupied, late for class three times. That morning, Willow had assumed Buffy was probably upset, for she had heard that there were more cattle killings last night; she knew both Buffy and Giles were worried about it because it was unfamiliar to them, and therefore posed a greater danger if it was something supernatural. But as the day wore on, Willow gave up on that theory as her insides slowly clenched, first with the emotional pain she felt, then with anger. Buffy was just avoiding her, that was all, and acting the way she did—preoccupied and busy—just made it easier.

Willow was alone in the hall, outside the closed doors of classes in session. She'd just come from her American literature class after finishing a quiz. The teacher, Mrs. Youngblood, had decided a quiz would serve as a good studying tool for next week's exams. "If you find that you are unable to answer these questions with some ease," Mrs. Youngblood had said, "then you should increase the intensity of your studying between now and next Tuesday." That was about the time Buffy arrived, and everything had to be explained to her. Although Willow tried, Buffy made no eye contact with her, just went straight to work on the printed-out quiz. Willow was pleased to see that the questions on the quiz posed no problem at all for her, and she finished long before everyone else. After looking over the paper, Mrs. Youngblood told her, in a whisper, that she could go.

In the hall, a door opened and Willow saw someone carrying a rolled-up poster. It was the new guidance counselor, Promila Daruwalla. Well, she wasn't exactly new, because she'd been doing part-time work in the school's main office for over a year. But that job had kept her pretty much invisible to the students. When the previous guidance counselor, Mr. Platt, was killed last month, Ms. Daruwalla filled in for him temporarily, until it was learned that she was fully qualified for the job, at which time she went from temporary to permanent within an afternoon.

Willow had never spoken with Mr. Platt, but Buffy had been very fond of him. Willow hadn't met Ms. Daruwalla yet, either, and neither had anyone she knew.

But she was well aware of the guidance counselor's popularity.

Promila Daruwalla was originally from India, and she was stunningly beautiful. She was tall—five-nine, maybe taller—and looked and moved like a model, as if maybe she'd spent some time modeling in her past. Her curves and long legs, combined with skin the color of chocolate milk, thick shiny black hair that fell nearly to her waist, and a perfectly sculpted face, sent most of the male students of Sunnydale High facedown on the tile whenever she walked by. Wherever she went on the high school's campus, Ms. Daruwalla left behind her a wake of whispered comments that ranged from affectionately admiring to shockingly obscene.

The poster Ms. Daruwalla was tacking to the corkboard just outside her office showed simply a spilled pack of cigarettes. Above was the word Think. At the bottom: Don't Smoke.

As Willow walked by, Ms. Daruwalla's back was to her.

"You certainly look down," Ms. Daruwalla said a moment after Willow passed her.

Willow stopped and turned to the woman. "I'm sorry?"

"You look like someone just stole your puppy dog." The couselor's smile was bright and disarming. "Is everything okay?"

"Oh, uh, well, um . . ." Willow shrugged and smiled back, knowing her smile was a pale imitation of the guidance counselor's. "Everything's fine," she said, nodding. Her smile fell away and her head stopped abruptly and she added, "No, um, everything's not fine, but . . . I'll be okay." She smiled again, but with less conviction than before.

"If you're not in a hurry to get somewhere, would you like to talk about it?" Her accent was slight, but gave her voice a musical quality. When Willow hesitated, Ms. Daruwalla said, "I'm free at the moment. You have nothing urgent, do you? We can have tea. I just now brewed a fresh pot."

It was tempting. Willow had been craving someone to talk to. But if she told Ms. Daruwalla what was bothering her, she would sound exactly the way she did not want to sound: whiney and self-pitying. Of course, she didn't have to talk about that if she didn't want to.

"Okay," Willow said.

The office was bright with sunshine that came in through the open blinds over the window behind a large desk. It was a very neat office, with a touch of Ms. Daruwalla's native Indian culture in the decor. A large peacock-blue silk scarf was stretched over the surface of a sideboard to the right of the desk; beautiful gold designs that looked hand-painted curled and swirled over the scarf. On top of the scarf were some small statues, and above, on the wall, were two watercolor paintings, one of a palace, and one of some elephants wearing elaborately decorated saddles.

"Have a seat," Ms. Daruwalla said.

Willow seated herself in a black, vinyl-upholstered chair in front of the desk as Ms. Daruwalla got two delicate-looking teacups from a cupboard, then took her seat behind the desk. There was a Mrs. Tea on one corner of the desk and the pot was full. She poured them each a cup and Willow took a sip. It was strong, but delicious.

"What has you feeling so down?" Ms. Daruwalla asked.

"Oh, well . . . lots of things, really. Nothing in particular."

"You'll pardon me, but I don't know your name."

"I'm Willow."

"Ah, Willow Rosenberg," Ms. Daruwalla said, her eyes brightening. "I've heard of you."

Willow's eyes widened. "You . . . you have? What, um, have you heard?"

"I have heard that you are an exceptional student. You are spoken of very highly."

Relaxing a little, Willow said, "Oh. Well, that's nice."

"Of course, that sort of thing can make it difficult for people."

A frown grew slowly on Willow's brow. "What do you mean?"

"Once you become known as an exceptional student who always does well, it's sometimes difficult for people to see you as anything else. It looks to them like your good grades come easily, because they usually fail to think of the work you put into getting them. This can lead them to think that everything comes easily to you, so they cease to see you as a person who has the same doubts and fears as they. But perhaps I am being presumptuous."

By then, Willow's frown was gone and her mouth and eyes were open wide. "No, no, Ms. Daruwalla, you aren't!"

"Oh, Willow, please . . . call me Mila."

"Mila?"

"Yes, it's short for Promila. I know Principal Snyder thinks that all students should address their elders as Mr. or Mrs. or Ms., but I prefer to be called Mila. Otherwise, I get the feeling people are confusing me with my mother." She leaned forward and folded her arms on the desktop. "So, I'll call you Willow, and you call me Mila."

Willow felt her grin getting out of hand, as if the corners of her mouth might split open up to her cheekbones. "Sure . . . Mila."

"So, you were saying?"

"Oh, yeah, I was saying that you're right. Sometimes people do forget those things. About me, I mean. Like, that I've got the same doubts . . . and fears . . ." Suddenly, she didn't want to talk about herself, and especially not about her problems. She wanted to get to know Mila more, because the way Willow saw it, Mila was the first real human being to get a job at Sunnydale High School since Giles had been hired. "So, how do you like being a guidance counselor?"

Mila laughed. "I like it. I enjoy working with students. It is so easy for the faculty—any faculty at any school, really—to forget that they are not the only people on the campus. That students are people as well, not just another part of their job, like chalk and erasers, and grading papers."

Willow was surprised to hear herself release a burst of happy laughter. "Are you for real? I mean, I feel like I'm suddenly playing a bit part in Must-See TV, or something, because real faculty people, I mean, they don't talk like that!"

Mila laughed again. "I'm just telling you how I feel." She leaned forward and lowered her voice to a conspiratorial whisper. "If word gets out, I have a feeling I won't be holding this position for long, so enjoy it while you can."

They both laughed.

"But Willow, I've not yet heard about you. You're

smiling now, and that's good, but out in the hall, you looked so down. So unhappy. Why?"

Willow talked for a while, taking the lead from Mila about everyone thinking that someone who gets such good grades couldn't possibly have the same doubts and fears they felt. Willow told her nothing of her *real* problems. If she told Mila anything about them, it might lead to further questions about the true Sunnydale. But even though she didn't bring up her feelings of loneliness and neglect or the inexplicable coldness between herself and her best friend, it felt good just to talk with Mila. Finally, after going on about herself for several minutes, she decided it was time to shift the conversation to something else.

"Those are beautiful," Willow said, gesturing to the statues on the sideboard. "What are they?"

"Ah, you mean my brother's work?"

"Your brother?"

"Yes, he is a sculptor. Come, I'll show you."

They went to the sideboard together and Mila picked up one of the statues. "This is Vishnu, the highest of the Hindu gods." She ran her fingertips over one of the statues' four intricately carved hands. Each hand held something: a shell, a ring or hoop of some kind, a club, and a lotus.

Willow touched the smooth, blue stone figure. "Your brother is very talented," she said.

"And quite popular in India. He was a cab driver for six years and did these in his spare time. Then he met a gallery owner through a friend, and suddenly, he's a sought-after sculptor, selling his pieces for exorbitant prices. Now he does it full time, and he's very happy. I'm very lucky, of course, because he makes something for my birthday every year. He has since he was a boy."

She put the statue of Vishnu down and picked up another. "This is Rama, one of the avatars of Vishnu."

"Avatar?" Willow asked. "Sounds like a new car. The Chevy Avatar. The new Avatar, from Volvo."

Mila laughed. "Yes, it does, doesn't it? But it's not. You see, Hindu gods often appear in many different incarnations, or avatars. Rama is one of the many incarnations of Vishnu, a very heroic god who saved Sita, his wife and the daughter of King Janaka, from the powerful demon Ravana."

"Sounds like the Hindu religion has a big cast."

"An enormous cast."

Willow liked the statue of Rama even more than the first, partly because it looked like a normal man, slender, with muscular arms, standing with both fists in the air, eyes turned upward, victorious. He stood in a very intricately carved archway on a round, flat base.

Next on the sideboard were four elephants, a large one leading three small ones.

"Elephants are sacred in the Hindu religion," Mila said, "so they are the subject of a great deal of our art."

"Did your brother paint the pictures, too?"

"No. He tried painting for a while, but he was really quite dreadful. Everyone advised him to stick with sculpting."

The bell rang, echoing in the hall outside the office.

Mila glanced at her watch and said, "I'm afraid I have an appointment now, Willow. I hope you feel better than you did earlier."

"Oh, I do, Mila. Thanks for talking. I really appreciate it."

"You're welcome in my office anytime. I hope you won't hesitate to come see me again soon."

Out in the hall, Willow felt much better than she

had before her visit with Mila. Of course, that might have been due, in part, to the busy hallway. It was noisy and crowded and people were hurrying in both directions. With all those people and all that activity and noise, it was easier than usual to put aside feelings of loneliness. But that wasn't the reason. The time she'd spent with Mila had made her feel better about herself.

Promila Daruwalla was a fascinating woman. Sure, it was her job to talk with students, but she didn't *have* to invite Willow into her office and serve her tea and spend nearly half an hour talking with her. That made Willow think that maybe the problem she was having with her friends—especially Buffy—was not her problem, that maybe there was nothing wrong with her after all.

She stepped into the busy foot traffic in the hall and headed for her next class. She was almost able to dismiss her worries about her relationships with her friends.

Almost. Not quite. She was still bothered by the coldness in Buffy's eyes whenever she looked at her friend.

After school that day, Buffy headed straight home. Normally, she went to the library to check in with Giles and hang out with the others. But not today. If Giles had come up with something about the cattle-eating whatever-it-was, he would track her down and let her know. As for the others . . . she just wasn't in the mood for hanging out.

And Willow would probably be there.

Buffy looked up at the sky as she went down the sidewalk. There were still patches of blue, but the dark clouds were moving back in for the night. They complemented Buffy's mood much better than the blue sky and bright sunshine.

She didn't understand her feelings about Willow. They didn't make sense. Maybe it had nothing to do with Willow at all. Maybe it was just the pressure of too much slayage in too short a time, and from worrying about exams because she wasn't prepared for them. Normally, she would go to Willow for help with that, but . . .

"What's wrong with me?" she muttered.

Her words were buried by the sound of a lawnmower being pushed by a man to her left. He smiled and waved at her; she waved back and smiled as best she could.

When Buffy got home, she saw an unfamiliar woman standing on the porch, talking to her mother, who stood in the open doorway. Her mother did not look happy. The woman was wearing a plain green housedress, no stockings, and sneakers on her feet. She was rather dumpy looking, overweight and sloppy, even lumpy, somewhere in her late forties, early fifties, with mousy brown hair shot with gray that reached just past her shoulder blades, frizzy and unbrushed, knotted in places.

"No, you don't seem to understand," Joyce said, obviously frustrated but trying hard to remain civil. "We have decided we do not want—" She stopped and smiled as Buffy approached.

"Excuse me," Buffy said.

The woman glanced at Buffy and stepped aside so she could pass.

"This is my daughter, Buffy," Joyce said, putting an arm across Buffy's shoulders.

The woman's face matched her body: round and lumpy. Her pasty, thick-fingered hands clutched the handle of her handbag in front of her so tightly that the skin over her knuckles had become even whiter. Her lips were paper-thin and her eyes were squinty. She had a faint mustache, and a mole on her chin that was small but vivid against her doughy skin. The mole, however, did not stand out as much as the bruise around her right eye.

She looked at Buffy and attempted a smile, but it came across as nothing more than a prolonged twitching of her lips. "Nice to meet you," she said distractedly. She sounded as if she had a cold.

"By the way, Miss Lovecraft," Joyce said, frowning, "what happened to your eye?"

Lovecraft? Buffy thought. That sounds familiar.

"Oh, that, uh . . ." She reached up and touched her fingertips to her cheek, just below the bruise. "It's, um . . . nothing, just a-a-a little . . . accident." She looked up at Joyce pleadingly and her voice trembled when she spoke. "Mrs. Summers, I-I . . . I can't tell you how very important this is to me."

Joyce said, "As I was saying, we—"

"Ten days, a week, that's all I ask," Miss Lovecraft continued. "You wouldn't even have to display them prominently, really, if you could just—"

"I'm sorry, Miss Lovecraft, but we've decided we don't want to exhibit the collection."

"*Who* doesn't want to?" asked Miss Lovecraft, sounding almost frantic. "I-is there someone else I should talk to?"

"No. We all decided. And that's our final answer. Okay?"

The woman said nothing for a moment.

"Okay?" Joyce said. "Now, I have to go, so you have a good day."

Joyce closed the front door.

As they headed into the kitchen, Buffy asked, "And that was . . . ?"

"Oh, that was the crazy woman who wants us to exhibit her collection," Joyce replied, flopping into a chair at the kitchen table with a steaming cup of coffee in front of her. "I don't even know how she found out where I live. She followed me, for all I know."

"Maybe she is crazy," Buffy said, getting a diet soda from the refrigerator. She sat down at the table across from her mother.

"Oh, yes, I'm starting to think she is," Joyce said. "Before, I was trying to be polite. But now . . . I'm really starting to think she may be a nut. She's so wide-eyed and desperate about getting that stuff in a gallery. I can't imagine any gallery taking it." She sipped her coffee.

"What's her name? Lovecraft?"

"Yes. Phyllis Lovecraft."

"Lovecraft. That sounds familiar." Buffy frowned, trying to place the name in her memory.

"You're probably thinking of the writer."

"No, not the writer." Where had she heard the name before? She couldn't remember . . . but it seemed to have something to do with Giles. Maybe he'd mentioned the name to her at some point. It felt important to her somehow . . . but she didn't know why. She made a mental note to ask Giles about it the next time she saw him.

"You're home a little early, aren't you?" Joyce asked.

"You, too."

"Oh, no, not really. I have to go back. But you . . . is everything okay?"

Buffy nodded. "Everything's fine. I just need to study for exams."

"That's good," Joyce said. "I like that. Studying. It sounds so . . . so . . ."

"Normal?"

"Yes! So normal!"

Buffy nodded again. "Well, don't get too attached to it, Mom, okay?"

Joyce lowered her eyes. "Of course not." She took another sip of her coffee, tipping the mug way back, finishing it off. Standing, she rinsed the mug, put it on the counter, and dried her hands on a paper towel. "Well, I'm off now."

"See ya, Mom."

Joyce leaned down and kissed Buffy's cheek, then backed up a bit and smiled. "Study hard."

"I'll try."

After her mother left, Buffy opened a textbook on the kitchen table. She usually studied in her bedroom, but she was afraid that if she went there, the temptation to nap would be too great. She would have that dream/nightmare again. She didn't want to . . . she was already upset enough. And for no reason she could fathom.

Buffy studied for a while, focusing all her attention on the books in front of her, making a few notes, trying to burn short but pertinent facts into her memory. After about thirty minutes or so, though, her concentration began to get clogged up with thoughts of Giles. Had he found anything? Did he at least have some idea of what they were looking for now?

She decided she'd done enough studying for the time being, gathered up her books, and went to her bedroom. Before changing her clothes, she clicked on the clock radio and caught the end of the latest song by the New Radicals. By the time she'd put on a pair of cargo pants and a black sweater, two commercials had fought for her attention and the local news had begun. Buffy was reaching down to turn off the radio when she heard something that made her freeze.

"Oh, God," she whispered as she listened.

She had to tell Giles.

Chapter 7

"CATTLE MUTILATIONS," WILLOW SAID, CLICKING HER mouse. "That's all I'm coming up—oh, wait, here's a Web site that sells life-size fiberglass cows. Other than that, just cattle mutilations."

Giles sighed as he paced slowly behind Willow. Oz stood beside Willow, hip leaning against the edge of the table, arms folded, watching the computer screen.

Xander and Cordelia were behind him in a couple of folding chairs they'd placed close together, Xander's arm around Cordelia's shoulders.

Oz leaned forward and nodded grimly as he scanned the screen. "That's some serious mutilation."

"Tongue, eyes, some internal organs removed with surgical precision," Willow said. "And there's never a drop of spilled blood found at the site."

"Space aliens," Xander said.

"Oh, puh-leeze," Cordelia groaned.

"No, really," Xander went on. "They use all that stuff from the cows in experiments and tests."

"Or for alien hot dogs," Oz muttered.

Cordelia pulled away from Xander a bit and turned to face him. "What kind of tests would need all that stuff?"

He shrugged. "Hey, if I thought it would help with exams, I'd go out and get a cow's tongue myself."

"Not a bad idea," Cordelia muttered. "You might find something you're good at."

"I'm quite familiar with the phenomenon of cattle mutilations, thank you," Giles said, still pacing slowly, hands locked behind him. "What happened here was not the same."

Willow turned and propped an elbow up on the back of her chair to look at Giles. "I think you were right yesterday," she said. "We're just going to have to wait and see what happens next."

"Have you tried the Sci-Fi Channel's Web site?" Cordelia asked, rolling her eyes as she stood.

"Hey, for some real scares," Xander said, "let's go to Cordy's Web site."

"You have a Web site, Cordelia?" Willow asked.

Xander stood, grinning. "Sure she does. Shrew dot com."

Cordelia turned to him slowly with eyes narrowed icily. "Why don't you www dot bite me dot com?"

Xander leaned over until he and Cordelia were almost pressed together, took both of her hands in his, and whispered, "I love it when you talk Internet to me."

One corner of Cordelia's mouth slowly curled upward. Xander kissed her on the lips, gently at first, but it quickly became more intense.

Oz cleared his throat. "Download otherwhere?"

Giles stopped pacing, faced them, and asked, "Does anyone know of Buffy's whereabouts?"

Xander pulled back slightly from Cordelia. "I saw her for a minute right after school," he said. "She was going home to study. At least, that's what she told me." Then he smiled as he put his arms around Cordelia and started to kiss her again, but she put both hands on his chest and held him back.

"Error, computer boy," she said. "Your server's down. Try again later."

"What's the matter?"

She lowered her voice, as if the others wouldn't hear. "You want to make out with other people around?"

"You've never minded before," Xander said, dropping his arms to his sides.

"Not now. It's rude."

He folded his arms across his chest. "Oh, and that's never stopped you before."

Cordelia shook her head, annoyed, and leaned back in her chair again. Xander sat in his chair, too. Cordelia scooted her chair a couple feet away from him.

There were some hurried sounds in the front part of the library, and Buffy joined them, stopping abruptly in front of Giles. She was winded, as if she'd been running, and her hair and clothes were wet. Everyone said hi, but she ignored them, focusing on Giles.

"It's happened again," she said.

Giles said, "You mean more cattle have been—"

"No," she interrupted. "Not cattle this time. A person."

On the radio earlier, Buffy had heard that seventy-one-year-old Tom Niles had killed seventy-year-old Delbert Kepley with his riding lawnmower. Kepley's sixty-eight-year-old wife had witnessed the grisly murder. Niles had casually driven his mower into his garage immediately afterward, then gone into his house.

Buffy pulled an empty chair away from one of the tables and flopped into it, flicking a strand of wet hair away from her eye.

"Is that the whole story," Xander asked, "or are you trying to build suspense?"

"There's more, there's more," she said wearily. "It wasn't raining when I left the house, so I didn't bring an umbrella. It started a couple blocks later and I got soaked. Then I had to make a few points with a bunch of vampires on the way through the cemetery. About two seconds after dusk, too, like they can't wait to get out and raise hell. No stretching, no taking time to wake up . . . just out of the ground and off to work."

Giles moved a chair and seated himself in front of her. He leaned forward, elbows on his knees, and said uncertainly, "Uh, Buffy, you did say there was more?"

She nodded. "When the police knocked on the killer's door, they got no answer."

"Duh," Xander said with a chuckle. "Most people who puree their next-door neighbor don't sit around waiting for guests."

"He was there," Buffy went on. "He just didn't answer the door. The police searched the house for him and finally found him in the attic. I mean . . . they found what was left of him." She turned her eyes to Giles. "From the description on the radio, he was just like the cattle. Eaten to the bone."

"Are they sure it was the same man?" Giles asked.

"He was identified with dental records this afternoon. Or denture records, whatever. It was Tom Niles, the lawnmower killer."

Giles stood, walked around his chair, and leaned forward with both hands clutching the back of it. He looked tense as he lowered his head slowly.

"A person," he said quietly. "Eaten. But why? And by what?"

"Little chance he got attacked by a mountain lion in his attic," Xander said.

"Or by any other form of wildlife I can think of," Willow said.

Buffy spoke up: "You mean *natural* wildlife."

Giles stood up straight. "Are you absolutely certain it was exactly the same as with the cattle? Were there any comparisons made in the report you heard?"

"No," she replied. "Not yet."

Willow turned to the computer and began clicking the mouse and tapping the keys.

"The radio," Giles said as he spun and walked briskly to his office. He continued speaking along the way: "We must find out all the facts before we panic." He got the radio, clicked it on, and turned the dial on his way back. "The remains could be different in some way." Giles frowned at the radio as he found one music station after another. "Those cows were found in a very distinct condition, and if this man was not found in that exact—oh, here, Buffy, find the station, would you?"

Buffy found it in a couple seconds, just in time for the sports report.

"It's in the afternoon paper," Willow said, looking at the screen, scrolling with the mouse. "It's not a very long article, but it's something."

"Do print that for me, Willow," Giles said.

"Okay. What else can I do to help?"

"You should catch up on your studying."

When no one else asked to study with her—or said anything at all, for that matter—Willow sighed quietly.

A copy of the newspaper article slid out of the printer and Willow handed it to Giles. His eyes ran down the page quickly, darting back and forth.

"Yes, it is short on details," he said. "Perhaps there will be more tomorrow. For now, I'd like to consult some books I have at home."

"That means we have to leave?" Cordelia asked, looking disappointed.

Giles headed for his office, saying, "Would you like to stay here?"

Xander lifted his arms in defeat and said, "He's right. No television." He turned to Cordelia. "What do you say we go someplace and study together?"

"I don't think so," Cordelia said. She stepped around him and headed for the door.

"You've got something better to do?" Xander called.

She looked back over her shoulder. "If it were the loneliest, most depressing night of my life, I'd have something better to do." She went out the door.

"Hey!" Xander hurried out of the library after her.

Buffy went to the front desk and announced, "I'm going out on patrol, Giles."

Giles was shuffling around in his office. "Very good, Buffy. And be on your guard." He came out of the office as he slipped on his long, gray coat. "If something unique is out and about, you're likely to be the first person to encounter it."

" 'Bye, Buff!" Willow called. But the library door had already swung shut behind Buffy.

"I'm going to stay and talk to Giles," she told Oz. "I'll call you later?"

Her boyfriend kissed her. "I'm good," he said and headed out.

Willow picked up her books from the computer table and went up to the front of the library. Giles was switching off the lights.

"Giles, could we, you know, have a little talk? There's something I really need to talk about."

He thumbed through the keys on his ring, looking for the right one. "I'm terribly sorry, Willow, but I'm afraid I'm very preoccupied right now, what with . . ." He found the key, flipped off the last light, and ushered Willow out into the hall. "What with this new oddity we seem to be facing, you understand, don't you?" He closed and locked the door and they started down the hall. "I've got some things I must do right now if I ever hope to sleep tonight, so I'm afraid I'll be—"

"I know, Giles, but, see, this is something I've been trying to tell—"

"How about tomorrow? Would that be all right?"

Willow brightened. "That would be great! What time?"

"Oh, time? Actually, I wasn't being that specific. I meant sometime . . . in the general area of tomorrow. Sometime."

Willow's smile wilted as they stopped at the doors and faced one another.

"Uh, can I give you a lift somewhere?" Giles asked.

He'll have to listen to me in the car, Willow thought as her smile quickly returned. She nodded and said, "Sure. Thanks."

Rain pounded on Giles's car in the faculty parking lot. He and Willow had been sitting in the car for nearly ten minutes. Giles had started the car and was about to pull out of his parking spot when Willow told him about the spell with which she'd tried to cure Oz's lycanthropy. He'd put the gearshift back in park, killed the engine, and stared at her intensely until she finished.

Willow fidgeted silently, waiting for Giles to say something, to respond, to get angry . . . something. Too much time passed and she took in a breath to speak, but he beat her to it.

"Willow, why on earth didn't you tell me about this sooner?" Giles blurted.

"I tried, Giles, really, I did, but you were—"

He closed his eyes and nodded emphatically. "Yes, yes, you're quite correct, I've been terribly busy and I kept putting you off, I realize that now, and I'm sorry, but Willow, do you realize what you might have done?"

"Yes, that's why I wanted to tell you."

"Well, I'm afraid you'll have to put off your studying for now."

"Why?"

He took the key from the ignition. "We're going back into the library. I want you to show me the exact spell you used, every last detail of it. If it is responsible for what happened to those cattle and to that unfortunate man today, I hope we're able to reverse it."

Buffy heard them before she even reached the edge of the cemetery.

Her hair and clothes were soaked, and her shoes squished loudly with each step. She'd considered getting an umbrella from Giles back at the library but decided to hope the rain would pass. The umbrella would probably weigh her down, anyway. And from the sounds she heard beyond the wrought-iron fence surrounding the cemetery, she didn't need anything to do that.

Just beneath the sound of the falling rain were sounds of movement. And a few other sounds, like grunts and throaty gurglings.

Buffy walked along the fence to the double gates. A padlocked chain held the two gates together, but not very closely together, because the chain was loosely wrapped. She squeezed through the opening easily, and into the cemetery.

Buffy's eyes had had plenty of time to adjust to the dark, but the darkness in the cemetery seemed a little deeper . . . to have a little more dimension.

And something in the darkness moved.

She walked along the cobblestone path, which was bordered, in places, by rose bushes and a couple weathered stone benches. There were tall oaks all around the cemetery, and Buffy was conscious of their branches overhead, listening for the slightest hint of additional movement.

To another person, Buffy would appear to be nothing more than a young woman taking a shortcut, a young woman who apparently didn't mind that it happened to be through the cemetery.

But the movement in the dark knew better.

Buffy heard something overhead, on its way down. She took one quick step and stopped at the same instant its feet clumped on the cobblestones directly behind her. As she spun around, her foot found the target half a second before her eyes and crushed a cheekbone. She tried to follow through with her hands, but the thing grabbed her right forearm and threw her off balance.

The vampire jerked Buffy toward it and twisted her

right arm behind her, clutched her throat tightly with its right hand, and held her close. Its face encompassed her field of vision. Male, dark . . . maybe even handsome once. But not anymore.

"Slayer's blood," the creature snarled through a grin of needles, squeezing her throat tighter.

"Not tonight," Buffy said in a strangled whisper. "You've had enough. Time to go home."

She brought her knee up hard between the vampire's legs and stepped back. She had taken a stake from her belt a moment earlier with her free hand. As he bent forward in momentary pain, Buffy swung the spike up into his heart. The power of her swing stood the vampire upright again, its mouth yawning open, eyes burning with hatred.

A split second after Buffy jerked the stake back, the creature vanished in a sucking whoosh of dust.

Something running through the grass. To the right. Closing fast.

Buffy hurried toward the sound, stepped aside, and held out her right arm. She clotheslined the vampire—a female with long silver-and-black hair. The ground hit the vampire in the back, and Buffy staked it in the front.

Two coming up from behind. Hardly time to turn around.

A kick in the face for one, the edge of a hand to the throat for the other. Then she danced with them. It was a dance her Watcher had taught her, and one she was born to repeat, over and over. She used every part of her body as a weapon: twisting, jumping, kicking, hitting. Finally, staking. Both at once with a stake in each hand.

But others filled their place, and others after them.

They kept coming. Too many for one cemetery. Had others come from different cemeteries to wait for her? But how had they known where she would be?

They don't know, not necessarily, Buffy thought, after staking a vampire on its way out of its grave. *They're just ... more active tonight, more stirred up than usual. Out and about, restless.*

They came from the darkness with slightly blurred speed, like undead missiles fired at Buffy by the night. One after another, their hands clawed at her and clutched her, their feet kicked her, their weight fell on her, and they tried to close their jaws on her flesh so they could drink from her veins.

Buffy fought them off as she moved through the cemetery, as many as four at a time, and staked every single one, except for the two who ran away. She came to a break in the violence when she was about fifty yards from the gates on the far end of the cemetery. She was beginning to feel weary. Not a good feeling for a Slayer, especially one who seemed to be surrounded by vampires.

Buffy made a run for the gates with her heart thudding in her ears. That sound was just distracting enough to keep her from hearing the small sounds above her.

Their feet hit the ground at the same instant, all five of them. In that same instant, they were on her. She took a blow to the face, a kick in the stomach, and two kidney punches within the space of a second. She managed to get in a kick, a punch, but the kick in the stomach emptied her, and she went down.

Buffy felt knees pinning her arms and legs painfully to the cobblestones, and a weight fell across her middle. A male face oozed out of the darkness, came close.

His dreadlocks fell down around her face. His fangs were moist and dripping.

"You've been a busy little bee," the vampire rasped.

Buffy tried to kick, to free an arm, to move, but she could not.

The vampire closed in on her throat as he said, "I've come for the honey."

Chapter 8

GILES AND WILLOW HUNKERED OVER A LARGE, OPEN book on a table. Willow wrote on a yellow legal pad, assembling each piece of the spell she had cast.

Giles paced across the table from her; his left hand clutched his right wrist behind him, and his right hand clenched into a fist repeatedly.

He was angry. Willow wasn't looking at him, but she could feel it. His silence was suddenly more . . . silent than usual. But what would he say if he started talking? Maybe the silence was better.

Willow felt awful. Giles had told her before to put away the magic unless she consulted him first. And now she was dumping it on him at a very stressful time. But she'd had no choice, because her spell could be the cause of that stressful time.

The pacing stopped and Willow lifted her head. Giles leaned over the table on his palms and said, "We've discussed it before, Willow." His anger often came out sounding more like frustration, and that was how he sounded. Frustrated. "What were you *thinking?* Why didn't you speak to me first?"

Willow's voice sounded a bit weak when she spoke, slowly lowering her head. "I wanted it to be something, y'know, special for Oz. Really special. Something—" She cocked her head and lifted a shoulder briefly. "Something only the two of us would know about. I was trying to be romantic." She raised her head and looked Giles in the eyes. "Now I'm being punished for it."

He pulled a chair over and sat on the edge, still leaning forward. "Magic isn't a thing for romance, Willow. A bouquet of roses and a box of chocolates can't do any damage like magic can. Roses and chocolates don't change the weather or wipe out lives or warp time. Willow, I'm begging you, stick to pinned sweaters and ID bracelets, or . . . or whatever it is you young people do these days."

Anger. It appeared from nowhere and settled snugly around her lungs, then began to make its way slowly up into her throat. Momentarily confused, she swallowed it, held it back.

Giles lowered his voice to a tense whisper. "Willow, in doing something for Oz, no matter how loving your intention, you could kill him."

"And you couldn't?" Willow snapped.

His eyes narrowed behind his glasses. "I'm sorry?"

"You couldn't kill Oz? Or somebody else? Just as easily as I could?" Her back was stiff and her hand held the pen so tightly her fingers were white. "You could, couldn't you?"

Giles shot to his feet. "Absolutely not!" he shouted as his palm crashed down onto the tabletop.

Willow stood up, too, and her voice rose as she

spoke. "It's because I'm a teenager, isn't it? You don't think I can understand it because to you I'm just a kid, and I don't—"

"I've had years of training and experience. How could you possibly suggest that a teenager could grasp the ... the ..."

They fell silent, didn't move, and stared at one another. The silence of the library, which just moments earlier had carried a heaviness, suddenly was airy and light.

Giles bowed his head a moment, adjusted his glasses, then said, "Willow, I am terribly sorry for shouting at you like that."

"Oh, no, I shouldn't have gotten so angry, I'm sor—"

"No, no, no, it was wrong of me to shout like that, and I am sorry."

"Me, too," Willow said with a sigh.

They both took their seats, and Willow started writing again. "I'll be done with this in just a minute."

"Willow, I hope you understand what I was trying to tell you," Giles said with gentle urgency. "Magic is not something you learn. If you devoted a whole, long life to studying it, it would still confuse and bewilder you. It is not something we do, Willow, it is something we harness, a monstrously powerful force. Each time you cast a spell, you tap it on the back. And you never know what kind of mood it will be in."

She kept writing for a few seconds, tapped a period at the end of the last sentence, and looked at Giles. "I know. I should've come to you." She was so drained from the sudden surge of anger between them that her voice was very soft. Willow hoped she sounded sincere, because she was. "And everything you said about magic, I know you're right. I need to show it more respect."

"Possibly. But not before you come to me."

Giles was sincere all over the place, but his voice was about to turn into a whine. Willow found it funny and almost laughed, but held it back with a broad but tight smile. "I promise, Giles." She handed him the legal pad.

He stood as he took it. "And I hope you understand . . . I hope you believe that I know you could tackle and grasp and overcome anything you put your mind to, teenager or not."

"Thank you Giles. But I won't be able to do any of that stuff if I don't get home and study so I can go to bed." Willow stood.

"Yes, we should move on." He tucked the legal pad under his arm. "I'll look over this spell tonight and see if there's any link."

They left the library and went down the hall.

"Giles, what happened back there, when we got so angry, could that be a thing?"

Giles lowered his voice to a whisper. "I wondered precisely the same thing, Willow. It was quite . . . odd. A sudden, swift rush of anger that lasted a short time, then dissipated. Is that what you experienced?" He glanced at Willow and she nodded. Giles sighed. "It seems I shall be up with those books later than I thought."

The vampire took its time with Buffy, whose attempts to resist all failed. He ran his tongue up her neck to her ear, carefully ran the tips of his fangs down her skin, then lifted his head and peeled his lips back over dark, ridged gums.

Then it was gone. Something had shot by Buffy's face, less than an inch from her nose, made solid contact, and the vampire was gone.

More sounds of harsh, hard contact . . . and the weight on Buffy lessened. She took advantage of it immediately. In a second, she was on her feet and swinging. Her fists and heels met with flesh and bone, and her stake broke vampire hearts.

Someone fought beside her. Buffy couldn't see, but she didn't need to. The movements were too fast and lethal to be just anybody.

"Stake!" Buffy called, tossing one to Angel.

He plucked it out of the air, slammed his elbow into a vampire's face, and the stake into its chest.

Vampire after vampire disintegrated into explosive bursts of dust, which continued to disintegrate on its way down to the ground, vanishing. More fanged grins and clawed fingers came at them out of the darkness.

Then, as if they'd reached a silent agreement, the remaining vampires suddenly began to retreat. Buffy and Angel staked the last two, then turned to look all around them, knees slightly bent, arms up and ready.

The vampires were gone.

The rain had lightened to a light drizzle, but neither of them knew when; they hadn't been paying attention to the weather.

Angel moved close to Buffy and put a hand on her upper arm. "Are you all right?"

Buffy ran a quick mental check of herself and nodded. "All right, but . . . really tired. Is there a national convention of vampires in town, or something? We've got enough as it is around here, but that was like an

Elmo sale on Christmas Eve! How many of them were there?"

Angel shook his head. "There aren't any more of them than usual. They're just getting braver."

"What?"

"They're more active, more . . . agressive."

"You think maybe they hired one of those motivational speakers?" Buffy propped a hand on her hip.

"Don't you feel it, too? I thought you would."

Buffy touched her lower lip to her upper teeth and almost asked, Feel what? Instead, she asked the question of herself, silently, and quickly found some answers in herself.

Nothing felt right. Nothing she did seemed even adequate. It had been going on for a few days now, as if each day had its own bad mood, and each one was a little worse than the last. Did it have anything to do with her recent feelings toward Willow, feelings ranging from awkwardness to bursts of directionless hostility from nowhere? Possibly. She'd been feeling it without even knowing it.

"Yes," she said, "I do." She told Angel about the slaughtered and eaten cattle, and about the old man who had met the same ugly end.

"You don't know what's doing it?"

"Not yet. We're working on it."

"Maybe that's what's causing this. Maybe they sense it, and it's agitated them."

"Or . . . maybe not. If you hear anything on the vampire grapevine . . ."

He nodded, and even though it was dark, she could see his smile, because he was so close. His hand moved up to her shoulder and quickened her heartbeat.

"Should I stick around awhile, in case—"

Not far from where they stood, a woman screamed. It was a ragged, painful scream that stopped abruptly, but echoed in the night like a ghost.

Buffy said, "That sounded important." She hopped up onto a large, boxy gravestone, propelled herself upward, grabbed an oak branch, and swung herself through the air, over the fence, and onto the sidewalk.

Angel was already there, pointing at a house across the street. "Over there."

They ran diagonally across the street to the house, and slowed to a cautious walk in the gravel driveway. It led under an old oak tree and along the side of the house to a rickety-looking carport in the back, which sheltered a small pickup truck.

"I'll go around the other side," Angel whispered. He crossed the unfenced lawn to the far side of the house and disappeared around the corner.

Buffy walked silently down the long, narrow driveway beside the house. Light came from a window at that end of the house; sound came from it, too—a rhythmic thumping sound. Buffy crouched slightly as she approached the window, careful to keep out of sight from inside.

Beneath the window, Buffy slowly raised her head until she could see just above the bottom of the sash. It was a tiled room. Bathroom? Nope. Laundry room. Clothes hanging on a rack. A water heater in the corner. The thumping came from a washing machine working on a load of laundry.

Buffy stood up a little higher. A white wicker clothes hamper lay on its side and its lid lay in the half-open doorway. Beside the hamper was something that did not, at first, make visual sense to Buffy. Strangely neat angles, wet, dripping in some places, and a few inches away on the floor, a meat cleaver, the blade's shine dulled by a dark half-moon–shaped stain. She gasped with realization.

The blood-streaked bones were moving, slowly, until the remains slumped to one side. It was settling. It had just happened, the scream was when it started. Whatever had eaten the flesh from those bones had worked fast, and was still close.

Buffy stood and ran to the back of the house, toward the carport. She jumped the six-foot fence surrounding the backyard, and when her feet hit the grass, she hunkered down, became still, and absorbed her surroundings.

Quiet except for the hushed breath of the drizzle and the muted thumping of the washer. But there was an aura of activity. Something had just been through that backyard.

Across the yard, at the corner of the house, something squeaked. Rusted metal and cranky wood complaining together.

Buffy raced across the yard and found a gate so old and uncared for it was too crooked on its hinges to close properly.

And something had just gone through it.

From the gate was a narrow strip of grass that led between the side of the house and the rest of the six-foot fence. To the front yard. And the street.

Buffy ran along the house to the front yard. Angel was standing on the sidewalk, staring up the street. And children were laughing somewhere.

When Angel saw Buffy, he waved for her to come quickly.

"I was running down the side of the house, toward that old gate," Angel whispered. "And then I heard them. Laughing. They cut across the front yard here and there they went up the street. Still laughing and talking. Like they just got out of a bar." He pointed.

They were at the end of the block, waiting for a Don't Walk sign to change, even though there was no traffic at all, not even the sound of traffic in the distance. Maybe six or seven of them, all about the same height, maybe eight or nine years old. It was impossible to tell if they were all male, female, or mixed.

"Why didn't you stop them?" Buffy asked.

"I didn't know what to do. I mean . . . they're children."

A little more than halfway across the street, the giggling, laughing children stopped and fell silent in the crosswalk, bathed in the glow of the streetlight on the corner they'd been approaching. They turned, all at once, and stared at Buffy and Angel. The glow from overhead shadowed the top halves of their faces, but their mouths were visible. None of the children were smiling, but their mouths were moving. They were . . . whispering to one another.

"No," Buffy said. "They're not children."

She broke into a run, heading straight for them. The children turned and ran away from her, onto the sidewalk, down the side street, and out of sight for a moment. Buffy picked up her pace, hit the sidewalk, followed their path for several yards, then stopped.

Up ahead, the sidewalk was empty, all the way up to the next streetlight and beyond. They were gone. Hiding in a yard? In a house? Buffy didn't think so. She suspected they were truly gone.

Jogging footsteps slapped on the wet sidewalk behind her, and she turned around to see Angel.

"They weren't real children," she said. "Haven't you

ever seen them in the streets on Halloween? They yell a lot, to each other, to strangers. They spew profanity. They threaten to egg-bomb people's houses. But they don't walk around laughing all the time like they're in a Kool-Aid commercial. The things we saw . . . they wanted us to *think* they were children."

"Why?"

Buffy thought about it a moment. "Because they knew we'd be less likely to harm children," she said. "Just like you were."

Angel shrugged as he looked around, searching for some sign of the small figures they'd seen.

"C'mon," Buffy said, walking. "There's a gas station around the corner up here. I want to call Giles and tell him what happened. He'll want to know."

At the gas station, Buffy entered the phone booth, fed some change to the telephone, and called Giles at home. She told him about the remains she'd seen through the laundry room window, and the laughing children.

"You think the children did it?" Giles asked.

"I know they did," she replied. "They came from the house. Angel saw them. But they weren't children. I mean, they looked like children, but they disappeared too fast and they were just . . . weird. All kids can be weird but these were just unnatural!"

"Angel is there with you?"

"Yes."

There was a noticeable pause on Giles's end.

"He's helping me," Buffy explained. "It's like a vampire riot out here tonight. Something's really stirred them up. I mean, they're bolder than usual."

"Do you think it could have something to do with our problem?" Giles asked.

"I don't know. Maybe."

"All right. I will see if the presence of these odd children at the site of another killing will help turn up anything in my books. Good work, Buffy. And keep your eyes open. Anything you see could be the clue we need to find out what we're dealing with. If anything else turns up, don't hesitate to call me again. I'll be up late."

"Late? What's late to you? I mean, are we talking Conan O'Brien late, or are we talking that infomercial with the guy in all the ugly sweaters who gets excited by kitchen appliances late?"

"Er, just anytime of the night or morning, Buffy. Anytime."

After Buffy hung up, she and Angel headed for the next cemetery. As they walked, they speculated on the origin and purpose of the children they'd seen, until they heard a car coming up behind them. Normally, Buffy would have paid no attention to it, but it was moving so slowly that it got her attention. She looked over her shoulder.

A glimmering white limousine cut through the night like a shark through water. It was wet from the rain and beads of water sparkled on the tinted glass. As it passed them, it slowed down even more, nearly coming to a stop.

She could see no one through the glass, but Buffy sensed eyes watching her closely from inside the car. After a long moment, it picked up a little speed and drove on, turning right at the next corner.

Something about it bothered Buffy, but she didn't let on. Instead, she muttered, "Well, there goes the neighborhood," as she and Angel walked on.

Chapter 9

WILLOW WALKED TO SCHOOL UNDER A SKY THE COLOR of steel, a small collapsible umbrella in her bag just in case it started to rain again. She'd hoped to get a ride with Oz, but there'd been no answer at his house. *Probably had band practice,* she thought, and headed for the library first to see if there had been any news.

The library was dark and felt empty. Willow turned on a couple of lights, letting the door swing closed behind her.

"Giles? Buffy?" Her raised voice intruded on the book-padded silence.

It was empty. Apparently, Giles hadn't even arrived yet. Probably stayed up most of the night with his books.

Willow didn't turn off the lights. The library was such a sad place when it was dark; she didn't want to leave it that way.

"Hey!" Xander called as Willow walked away from the library. "What're you sneaking around for?" He was walking close to Cordelia, playing one of their games of slap and tickle. He put his arm around her waist and dropped his hand to her behind, and she knocked his arm away with a sharp elbow and an insult.

"I'm not sneaking around," Willow said, following down the hallway.

"You look like you're sneaking. Like some secret agent. Y'know, like La Femme Nikita. So, what're you doing today? Foiling terrorists? Infiltrating a dictatorship? Making sure people with ten items or more stay the heck outta the nine-items-or-less lane?"

"Just looking for Giles. He's not here yet," Willow responded as she leaned against a locker.

"I wonder if he's heard the news," Cordelia said.

"What news?" Willow asked.

Xander seemed surprised. "You haven't heard yet? A murder sometime late last night . . . and the suspected killer was found, uh . . . y'know, like the guy with the lawnmower."

Willow's chest tightened, as if she were pinned against a wall and someone were pressing with great strength on her chest, crushing her lungs. Was it her botched spell again? Maybe that was why Giles hadn't arrived yet. Maybe he was working on something, on the verge of finding a way to reverse the spell.

Or maybe, as so often seemed to be the case, something bad had happened.

"Willow!"

Surprised that someone was calling her, Willow looked around until she saw Mila coming out of the teachers' lounge with Miss Gasteyer and Mrs. Truman. They were Sunnydale High School's art teachers. New students often thought they were sisters because they were almost always together and even shared an office upstairs, but they weren't related at all. Both were in their mid-forties. Mrs. Truman—short, plump, and rosy-cheeked, with short light-brown hair—had been widowed years ago when a car fell off a jack onto her mechanic husband. Mrs. Truman wore a sailor-style outfit with navy blue skirt and blue and white top; her clothes were typically on the silly side. Miss Gasteyer, on the other hand, had never married; she was four or five inches taller, not really fat but very sturdy, with slightly buck teeth, large round glasses, and long strawberry-blond hair that she kept in a braid or bun. Today, Miss Gasteyer's hair was in a braid, and she wore her usual, a plain blouse and a pair of baggy chinos; as always, a large bag hung from her left shoulder by a strap and her hands were stained with paint.

Xander pointed at Mrs. Truman and whispered, "Oh, look! The fleet's in!"

Willow smiled, happy to see Mila.

"Come to my office sometime today," Mila said. "I have something for you."

"Really? Okay!" She grinned.

"Have a good day, Willow!"

"Thank you, you too!"

Xander and Cordelia turned and looked at Willow curiously.

"I saw you with her yesterday, too," Xander said. "Are you becoming friendly with the most beautiful woman in the world?"

Cordelia rolled her eyes up into her forehead. "Oh, Xander, she is not the most beautiful woman in the world. That is such a . . . boy thing to say."

"Boy thing? What the hell does that mean? I am a

boy, that's what I'm supposed to say. What'd you expect me to do, admire her shoes? That's your job. You notice what she's wearing, and I'll notice what's in it."

"The real tear-jerker," Cordelia said, "is that she doesn't even dress that well."

Xander started to say something very emphatically, but stopped himself. "Okay, look, I'm not even gonna argue with you about this. I'm not."

"Well, good. It's ridiculous. Just because she's from India and has a little accent, every guy on campus thinks she's beautiful and exotic. It's just sillier than putty and I'm sick of hearing about it."

"See? That's what I mean. I can't argue this with you, because there is no argument. It's like arguing about gravity. I know she's beautiful, everybody I know says she's beautiful, and if you push this anymore, you're gonna turn a bright shade of green."

"Green is a good color for me."

"Not for your skin, it isn't. I meant you'll be green with envy. You're just jealous, that's all."

Cordelia made a breathy sound of shock, but Willow spoke up before she could say anything.

"Well, whatever else she is," Willow said, "she's very nice."

Xander and Cordelia said nothing more as they headed for their first class.

"I can't believe it," Buffy said with genuine shock. "You overslept?"

Giles stood in the half-open door of his apartment wearing a gray and black terrycloth bathrobe. Somehow, he managed to look groggy and frantic at the same time.

"Well, it appears that my alarm no longer functions," he said, pausing to yawn. "And I fell into such a deep sleep . . . I only got two hours as it is."

Buffy pushed her way past him into the apartment. "Time to rise and shine, Giles. I'll make the coffee while you dress."

"Why don't I meet you at school, Buffy? I'm going to—"

She turned to him and interrupted. "What I saw last night? Well, it's on the radio now. And television, probably."

"That's hardly surprising."

"Yeah, but it's the second one, and now that it's out, people are going to start worrying, and they're going to keep an eye out for something, anything. And that's going to make my job difficult. There's nothing more dangerous than amateurs crashing a Slaying."

He nodded, tugging thoughtfully at his chin. "I see what you mean, Buffy."

"You said you might need to talk to the wife of that guy who got killed by the mower? I think we should do it right now."

"What, you mean this morning?"

"As soon as you slip into something probably even more ancient than that robe."

He rubbed his forehead as he tried to come up with some argument. Instead, he said, "Buffy, I'll have you know, this is a brand-new robe."

"Really?" She crossed her chest with her left forearm, rested her right elbow on her wrist and walked around Giles slowly, tugging on her lips thoughtfully, narrowing her eyes as she inspected the robe. "Did they have a clearance sale at Fifties-R-Us? You look like Ward Cleaver. Did it come with a pipe?"

"Ward . . . who?" he asked.

"Never mind. Too early for pop culture references."

"Buffy, should you be missing any school so close to exams?"

"Don't worry about that. I've been studying." Buffy wondered if she managed to keep her doubt from her voice.

"That was a rhetorical question," Giles said. "Go to school, Buffy, I insist."

"If we go now, I'll miss maybe fifteen minutes of my first class. We could—"

"We have no idea how long this will take. Besides, the woman probably has a houseful of relatives. It's too early for a stranger to pop in and start asking questions. I'll go later in the morning."

"Okay. I'll go with you then, but I still think we should go right now."

Giles frowned. "Buffy, it's not necessary for you to accompany me."

"It's not necessary, but I want to, Giles. And I want to do it as soon as possible." She talked gradually faster as she continued. "Whatever this thing is, it seems to be getting worse. I have this feeling of . . . urgency about it. The less time we waste, the less chance another person shows up looking like yesterday's buffet."

He nibbled at his lower lip as he stared at her a moment. "Very well, then, Buffy. I'll be as quick as I can."

"And I'll make coffee," Buffy said as Giles disappeared down the hall. She went into the kitchen, talking to no one in particular. "Everybody would save a whooole lotta time if they'd just agree with me in the first place."

* * *

Madge Kepley came to the door alone, and from the looks of it, she was alone in the house, too. There were no cars parked bumper to bumper at the curb, no people dressed in black carrying casserole dishes and foil-covered baking pans to the door.

"I realize this is going to seem quite irregular," Giles said, "but I am here to ask you a few questions about your husband."

Her eyes looked exhausted and physically worn from having tears wiped from them. But they brightened a little at the mention of her husband, for just a moment, and she even tried to smile.

"Did you know him?" she asked.

"I regret to say I did not."

"Hello, young lady," she said, her smile growing a little for Buffy. She looked at Giles again. "Oh, you must be from the church, then." She stepped back and pulled her front door all the way open. "Please come in."

Buffy felt bad for the woman. There were still a few bits of yellow crime scene tape stuck to the outside of the fence. In her state of mind, Mrs. Kepley probably hadn't noticed the tape . . . but hadn't anyone been by lately, anyone who cared enough to snatch those remaining pieces of tape from the fence? She smiled at the old woman as she entered. Giles followed her uncertainly.

"I have a pot of hot coffee in the kitchen," Mrs. Kepley said, heading out of the living room through an archway. "Why don't you come in and have a seat?"

They followed her into a small but very well-appointed kitchen with yellow-and-white-checkerboard curtains and a sunflower clock on the wall. The smell of coffee hung in the air, and a weary, old-looking black-and-white cat was draped bonelessly over the edge of the windowsill over the sink. They took a seat at a small oval table with a blue Formica top and chrome legs, and exchanged a glance of surprise. They had both expected the whole thing to be much more difficult.

Mrs. Kepley went about getting coffee at the counter. "We used to eat most meals at that table," she said. "It was meant for breakfast, but that's not what happened. Funny, really. We have a lovely old oak dining set in the living room. It was left to us by Del's mom. But we've only used it for holidays." She turned to them with a small tray with three cups of coffee on it. There were already a cream pitcher and a little bowl of sugar cubes in the middle of the table, flanking a small arrangement of silk flowers in a narrow vase. She smiled and said quietly, as she seated herself, "Funny how things turn out like that."

"It's terribly generous of you to do this, Mrs. Kepley," Giles said. "I just wanted to ask you a few questions. It wasn't necessary—"

Mrs. Kepley absently waved a hand at him. "Oh, please. It's little things like making a cup of coffee or baking muffins or even washing dishes that are keeping me alive right now." She poured some cream in her coffee and stirred. "Now, you say you didn't know Del?"

"No, I-I-I didn't, I'm afraid. I'm a librarian at—"

Mrs. Kepley frowned and stiffened her neck. "Was Del checking books out of the library?" she asked, surprised at the thought. "I hope none of them are overdue!"

"Oh, no," Giles said. "Nothing like that."

"It wouldn't surprise me. Del and I are both avid readers. He doesn't like my spooky books by Stephen King and Dean Koontz. But he'll go through several detective novels a week." She stared between Buffy and Giles silently, long enough for them to look at one another cautiously. "I'm sorry," she said, smiling then. Unspilled tears were starting to glimmer in her eyes. "It's just that . . . well, it's only been a day, and—"

"No need to apologize, Mrs. Kepley," Giles said. "We understand that this is a very difficult time for you."

"You're very nice," she said, dabbing at her eyes with wadded tissue she'd taken from the pocket of her housecoat.

"If you could just answer a few questions," he went on, "we'll be out of your way in no time."

She was staring between them again. She shook her head very slowly and clicked her tongue once. "To lose both of them at once like this . . . that makes it so much harder."

Buffy and Giles frowned at each other.

"Both of who, Mrs. Kepley?" Buffy asked quietly.

"Del and Tom."

Giles asked, "You mean . . . your neighbor?"

"Hardly. He was over here most of the time. We might as well have joined the houses. I've never seen two men as close to one another as Del and Tom."

"They were good friends, then?" Giles asked.

"We both moved into these houses at the same time, right after the war, Del and me, and Tom and Fran. From then on, we were inseperable. Fran was the best friend I've ever had, Tom was the best friend Del ever had. It was perfect. It changed, though, after Fran found that lump in her breast. That was the biggest loss in my life since my mother died."

Giles leaned forward. "Can you tell me, Mrs. Kepley,

why that man might have . . . done what he did to your husband?"

"There it is," Mrs. Kepley said, as if Giles had suddenly discovered a misplaced earring. "That is the thing that disturbs my sleep the most. Why?"

"Were they having a fight, or something?" Buffy asked.

"A fight? For over fifty years! They fought all the time. Over everything. The radio, the television, sports, food, movies, politics. They were constantly fighting, like two six-year-olds over a box of toys. But all the while, each one would've laid down and died for the other." She fingered a strand of her gray hair as she frowned at the tabletop. "The only thing I can think of . . . maybe they were talking over the fence—I'd heard Del shouting just before it happened—and then maybe something happened to Tom. I don't know, a stroke? An embolism? Something to make him lose control of himself, and of the mower. Maybe Del thought Tom was joking and would turn away at the last minute, so he didn't run. Afterward, Tom was somehow able to get into his house, and die there."

Buffy cleared her throat. Her quiet voice trembled slightly as she asked, "What about . . . what happened to him in his house?"

Mrs. Kepley put a hand over her mouth and sighed through her nose. She took her hand away as tears began to drop onto her cheeks and make their way down. "That was . . . so horrible. I saw his daughter just last night. They said there wasn't enough left to do an autopsy. Mostly bones and some blood. Such a horrible thing. People in the neighborhood are scared. They think it might be some kind of wild animal or something. I have no idea how that could have happened." Her entire face clenched and she began to sob.

Giles went to her side and put his hands on her shoulders. He looked tremendously uncomfortable, but his voice was comforting. "My apologies, Mrs. Kepley. We've bothered you too long, I'm afraid. We'll be going." He nodded at Buffy and she stood after one last sip of her coffee.

Mrs. Kepley put one of her hands on one of his. "Oh, but it was so nice of you to drop by. I hope you'll come back sometime. Maybe I'll be more cheerful. I usually am, you know." She laughed as she stood. "All the children in the neighborhood call me Grandma."

"Thank you so much for the coffee," Giles said.

"But weren't you going to ask some questions?" she asked Giles.

"You've answered our questions. Perhaps you should get some rest."

"Why, that's so sweet of you to think of me like that," Mrs. Kepley said, as she led them to the door.

They drove a few blocks in silence after leaving Mrs. Kepley. Then Buffy said, "Well, it's a shame . . . but it doesn't help us."

"We don't know yet. It might."

"So, what do we do next, Holmes?"

"Keep an eye on the news and see what details are available about the remains you saw last night."

"There was a meat cleaver beside the remains. And the blade was stained."

"Are you quite serious, Buffy?" Giles took his eyes off the road long enough to look at her.

"It was on the floor, near the . . . the . . ." She waggled her hand indecisively. "Leftovers."

"If you don't mind, Buffy," Giles said, "I would prefer to use the word 'remains.' "

After Giles parked the car at the school, they agreed to meet at lunch and went their separate ways.

"And go straight to class!" Giles shouted over his shoulder.

She did.

Chapter 10

EVER SINCE WILLOW HAD STARTED DATING OZ, cafeteria food always reminded her of horror movies. Not that the food was horrible; it wasn't great, of course, but it wasn't horrible. Willow and Oz sometimes watched horror movies together, and every time a slimy, disgusting monster appeared, or someone's face got ripped off, or someone's head exploded, they would point to the screen and scream, "Cafeteria food!" Now, every time she saw cafeteria food, she was tempted to point at it and scream, "Cafeteria food!" Or would it make more sense to point at the cafeteria food and scream, "Horror movie!"? She couldn't decide.

Willow left the line, carrying her tray of food, and joined Oz, Xander, and Cordelia at a table. Oz gave her a kiss on the cheek and it made her smile.

"You are so wrong," Xander said, pointing a finger at Oz. "You are the essence of wrong."

Oz said, "I'm going with the strength, rage, and desperation to kick some serious ass. She wouldn't stand a chance."

"Who wouldn't stand a chance?" Willow asked. "Doing what?"

Cordelia explained. "They're arguing over who would win in a fight, Alanis Morissette or Jewel. Can you believe it?" She sighed. "I've known rabid Xena fans who were less annoying."

"Alanis," Oz said.

"Just because Jewel is so delicate-looking," Xander said with a scoffing chuckle. "Beneath that waiflike exterior is a woman of tremendous strength."

"Alanis," Oz said again.

Willow said, "I lost interest in Alanis after she read her high school yearbook—or whatever that was—out loud and sort of put it to music but not quite."

"Jewel," Oz muttered to Willow, "sings her own poetry."

"Hey, I heard that," Xander said defensively. "Jewel is a very deep chick."

Cordelia laughed derisively. "Deep chick? You wouldn't know deep if somebody threw you into it."

"That's funny coming from the intellectual equivalent of the Grand Canyon," Xander said. "Great depth, very little content."

Cordelia's mouth dropped open as she turned to face Xander. "Little content? What's that supposed to mean?"

"You know, some shrubs here and there, maybe a few wild goats."

Willow sighed. *This is getting old.*

"At least I don't go around pretending to be something I'm not," Cordelia replied.

"Oh, like I do?" Xander asked. "What do I pretend to be that I'm not?"

"A biped."

"Hello, Willow."

Everyone looked up, including Willow, as Mila stopped at the table.

"You hadn't come to my office yet, Willow, so when I saw you here, I thought I'd give you this." She pulled an empty chair from the next table and seated herself beside Willow. From her purse, Mila removed a tiny red box and handed it to her.

"Thank you, Ms., I mean, Mila." She opened the box and removed a wad of tissue, which was wrapped around a miniature version of one of the statues she'd seen in Mila's office.

"My brother makes miniatures as well," Mila said. "You admired the statue of Rama in my office, so I thought I'd give you one of the little ones."

Willow was stunned by the intricate detail of the piece. It was every bit as vivid as the one she'd seen in Mila's office, only much smaller. There was a tiny loop atop the head for a chain.

"This is so beautiful, Mila! Thank you!"

"I thought it would make you smile. That's why I brought it." Mila stood. "Feel free to drop by the office, anyway."

Willow thanked her again, then Mila left. When Willow turned back to the table, still looking at her tiny gift, she lifted her head to see that Buffy had joined them. She sat across the table next to Xander, looking at the thing in Willow's hand.

"What's that?" Buffy asked.

"Oh, it's a gift from Mil—, Ms. Daruwalla." Willow handed the miniature to Buffy. "It's the Hindu god Rama. Her brother makes them. He's got, like . . . industrial-size talent. She has more in her office, and—"

"But why did she give it to you?" Buffy asked, frowning.

Willow froze. There was no anger or threat in Buffy's voice at all, it was just a simple question, but an iciness fell over Willow that made her feel defensive, on guard.

"*Because* she's a very nice person," Willow replied, "and *because* I was admiring the statues in her office."

"What were you doing in her office?" Buffy asked.

Willow took a deep breath, and when she spoke, a note of sternness crept into her voice. "She invited me in. We talked awhile, had some tea, and looked at her brother's statues."

"Oh." Buffy shrugged dismissively. "That's weird."

"What's weird about it?" Willow asked defensively.

"Well, I mean, what are you doing?" Buffy asked. "Becoming friends with the faculty or something?"

Willow felt her heart machine-gunning her ribs. "It just so happens that I think she's too cool to be faculty. And besides"—she stood and put the miniature sculpture in her purse—"maybe sometimes people have to look for friends in weird places, because the friendships they've already got have gone cold." Willow spun around and nearly knocked her chair over hurrying away.

"Hey, what's that supposed to mean?" Buffy called defensively.

Willow didn't reply as she crossed the cafeteria and pushed the door open hard with a stiffened arm as she left.

Oz scratched the back of his head and screwed up his face before asking, " Little too Waco?"

"What?" Buffy asked. "I was just asking. She was the one who went all Carrie."

"I think you're all weird," Cordelia said.

"By a show of hands, please," Xander said. "Who gives a monkey on a rock what Cordelia thinks?"

No one raised a hand.

Cordelia clicked her tongue and exhaled explosively. "You know, I don't have to sit here and take this."

"Oh, I know," Xander said with a nod. "You sit here and take it because you really like it." He grinned.

"That's it," Cordelia said. She scooted her chair back, stood, and picked up her lunch tray. "I'm going someplace where I can digest my food." Cordelia walked briskly away from the table.

Oz and Buffy stared at Xander as he resumed eating his lunch. Finally, he put his fork down. "Okay, okay, I'll go talk to her." He grinned at them both, picked up his tray, and followed Cordelia.

As Buffy watched him go, she said, "That's not a relationship. It's a two-person soccer-fan riot."

Oz took a bite of food, chewed it slowly, swallowed. "What's the sitch?"

She frowned. "What do you mean?"

"You've seemed . . . different lately. Willow, too. Both distant."

"Maybe it's the exams," she said with a shrug. "Or this thing that's eating the meat off bones. I don't know. I didn't realize I seemed any different."

Oz took a couple more bites of food and chewed fast this time. "I should go find Willow."

"Yeah, well . . . she needs a thicker skin, I guess."

Oz frowned as he pointed to Buffy with his fork. "That's what I mean."

The corners of Buffy's mouth turned downward very slowly as her eyebrows rose. She looked at the clock on the wall. "I've gotta go to the library and meet with

Giles. I just came here to pick up a portable lunch." She stood, but before she could say anything more, there was an explosion of sound on the other side of the cafeteria.

Buffy looked in the direction of the sound. Several people suddenly shot to their feet to get out of the way of something. A fight.

Oz stood in time to see a folding chair fly through the air and crash onto a table. A tight group of students scattered to avoid the chair as it skipped off the table and clattered onto the floor.

"One little mistake and you won't let me forget it!" a voice shouted. It sounded female, but it was so ragged with anger that it was difficult to tell.

Buffy and Oz moved toward the racket.

"One mistake?" another voice shouted back. This one sounded female, too. "You do it all the time!"

More crashing, a few startled cries from onlookers.

When they got a better view of the brawl, Buffy stammered, "Is that . . . no, that couldn't be . . . is it?"

Oz's mouth dropped open for a moment. "Get ready to believe."

Miss Gasteyer and Mrs. Truman, Sunnydale High School's two art teachers—their faces bloodied and hair splayed in all directions, Miss Gasteyer's fat bag swinging violently from her shoulder—were fighting with fists, feet, teeth, and nails. And if the animal-like savagery in their faces was any indication, they intended it to be a fight to the death.

Willow felt foolish the second she sat down in front of Mila's desk. Her throat stung from crying on the way to the guidance counselor's office and her cheeks were sticky with tears. She rubbed a hand downward over her face, then swept a knuckle across each closed eye.

"Willow, what's wrong?" Mila asked.

"I don't know," Willow replied with a sniffle. "I wish I did. I mean, if I knew, there wouldn't be anything wrong because maybe then I could fix it."

Mila leaned forward and locked her hands together on the desktop. "You seemed just fine in the cafeteria a few minutes ago. Tell me, Willow, what is the matter?"

"My friend," Willow said, trying not to cry anymore. "My best friend in the whole world, Buffy." She stopped to wipe more tears from her eyes.

"Have you two had a fight?"

"Well, that's just it. We haven't. But for some reason, it feels like we have. There's so much tension between us all the time. In fact, all my friends seem . . . well, preoccupied. But with Buffy, it's different. Worse."

"Perhaps they are all just concerned about the tests coming up," Mila said. She smiled encouragingly. "With that many tests all at once, most students tend to become preoccupied."

"That's what I thought at first," Willow said, nodding. "And that may be the case with the others. But with Buffy, it's something different. And what's worse is . . . well, I sometimes find myself . . . y'know, getting, um . . . getting really angry with her. Like just now in the cafeteria. She said something about the gift you gave me, and I snapped at her, and she seemed to get angrier, and . . . I don't know." She bowed her head and let more tears fall.

Mila took a tissue from an ornate wooden box and handed it Willow, who dabbed at her eyes, then blew her nose. She tossed the tissue into a small wastebasket at the end of Mila's desk, then stood.

"I'm sorry," Willow said. "For bothering you with this, I mean. It's silly, and I should probably—"

"No, no, Willow," Mila said. She stood, too, and came around the desk. Sitting on the front edge of the desk, she took Willow's hand in hers. "Nothing is silly that makes you hurt this much, so you mustn't talk that way. I'm glad you felt you could come to me with this. And I'm going to give you a piece of advice, so listen up." She grinned. "The only thing that will solve this between you and your friend is communication. You must talk to one another with no interruptions, with nothing to get in the way. You can do that whenever you wish, of course. But I think you should do it right now. Go back to the cafeteria, find Buffy, and go someplace quiet where you can talk. You've still got most of the lunch hour ahead of you."

Willow thought about it a moment, although she didn't really need to. She knew immediately that Mila was right. It wouldn't be easy, but she knew it was the only way to close the gap that had opened between her and Buffy.

Willow thanked Mila for talking to her, then headed for the cafeteria. She walked at a brisk pace, wanting to get it over with before she changed her mind or just plain chickened out. Things had become so tense between herself and Buffy that the idea of approaching her and asking to go someplace where they could talk was a bit unnerving . . . and the fact that they were best friends made that part, the unnerving part, disorienting, head-spinning. It felt so unnatural, so unreal to her, and yet it was very real.

As she neared the cafeteria, Willow frowned at the loud noises coming from inside. What sounded like cheering was accompanied by erratic clattering noises.

Something heavy slammed against the cafeteria's double doors; the safety glass in the left door shattered into tiny hail-like pieces and the leg of a chair appeared for just an instant, then fell away.

Uh, oh! Willow ran the rest of the way and pushed her way into the cafeteria.

A large group of kids were gathered in a semicircle, cheering and pumping their fists in the air. The broken door had brought an explosion of laughter from them, but their attention was not diverted for long.

They were cheering on a fight, and when Willow saw it, her eyes became almost as wide as her mouth. Miss Gasteyer and Mrs. Truman were fighting like a couple of punks in the street . . . and no one was stopping them! Mrs. Truman's left eye was swollen shut, Miss Gasteyer's lower lip was twice its normal size, and both of them bore bloody scratches and cuts on their faces.

Beyond the group of enthusiastic observers, Willow saw Buffy and Oz coming forward.

Miss Gasteyer got Mrs. Truman with a hard uppercut. Mrs. Truman's sensible shoes left the floor for a moment and she fell back onto a table. Miss Gasteyer grabbed something off the table, something shiny, and lifted it high, then brought it down.

"No!" Willow cried at the last instant.

Miss Gasteyer buried a fork halfway up the handle in Mrs. Truman's throat.

The second she saw the fork, Buffy yelled, "Stop her! Somebody stop her!"

But the students crowded around the two fighting women were too busy cheering and yelling to hear her.

Miss Gasteyer brought the fork down once, twice, a third time. As warm blood spattered from Mrs. Truman's gurgling throat and landed on some of the on-lookers, the voices died down. A girl screamed. Then another.

Buffy knocked her way through the crowd like a wrecking ball through an old concrete wall. By the time she got through, Miss Gasteyer was going out the door into the hallway. Buffy slapped a palm on the tabletop, vaulted over to the other side, and hit the floor running. Mrs. Truman was still alive on the table, but barely. Someone would try to help her, but Buffy knew they would not succeed. Blood spurted in rhythmic strings from Mrs. Truman's severed carotid artery, which Buffy knew could not be repaired.

She went through the doors and saw Miss Gasteyer nearing the corner at the end of the hall to her right, her bag slamming and rattling against her left hip as she ran. The woman disappeared around the corner in an instant.

Buffy ran at full speed. A couple of students—a confused-looking guy and a clearly annoyed girl—stood in the hall with their backs pressed to the wall, staring at the corner that Miss Gasteyer had just rounded. They turned to Buffy and watched her run by.

Buffy could hear Miss Gasteyer's running footsteps echoing away in the main hall around the corner. And something else . . . the jangling of keys. Half a second before she rounded the corner, she heard a door slam.

The hall was empty, which was typical at lunchtime. There was activity to be seen through the open doors of some faculty offices, but Buffy ignored it. That wasn't the kind of door she'd heard slam a moment ago. It was a heavier door, much more solid. She walked at a hurried pace, looking around frantically, then stopped in front of the stairwell. She turned around and walked back, slowly this time, and stopped in front of the door that led to the school's basement.

It was set back in a small rectangular niche, bathed in shadow. It was brown-painted steel, and it was locked.

But Miss Gasteyer might have a key, Buffy thought, remembering the jangle of keys she'd heard. She remembered the slam of the door, as well . . . solid, heavy, like this one.

As soon as Mr. Snyder heard of the soon-to-be broken basement door, he would no doubt find some way of tagging Buffy with it, and he would love doing it.

Buffy looked around to make sure she was alone as she muttered under her breath, "Oh, well, some things can't be helped."

Buffy slammed her foot into the door. The deadbolt gave, the door flew open and clanged into the wall on the other side. Buffy stepped through and quickly swung the door closed behind her. It wouldn't latch anymore, but she didn't have time to worry about that.

The temperature in the stairwell was cooler than in the hall, and it was darker than Buffy anticipated. She hadn't bothered to look for a light switch inside the door. At the bottom of the stairs, it was colder, but there was light coming from the other side of a tall set of shelves. She froze when she heard a sound and listened carefully.

It was more than one sound, actually. Somewhere, something was dripping steadily. A clock ticked. And something else, something wet and smacking and . . . was that a snarl?

Buffy started moving through the long shadows of the basement, following the sound.

Eating. Something was eating.

She moved faster, around the shelves, past several broken chalkboards leaning against a wall, around stacks of old wooden chairs with metal legs, past outdated classroom desks.

Slurping and sucking sounds and harsh, throaty grunting.

Sounds like more hellhounds.

Buffy tripped over several bright orange electrical cords and nearly fell facedown onto the concrete floor. She landed on her hands and knees, and her arms slipped into something coiled and pliable. She was in a dark shadow and couldn't make it out at first. Her arms were tangled in a long, coiled garden hose. Before she could start pulling her arms out, she realized the horrible sounds had stopped.

The wet chewing and grunting was suddenly replaced by rapid hissing whispers.

Buffy pulled and jerked her arms from their entanglements, got to her feet, and rounded another tall set of shelves. She skidded to a halt.

Overhead, two tubular flourescent lights glowed through an opaque plastic cover; one of the lights hummed and flickered. Buffy found herself in a corner that was blocked into a cubicle by the shelves. There were more cluttered shelves on the two cinder-block walls that met in the corner.

Something lay in the middle of the concrete floor within the makeshift cubicle. It was the remains of Miss Gasteyer. They hadn't quite finished with her. Nearly all of her body had been stripped of flesh, and blood dripped from her bare ribs. But most of the internal organs remained, and there was still skin on her fingers; her nails appeared to be clawing at the floor. The skin on her face and head was still intact, but her eyes were gone, and empty, bloodied sockets stared blindly upward.

Buffy looked around quickly: the shelves, the dark corner, the shadows, even the ceiling above the flickering flourescent light.

Where were they? They couldn't have gone out without getting past her. But the basement seemed to be empty except for Buffy.

She took two steps toward Miss Gasteyer and hunkered down to get a closer look. The woman's clothes were scattered over the floor in torn shreds. Her bag lay a couple feet away on its side, its contents spilled on the concrete.

They didn't get past me, she thought. *They're here. I can feel it in my*— She glanced at the skeleton, winced, then began to stand.

There was a rushing movement in the air and several feet hit the floor around her.

Small feet.

Children's feet.

Buffy rose to her full height and looked down on them, all six . . . no, all eight of them. Or were there more? They were dressed in blue jeans and polka-dot skirts and sneakers and pumps and a Daffy Duck T-shirt next to a *Jurassic Park* T-shirt . . . the way little kids dress. Except the small clothes didn't look right. They seemed to have no texture. It looked as if the clothes had been painted on the children's bodies.

They began to giggle, then laugh as they stared up at her.

They're not children! she reminded herself. *Now . . . hold that thought.*

Buffy spun around, kicked a leg up, and fell to the

floor with a gasp when her foot connected with nothing. They were gone. Just gone.

She got to her feet and stood tense, ready, because she knew they weren't really gone. They hadn't gone by her. Her skin prickled with the feeling of being watched. She knew they weren't children, but whatever they were, she would have felt them go by. She looked all around Miss Gasteyer's remains at the places where the children had been standing.

In the dark corner, the cinder-block wall rippled like the surface of a pond. The gray metal shelves did the same. No, that wasn't it . . . those things hadn't actually rippled. But something had moved.

There was a rush of movement in the air around her and colors and shadows blurred and blended like spilled drinks. Something bumped into Buffy on her right side, her left side, and she spun around twice before stopping to listen.

Footsteps ran through the basement, and children giggled. The sounds were getting farther away very quickly. Buffy ran after them, back around the shelves and past the desks and chalkboards and endless boxes, over the coiled-up hose without incident this time, and to the stairs.

She'd seen nothing coming back through the basement, hadn't even felt their presence. And she didn't feel it now as she stood at the foot of the stairs, looking around. Without waiting another second, she ran up the stairs and nearly pulled the already-broken door to the hall off its hinges on her way out.

There were several students standing around outside the door, talking quietly. Buffy looked in both directions for any sign of the . . . *What are they?*

Creatures, critters, beasties, monsters, whatever,

Buffy thought. *They're all under the same umbrella, and in the same Hellmouth town, of course.*

Buffy rushed to her left, toward the front of the building, looking for any sign of them. They were gone. And yet Buffy didn't feel they were gone. She stopped suddenly and ran a hand through her hair, frowning as she thought about those other students she'd seen outside the basement door.

Who were they? she asked herself. *Did they look familiar? I . . . I can't even remember their faces now.*

She spun around and ran back the way she'd come.

How did they get away so fast? she thought. *Did I really see them?* She knew she'd seen them. The fact that they were such a blurry memory convinced her of that. That was how they remained *un*seen . . . whatever they were.

As she ran down the main hall, Buffy looked around corners, peered into rooms and offices, but they weren't there. She ran back to the staircase and went up to the second floor to search for them. But she knew they were gone. She could no longer feel their presence. She returned to the stairs to head back down.

"Miss Summers."

Buffy froze on the fourth step down and turned around slowly.

Principal Snyder stood in the hall, hands joined behind him. He was wearing that reptilian look on his face: thin, tightly pressed lips pulled back into something that was supposed to be a smile; tiny, deep-set eyes staring flatly at her through glasses, all taking up surprisingly little room on that enormous, shiny head.

The vice principal, secretary, and two guidance counselors stood behind him, with worried looks on their faces. The secretary was crying.

"In case you hadn't noticed," he said, "this is the wrong building for physical education."

"Yeah, well, I'm in a hurry, that's all," she replied.

"In a hurry to your next class, I hope." He took a few slow steps toward her, stopping at the very top of the staircase until he was looking down on her. "I'm waiting for the police to arrive, but I would hate to learn at the end of next week you had failed any of your quarterly exams. I would feel somewhat responsible for not doing my part. Such as requiring you to repeat senior year."

The bell rang, ending lunch.

"Gotta run," Buffy said abruptly. "Don't wanna be late for class." *Not!* she thought.

He just stood there, watching her.

Sirens sounded in the distance.

Buffy turned away and hurried down the stairs. Snyder would love to see her flunk any or all of her exams. He'd eat it up like dessert. That started a nagging worry in her head. She hadn't studied as much as she needed to, and she'd missed some classes. And right now, she was about to miss, or at least be late for, another one. She needed those classes and more study time, but she didn't have time to stress over it.

Buffy needed to get to Giles and tell him what she'd just seen.

Chapter 11

THE CAFETERIA WAS QUICKLY CLEARED OUT AND THE police were called. Eyewitnesses were questioned in empty classrooms, including Willow, while Mrs. Truman's body was taken out to the coroner's van parked at the foot of the school's front steps. Willow told the officer everything she'd seen. It didn't take very long, but it felt like forever. Time had slowed to a crawl after Willow had seen that fork buried in Mrs. Truman's throat. It was vivid, but at the same time, it didn't seem real; it felt more like a sharp memory of something she'd seen in a movie a long time ago.

Snyder had reluctantly canceled classes for the rest of the day, and as soon as questioning was over, it was okay to go home. Willow felt nauseated as she went down the hall, hugging her books to her chest, head bowed. A door opened to her left, but she paid no attention to it until she heard Mila's voice.

"Are you all right, Willow?" she asked as she went from her office doorway to Willow's side.

Willow's eyebrows slowly raised high above her eyes in an expression of sadness and confusion. "Not now. But I will be."

Mila shook her head slowly, frowning at nothing in particular just to Willow's left. "Such a horrible thing. And I was just talking to them this morning. They seemed fine. No unusual behavior, no tension. And then . . . that happened." She shook her head again, then met Willow's eyes. "Have they found Miss Gasteyer yet?"

"Not that I've heard. There are still a lot of police here. I heard one say that her car is still in the parking lot."

Mila put a hand on Willow's shoulder and squeezed. "Listen, Willow, if you need to talk, don't hesitate to let me know. More counselors will be brought in tomorrow to meet with students, but you don't have to wait till then. You can call me anytime. I'm in the book."

"Thank you, Mila. I appreciate it."

"Hey."

Willow turned to see Oz approaching her with a couple of books tucked under his arm. He stopped beside her.

"Were you just questioned, too?" Willow asked.

Oz nodded his head. "You on your way out?"

"Yep." Willow turned to Mila, thanked her again, said goodbye, then she and Oz began walking together.

"Getting down with the faculty is a pretty serious offense," Oz offered in his low-key nonjudgmental way.

Willow heard him, but didn't reply. Instead, she whispered, as if to herself, "I don't know how Buffy deals with it."

"With what?"

"I don't know, the . . . y'know, the killing. The death. Or maybe . . . the undeath. In her line of work, I mean.

I guess it's different with vampires and demons. I mean, I've staked vampires and, no, it wasn't like seeing this. When I stepped into the cafeteria and saw that happening, it was like I couldn't scream loud enough. I couldn't scream at all. I'm still sick to my stomach. I guess Miss Gasteyer just ... I don't know, just snapped. Mila said they were fine this morning. I saw them and they were both smiling."

"Do you think this has something to do with Buffy and all the other strange stuff?"

"Oh, I don't know if it does or not. Do you think so?"

He nodded. "Two teachers who were right with each other get in a brawl? Fork in the throat? It's got Buffy written all over it."

Willow thought about it a moment. "You're right. I was so messed up from seeing it happen, it never even occurred to me to think about what it meant. Have you been to the library to see Giles?"

Oz shook his head.

"Then let's go. I wanna hear what he thinks of this."

They turned around and headed back the way they'd come.

"The Rakshasa," Giles said, sliding his glasses up his nose. He held a large, heavy book open on his arm; the edges of the cover were worn by age and use. "Often called Night Wanderers."

"That's a new one on me," Buffy said. There was interest in her voice, but weariness, as well.

"I've heard of them, but never dealt with them. They never occurred to me until just a little while ago."

When Buffy had arrived at the library several minutes ago, the halls outside had been eerily quiet. People were being gathered by the police to give their eye-witness accounts. Everybody who wasn't being questioned was wandering around in a kind of sickened daze, some laughing nervously, others whispering the details of the killing to one another as if they were telling dirty jokes.

She'd found Giles reading in his office and told him everything that had just happened, thoroughly but quickly.

Xander and Cordelia had arrived at the library a few minutes after Buffy, and had taken seats at the first table they came to.

"We figured when the weird stuff starts hitting the fan," Xander said, "this is probably the best place to be."

"You're the one who wanted to come here," Cordelia corrected him. "*I* wanted to go shopping."

Giles had brought his book out of his office. Buffy had been pacing when Giles paged through it to find a certain passage, but she'd stopped and faced him when he said the word "Rakshasa." She'd never heard of it before, but something about it made chips of ice skitter down her spine.

"What—or who—are they, Giles?" Buffy asked. "These Rak . . . Rak . . . shasta?"

"The Rakshasa," Giles repeated.

Xander said, "Sounds like a some new dance that would get old after about a week."

"There are many different kinds," Giles said. "Countless, really. Here." He began to read from the book. " 'They thrive on violence, division, and chaos. They take great delight in the brutal destruction of loving relationships, turning husband against wife, brother against sister, parent against child, friend against friend. They enjoy hiding in churches and turning people, particularly the clergy, away from their spiritual beliefs. When their work goes well, death is the result, with the Rakshasa eating the survivors. They also eat horses and cattle.' "

"Cattle," Buffy said, her eyes widening. "So the hell-hounds on wheels were just . . . a coincidence?"

Giles nodded, then continued reading. " 'The Rakshasa are shapeshifters and can assume any shape. Although not fond of great height, there is no limit to the Rakshasa's ability to mimic. One particular breed of Rakshasha, called the Pisacas, actually nests in a town's water supply and makes the locals waste away to skeletons ever so slowly, one person at a time.' "

"Shapeshifters!" Buffy exclaimed. "That's what those rugrats in the basement were. They . . . it's like they camouflaged themselves to blend in with the shelves and the cinder-block wall and they were right in front of me and I just couldn't quite see them."

"How many were there?" Xander asked nervously.

She walked over to the table and sat down with them. "It was weird. No matter how hard I tried, I just . . . couldn't . . . tell." Her right fist was clenched, frustration whitening the knuckles.

"Buffy, it's quite obviously not your fault," Giles said before reading more from the book. " 'The Rakshasa will use their shapeshifting abilities to attract food, hide from danger, or toy with humans. They are very intelligent, with an equally intelligent, if twisted, sense of humor. They draw strength as well as pleasure from the mayhem and chaos they create.' "

"How do we stop them?" Buffy asked.

Giles walked over to the table and set the heavy book down. "I only found this volume shortly before you arrived. I haven't gotten to dispelling and disarming techniques yet."

Buffy stood up and walked slowly around the table. "Why were those things down in the basement?" she asked, more to herself than to the others.

"Perhaps they saw Miss Gasteyer go down and followed her," Giles suggested.

Buffy nodded, thinking of the blurry teenagers she'd passed just outside the basement door. But the basement door had slammed only once, and Buffy had been only a few seconds behind Miss Gasteyer. Once the art teacher had gone through that door, no one else had gone in or come out until Buffy followed her. She stopped nodding and shook her head.

"Unless they can go through walls and doors," Buffy said, "they were already in that basement when Miss Gasteyer went down there."

Giles cocked his head. "Are you saying they were . . . waiting for her?"

"I don't know," Buffy said, throwing up her arms. "You're the one with the books, Giles. I just do the heavy lifting."

"Nonsense, Buffy. You're the Slayer. It is important for you to be able to think ahead of the problem and anticipate the next move of your adversary." He stepped closer to Buffy and closed the large book on the table. His voice was not quite stern, but there was urgency behind his words. "Your job is to extinguish these creatures and others like them, Buffy, but as you know, they seldom call ahead and make appointments with you so you can do that. You must use every resource at your disposal, including knowledge. The more you know about your adversary, the more powerful you are against it."

"Okay, then," Buffy said, folding her arms, "tell me what else I need to know."

Giles blinked several times. "Well, as I said, I haven't read much yet, you see, so I don't know—"

Buffy shrugged and said, "A lecture wasted."

"But there are things I can tell you." Giles went to the front desk and came back with the local paper. He put it on the table and pointed at it, as if it were guilty. "I read the story on Miriam Webber." He turned to Buffy. "She's the woman whose remains you saw through that window. The blade on the floor beside her had just been used by Miss Webber to kill one Miss Lena Tesich. Miss Tesich was in many pieces, and the cleaver carried Miss Webber's fingerprints alone."

"What did they have to say about Miss Webber's remains?" Buffy asked.

"Although Miss Webber is the prime suspect, the remains in her house have not yet been conclusively identified."

"So why are you so sure they are her remains?" Xander asked.

Next to Xander, Cordelia delicately filed her nails.

"Because Miss Webber and Miss Tesich have been friends since childhood," Giles said.

Buffy's neck felt stiff and she let her head roll around in a few slow circles as she massaged the back of her neck with her right hand. "You getting enough sleep, Giles? You're not staying up all hours watching BBC America on cable, are you?"

"Tom Niles and Delbert Kepley had known each other since they moved into neighboring houses more than forty years ago," Giles went on. "During that time, they and their wives were very close friends."

"Miss Gasteyer and Mrs. Truman were best friends

in college, and quite by coincidence ended up here, where they have worked together for almost twenty years without so much as a disagreement."

"Just like the book says." Buffy put it together. "They like to turn friends against each other and . . . then eat."

"That's what tipped me off to the Rakshasa," Giles said. "And it's valuable information, Buffy. You've just gone from knowing nothing about your adversary to knowing something that could enable you to prevent another killing. Or perhaps more."

"That's not really going to help," Buffy said, "until I know how they work, how they do whatever it is they do."

"Where do they come from?" Xander asked.

"They come from the mythology of the Hindu religion," Giles said.

Xander frowned. "You mean, Hindu as in . . . India?"

"Well, the religion itself," Giles said as he shrugged one shoulder, "is practiced all over the world, but yes, it originates in India."

Xander and Cordelia looked at one other for a moment, their eyes locked.

"What is it?" Buffy asked them.

Xander looked sheepish all of a sudden. "Well, I was thinking, um . . ." He turned to Cordelia, who rolled her eyes.

"He's talking about Ms. Daruwalla, the new guidance counselor," Cordelia said. She sounded as if she were explaining a dumb joke. "She's from India."

"What about her?" Buffy asked.

"Well, Willow's been spending a lot of time with her lately," Xander said nervously. "At least, it seems that way. I've seen them together a couple times. Willow came out of her office once, then Ms. Daruwalla came into the cafeteria today to give her that present."

"Present?" Giles asked. "What present?"

"I don't know, some little thing to wear around her neck, some kind of . . ." His nervousness faded and suddenly he looked genuinely concerned. "Some kind of . . . Indian god."

"Which Indian god?" Giles asked. The arm holding the closed book stiffened and pressed it closer to his side.

Xander slumped into his chair a bit. "I don't know," he said. "Really. I wouldn't know an Indian god from a Beanie Baby."

"It was carved by her brother, I think she said," Cordelia said quietly, more involved in her nails than the discussion.

Giles was paying no attention to them. He had the book open again and his eyes moved back and forth over the pages. "Whose brother?" he asked.

"Ms. Daruwalla's," Cordelia replied.

Buffy wandered over to a bookshelf with her back to the others, because she did not want them to see her face. Her teeth were clenched and her lips so tightly closed they were white. She did not want them to see her anger. It flared in her again and burned hot when she thought of Willow spending so much time with the new guidance counselor.

What is Willow up to, spending all that time with Ms. Daruwalla? Buffy wondered. High school students weren't supposed to hang out with faculty and/or staff between classes, it wasn't the natural order of things. *And, really, she should be* here *helping* us. The more she thought about it, the angrier she got, until she spun around and asked harshly:

"What does Willow think she's doing, hanging out with a guidance counselor?" She walked over to the front desk and picked up her books. With the books clutched to her chest, she walked back toward the others, her face dark. They watched her, puzzled. "It's like dogs mating with cats, or monkeys experimenting on scientists. It's upside down."

"Whoa, Buff," Xander said. "Your veins are showing. You look like that guy in *Scanners*. If your head's gonna explode, maybe you should go out in the hall."

Buffy propped a fist on her hip. "What's that supposed to mean, Xander?"

Xander's face wilted a bit, as if he were questioning the judgment of saying anything in the first place. "Well, it's just that you're . . . you're so . . . so tight, Buffy. You're about to explode into a bunch of Slinkies." He turned to Cordelia suddenly and leaned down to whisper in her ear. "That was a good one, remind me to tell that one to Oz."

"Well aren't you, Xander?" Buffy asked as he turned to her again. "These things are going around eating people. Doesn't that worry you just a little?"

"Sure it does," Xander said, nodding. "Most things worry me, it's a wonder I sleep at night. It just seemed you were a little overly upset about Willow seeing the most beautiful—" He gave his head a jerky shake. "Seeing Ms. Daruwalla."

Buffy walked over the to the table and dropped her books on it with a loud clap. "We should all be upset! Don't you understand, Xander, these things are Hindu. Ms. Daruwalla is probably the only person of Indian descent on staff at this school."

"Maybe so," Xander said. "But not the only one in school or in town."

Giles looked up from his book and said, "Buffy, that is a conclusion to which I do not recommend you jump."

"Such an economy with words, the English," Xander said to Cordelia.

One half of Cordelia's mouth curled into a sneer as she said, "Oh, what do you know, Metaphor Boy?"

"We don't know everything about these creatures yet, Buffy," Giles went on. "To attach Ms. Daruwalla to this so soon would be a dreadful mistake. She may very well be involved somehow, but no more so than anyone else at this point."

"Whatever," Buffy said quietly. She picked up her books. "I've gotta go. I want to study early so I can start patrolling early. It's a demonic jungle out—" Buffy turned toward the main doors and froze when she saw Willow walking slowly toward them, Oz a few steps behind her. There was a look of hurt on Willow's face, though she was struggling to conceal it.

"Giles, what were you saying? About Ms. Daruwalla?" Willow asked as she approached him.

"Hey, Willow," Xander said. "That's some kickass timing. Was there any magic involved in it?"

Surprised, Giles turned to Willow and closed his book. He tucked the book under his left arm and removed his glasses. His eyes were narrowed and crinkly in that way they got whenever he was concerned or worried. He was clearly concerned about how to tell Willow what he needed to tell her.

"Er, Willow," Giles said. "Come, uh, come have a seat." He gestured toward the table with his glasses in hand.

Buffy's head was bowed slightly and it didn't move, but her eyes followed Willow to the table and into a chair. *What a stupid thing to do,* she thought, the words hissing in her mind. *Getting friendly with a demon.* Her teeth crunched in her head like breaking concrete as her jaw ground them together. She'd been on her way out, but Buffy decided to stay and see what Willow had to say for herself.

Giles quickly told Willow everything they knew about the Rakshasa. At first, Willow's face wore an expression of great interest, but as Giles outlined the gruesome proclivities of the Rakshasa, her expression morphed into one of fear. When Giles mentioned the Rakshasa's origins in India, Willow's face slowly tightened in anger.

"So, exactly what are you trying to say, Giles?" Willow asked.

"I wasn't trying to say anything," he replied. "I simply wanted you to be aware of the facts we have thus far."

"Then what were you saying about Miss Daruwalla when I walked in?" Willow's voice rose slightly and became somewhat shrill. "That she might have something to do with this just because she's Indian?"

"No, not might. We were saying she *does*," Buffy said coldly. "Giles is just trying to be politically correct. What are you doing with this woman, anyway?"

Giles frowned as he turned to Buffy. "That's hardly relevant to—"

Buffy didn't let him finish. "I think it is. She gave Willow some kind of charm, didn't she? At least it looked like a charm." She turned to Willow. "So what's up with that?"

"It was just a gift," Willow insisted firmly. She stood and took slightly sidelong steps away from the table.

"You heard her. A tiny carving by her brother. He's a very popular sculptor in India."

"But why would she give you a gift? A guidance counselor? Giving a student gifts? Do you know how loopy that sounds? It's like Nazis trick-or-treating for UNICEF—it's too wonky for words." Buffy paced very slowly, going in the opposite direction of Willow's cautious sidestep, their eyes locked.

"I admired some of her brother's statues in her office," Willow explained, one fist clenched at her side, "so she gave me one of the miniatures he'd carved. That's all. There's nothing sinister about it."

"What were you doing in her office in the first place?" Buffy asked.

"She invited me in for tea."

"Oh, yeah, like that happens every day. I suppose when you get matching tattooes and start sharing an office, you'll say that's not weird and unusual, either."

Willow's mouth dropped open and she stopped moving. Buffy stopped as well, and they stared at one another across their imaginary ring.

Xander stepped forward, one finger pointing upward. "Overreacting for a hundred, Alex?"

"That's sick, Buffy!" Willow snapped. "That's just . . . stupid! It's nothing like that. I talked to Daruwalla because I needed to talk to someone, and that's her job."

"That still doesn't explain why she'd give you a gift."

Buffy and Willow moved straight toward one another as tension thickened the air in the library, slowly at first, but picking up speed. Buffy felt a tingling sensation in her shoulder, the voice of instinct telling her to start swinging.

Giles stepped between them abruptly. "Are you two ladies getting quite enough sleep?"

They froze, but glared at one another unflinchingly, just a few feet apart.

"We simply want you to be aware, Willow, of a possible relationship between Ms. Daruwalla and the problem at hand. Not likely, mind you . . . just possible." Giles turned to Buffy. "And Buffy, I must insist you stop referring with such conviction to a relationship we do not yet know exists."

Willow made a startling sound—a sob that managed to claw its way out in spite of her efforts to hold it back—as she spun around and swept her books up off the table. She stalked to the front of the library. "I can't believe you'd think that about her," she said angrily through her tears. She stopped for a moment and looked back at them. "Did it ever occur to you maybe she's just, like . . . a nice person?" Willow looked directly at Buffy. "You don't know what I needed to talk to her about, and you don't care. Jeez, you . . . you've been chasing monsters so long, you're becoming one, Buffy." She continued walking, but faster now.

Buffy's eyes widened. "What is that supposed to mean?"

Oz jogged up behind Willow, reaching her just before she got to the door. He put a hand on her shoulder.

"Not now," Willow snapped, jerking her shoulder away.

Oz stopped and watched her leave the library. He turned to Buffy with a serious look and went through the door after Willow.

"I suddenly feel like I'm in the wrong neighborhood," Xander said quietly.

Giles said, "Buffy, was that entirely necessary? If you know something I don't, I want to hear it."

The vicious anger was no longer trembling just beneath her skin and filling her throat with heat. It seemed to fold in on itself, getting smaller and smaller. Like that house in *Poltergeist*.

"What. Ever." She almost shouted the second word. She got her books and headed for the door.

"Buffy, where are you going?" Giles asked.

"I have work to do," she said stiffly over her shoulder. She was gone.

Giles felt a tightening in the back of his neck. It joined the tightness that already existed in his shoulders. But it was especially prominent in the frontal lobe of his brain, around which he was developing a quick headache. He knew what was causing it, though.

He was worried about Buffy and Willow. Their behavior had been uncharacteristic. It could, of course, be caused by any one or two of the dozens of problems teenagers faced every day, but he was not certain, and that was what worried him.

Tom Niles and Delbert Kepley, Mrs. Truman and Miss Gasteyer, Lena Tesich and Miriam Webber—all of them such good, longtime friends, so close they probably knew everything about each other. *But did they know something was wrong before the killings? Were there signs of trouble before the end? Or did it happen suddenly and without warning, that change in a person, suddenly deciding to kill someone you love? Actually doing it in some horrible way, and then running off and hiding in a place where you are . . . eaten.*

Giles rattled his head a little to shake it of the mental imagery. Oz was with Willow. He was a smart boy, but would he see the possible connection between the work of the Rakshasa and the sudden animosity between Buffy and Willow? He just might. Buffy, on the other hand, was alone. *I should have warned them,* Giles thought.

"Xander, could you go find Buffy?" Giles asked. "I'd like you to stay with her for a while."

"Stay with her?" Xander asked. "Uh, I don't know . . . she didn't look like she was going out to find company when she left here, Giles."

"This is important, Xander. I'm afraid Buffy and Willow may be in trouble."

Giles said firmly, "So far, three people have been eaten by the Rakshasa. But don't forget those same three people first killed their closest friend for no apparent reason. You saw the way Buffy and Willow just behaved. I'd like you to keep an eye on Buffy, Xander."

"Uh, wait, whoa, hold on." Xander scooted his chair back and stood. "Let's say something is wrong, that it's got something to do with those Roxannes, or whatever you call 'em. What if Buffy doesn't want an eye kept on her? I mean, don't forget, she's a Slayer, y'know?"

"What are you afraid of, Xander?" Cordelia asked, unable to keep a crust of contempt off her words.

He walked slowly around the table. "You wanna know? Huh? Okay, I'll tell you, if you wanna know." His head dipped a couple times, as if he were swallowing pills dry. "I'm afraid of Buffy getting worked up by them and taking it out on me, that's what I'm afraid of. I mean, you've seen her in action, right? She'd put me in a coma, I'd wake up just in time to have a mid-life crisis."

"Please, Xander, just do the best you can," Giles said. "I'd go myself, but I must continue reading.

Knowledge is a great weapon, and at the moment, we're virtually unarmed." He opened the book again and turned toward the front of the library.

"What am I supposed to do?" Cordelia asked.

Giles turned back to her with a momentary look of confusion. "Whatever you like, I suppose."

She thought about it a moment. "I'd like to go dancing."

"Sounds delightful, Cordelia, enjoy yourself," Giles said as he walked hurriedly to the front desk and went into his office.

Cordelia stood and took her purse and books off the table. "You have no idea how happy it makes me to know that I'm not needed around here. If I was, it would be, like, I'm one of you, or something, and then I'd have to hang myself from a ceiling fan." She turned to Xander. "Well, in spite of your lameness, I guess I'll go with you. Just in case you need some protection."

Chapter 12

THE DARKNESS AROUND BUFFY BREATHED, EVEN THOUGH the things inside the darkness did not. Dogs barked up and down the street, some forlornly and some with a viciousness typically reserved for certain marauding neighborhood cats. A car alarm went off somewhere. Glass broke in the distance. Sounds that were normal, sounds that even in the dark of night were probably nothing to worry about. But she could not be sure.

Buffy ignored them. They were distractions. She listened for the sounds beneath them, the sounds that hid between other sounds. And they were everywhere. Buffy considered herself a veteran when it came to patrolling. But she'd never had a night like tonight.

Some were just coming up out of their graves when she found them, and others dropped down out of the trees. But it wasn't just their activity that bothered Buffy. They were getting very bold.

The first ones Buffy had encountered that night had

been wandering along the sidewalk, peering into mail-boxes and then crushing them and knocking them into dark yards. A male and female appeared out of the misty darkness, their dark clothes crusted with mud and bits of grass, the ridges and creases of their vamp faces perfectly etched in deep shadow and the slightly yellowish glow from the streetlights above. They'd been so busy laughing and talking and looking into mailboxes before the strutting guy knocked them off their posts that they hadn't noticed her at first. "You expecting a package?" Buffy had asked before rough-ing them up and sending them on their way with a couple quick sticks of the stake.

The cemeteries teemed with them. They gathered in alleys and whispered their secret plans as they licked the remaining smears of blood from their teeth. But they walked the streets, too, as if they planned to do some shopping or had just gotten out of a movie, fangs glimmering wetly as they tilted their heads back and laughed or grinned dangerously. And none of them flinched when she brought out her stakes, as if their confidence were great enough to steady their gaze and ease their minds.

It's like vampire's night out, Buffy thought. She imagined a sign at the city limits: Vampire nite! No cover charge for vampires! Bring your mummy and get a free Bloody Mary!

But it wasn't funny. Something was up.

Could they know about the Rakshasa? Buffy won-dered as she crossed the street to the next cemetery's pedestrian entrance on the other side. *And if they do, how much do they know? Maybe I should start quizzing them before I stake 'em.* She shook her head slightly. *Mmm . . . nah.*

The cemetery's pedestrian entrance was a regular-size doorway in a large, ten-foot-tall stone wall.

Buffy froze a few feet from the stone doorway. She heard a soft, gritty sound above her, the sole of a shoe on wet cement. Half a heartbeat later, the sound was behind her. Buffy spun and threw herself toward the sound, punched, and connected with a flat stomach that gave way beneath her knuckles.

A sound burst from Xander like a tuba dislodging an obstruction as he stumbled backward and landed on his butt on the sidewalk.

Buffy and Cordelia rushed to him from different directions and knelt on either side of him.

"Xander!" Buffy said with a horrified squeak in her voice. "I'm so sorry! When did you get so quiet?"

"He usually never shuts up long enough to be quiet," Cordelia muttered.

Xander groaned and leaned forward with his arms crossed over his belly.

"Jeez, I'm glad that wasn't any harder," Buffy said.

"Harder?" Xander barked in a voice like grinding metal. He tried to say more, but gave up and went on groaning.

"Don't you dare throw up on me," Cordelia said sternly.

A minute or so later, Xander's breathing had stabilized and he was able to talk without sounding like the emergency brakes on a train. "I'll speak up next time," he said. He got to his feet slowly and walked in a circle, trying to straighten his body out.

Buffy heard the sound again—shoes crackling grit against a surface of concrete or stone—overhead. She looked up and took a stake from beneath her jacket almost in the same second.

A female hunkered atop the stone wall, hands dangling between her knees, fangs bared in a broad, black-lipped grin. Then she was a blur, coming down at Buffy.

Buffy took half a step back and plunged the stake forward the instant she heard the feet hit the sidewalk. The female was vaporized before she could make a move, or even a sound.

"C'mon, let's get away from this zombie Holiday Inn, okay?" Buffy said. She walked fast across the street and Xander and Cordelia tried to keep up. Xander was still hunched forward slightly and held a hand to his stomach, but he didn't lag behind.

"Are you late for a very important date?" Cordelia asked.

"I don't want to be so close to the cemetery if you're here," Buffy said distractedly. She looked over her shoulder at the cemetery across the street. "Too much activity. I can't be expected to talk to you guys and battle the Denizens of Hell, can I?"

A low rattling sound came from up the sidewalk—the plastic rumbling of a Big Wheel being driven by a child.

Buffy stopped and turned around. "Look, Xander, I'm really sorry I hit you, but what are you doing here, anyway?"

"We came to see how you are," he rasped out.

"How I am? You mean . . . as in, 'Hi, how are you?' "

The Big Wheel got closer, louder.

"Giles was worried," Cordelia said, then turned to Xander. "And I'm getting soaked from this drizzle. Can we go now?"

"Worried?" Buffy asked. "About me? Why?"

"You weren't exactly happy when you left," Xander said. "Giles was worried and concerned."

Another sound joined that of the Big Wheel as it drew closer: wet breathing, like a child with a cold trying to breathe through his nose.

"Look, I don't have time to talk now," Buffy said. "Go home. You hear me? It's dangerous out here. I'm not kidding."

The plastic wheels grew louder, the wet breathing became a snarl, and Buffy turned toward it as it launched itself out of its wobbly vehicle. Cordelia screamed as a round, childish, bat-like face with a runny nose swallowed up her field of vision.

Buffy's arm snatched out, her hand closed around the throat, and her body absorbed the impact as she brought the creature to a halt. The toddler's inhuman eyes glared at her as its tongue peeked out between its fangs.

"Way past your bedtime," Buffy said as the stake went in. The vampire child shrieked and became a part of the night. The Big Wheel bumped into Cordelia's leg and she kicked it aside with her foot.

"Look, kids, I'm serious here, okay?" Buffy said with no humor. "Go home. It's not safe to be out tonight. It's like it's getting worse every night." Her eyes darted all around Xander and Cordelia, looking for the slightest movement as she listened intensely for sounds from behind her. "If Giles wants to worry about anybody, he should worry about you guys."

Xander frowned. "Hey, what's going on? Is it that time of the month for the undead, or what?"

Buffy turned around slowly, watching, listening, her expression grim. "From what I've seen so far, I'd say they need to switch to decaffeinated. It's almost like they know something that's made them pretty sure of themselves."

"You think they know about the Racketeers?" Xander asked.

"You mean the Rakshasa?"

"What about them?" Cordelia asked.

"Do the vampires know anything about them?" Xander asked again, frustrated.

"Oh," Buffy said. "I don't know."

"No, they don't." Angel's voice came from Buffy's right.

She turned to see him coming from the darkness of a yard with a For Sale sign on it in front of a house with no curtains hanging in its dark, empty windows. He joined them on the sidewalk.

"Hey," Angel said.

Xander nodded once, but Cordelia's face brightened. Buffy watched Cordelia look Angel over as if she were considering bidding on him.

"Hi, Angel," Cordelia said with a bright smile.

Some people never learn, Buffy thought.

Angel focused on Buffy. "They don't know anything the way you're thinking of knowing. But they—we—sense something. A shift of something."

"What are you—" Buffy stopped and coughed dryly to clear her throat. Every time Angel looked directly into her eyes and spoke to her in that quiet, level voice, her own voice gave out on her like a bad lightbulb. "What are you talking about, Angel? A shift of what?"

He shrugged faintly and his eyes narrowed slightly. "A shift in the balance of power, maybe. Or maybe a shift in you."

Buffy felt her heart pierced, as if by one of her own stakes. "Are you saying I've gained weight?"

"Buffy, I'm being serious," Angel said.

"You think I'm joking here?" Buffy asked. "What do you mean?"

"Look, Buffy, you're not focused."

"What?"

"They do know," Angel went on. "You're not focused. You're spreading yourself thin because of those killings, or maybe because you've got personal stuff on your mind. But they sense your distraction and they're taking advantage of it."

"Meaning?"

"Meaning you need to solve your other problems so you can focus on your work."

Buffy sighed. "I have to do everything around here." She turned to Xander and Cordelia. "Why are you still here? Why aren't you on your way home?"

Xander spoke in a mocking, childish voice: "Can we stay up and watch Letterman, Mommy?"

Buffy rolled her eyes. "Do whatever you want. Just do it someplace else, okay? I've got vampires to take care of." She turned and headed back across the street to the cemetery's entrance.

Angel walked at her side. "Need a little company?"

"A little company?" Buffy chuckled. "Tonight I could use a whole multinational corporation."

At home, where Willow should have been studying, she was instead silently traveling the endless highways, biways, and subways of the Internet. Ninety minutes ago, she had typed "Rakshasa" into a search engine, and she'd been busy ever since.

There were countless Web sites that mentioned or made brief reference to the Rakshasa, but few with any of the real information she needed. So she'd gone to a

Web site she visited frequently called, Gods, Demons, and Mortals. It was a poorly laid-out site with text that tended to ramble, apparently manned by a single person who referred to himself only as Metaphysical Phil.

Willow had exchanged e-mails with him a couple of times. He was an old hippy who spent most of his time on the road in a motor home with his wife—known only as She, practitioner of a cross between Wicca and some kind of transcendental aerobics—traveling the country in search of things to add to their already enormous collection of supernatural lore, much of which was for sale in Phil's online store.

Phil once wrote in an e-mail to Willow, "The Internet is like a worldwide Woodstock for all the misfits and outcasts on the planet; only instead of mud we've got comfortable seats, and instead of bands we've got bandwidth, and instead of sex and drugs, we've got . . . well, sex. Sort of." Willow stayed off the Internet for days after that.

Metaphysical Phil might not know much about creating an attractive and organized Web site, but it turned out he knew a whole lot when it came to the Rakshasa. Willow read from the monitor as she printed.

The text included links that led to more text. She found everything Giles had told her easily enough, but there was much more. The Rakshasa had a king who, like them, was a shapeshifter, but a shapeshifter that was not like them at all. The king of all Rakshasa was named Ravana, and his shapeshifting powers were limitless. He could take the form of a large piece of granite jutting up from the earth, or a storm cloud in the sky, or a tuft of woodsmoke curling upward in the distance. He could create enormous storms at sea and tear a mountain down with his bare hands.

"Not that big a trick if you've got twenty hands," Willow muttered at the screen.

Ravana had ten heads, twenty arms, and twenty eyes that burned like the hottest fires. In the accompanying illustration, his thick neck sprouted a carousel of heads that allowed him to see in all directions at once. The arms extended from all around the upper body, ending in powerful-looking, black-clawed hands.

If he started spinning around, Willow thought, *he'd look like some kind of way-creepy carnival ride.*

Willow remembered Mila mentioning Ravana, but couldn't remember in what context until she read further. The stories of Ravana all intertwined with the stories of other Hindu gods, weaving a sprawling tapestry of interconnected tales of vengeance, love, betrayal, death, and sometimes murder among gods and demons.

Ravana gained his power through thousands of years of poverty, self-denial, and meditation. When he'd gathered enough power, he went to Brahma—one-third of the Hindu Trinity and creator, with his daughter Vak, of humankind—and asked for the boon of immortality. Brahma refused at first, but was willing to negotiate. Finally, Brahma decided to grant Ravana protection from all the elements, which made him, if not immortal, then virtually indestructible. There was one thing, however, from which Ravana did not want to receive protection. Because he felt such contempt for them and thought them to be less significant than the smallest fly humming around him, he left himself vulnerable to human beings.

Being indestructible made Ravana a boastful tyrant, and he expected women to fall at his feet, swept away by the very sight of him. When they did not, he dragged them by the hair to his harem, where they were forced to live only to please Ravana. When she got to Ravana's encounter with Rama, Willow put her hand to her chest and fingered the small hand-carved Rama beneath her shirt, hanging from a delicate silver chain.

Mila kept coming to mind as Willow read. She did not want to consider even the possibility that Mila was involved somehow with the killings in town, but she couldn't avoid it. It gave her slight feeling of nausea that made her nose wrinkle and her upper lip curl unpleasantly.

Rama, a mortal, was a god incarnate. He was a great hero whose exploits were renowned, and he was happily married to the beautiful Sita. Ravana, an indestructible demon who even had a flying chariot, was never content and always hungered for more of everything. His envy of Rama had long ago turned to a burning hatred after years of fantasizing about how he could reduce Rama to nothing and take all he had. When Ravana heard that Rama had encountered and insulted Ravana's own sister (who was skanky in ways only the sister of a demon could be), he decided it was time to make his fantasies real.

Ravana kidnapped Sita, dragging her back to Lanka by the hair in his flying chariot. No matter what he did, no matter what form he took or what he said, no matter if he was kind and charming or showed her the storming, shrieking monster he was, Sita resisted him. Given Ravana's tremendous powers, Willow assumed that meant Sita was pretty damned strong herself.

"You go, girlfriend," Willow muttered.

Rama went on a long journey and faced many perils to search everywhere for Sita, and it finally ended on the island of Lanka. But to get to Ravana and Sita, Rama first had to pass through a vast forest that was alive with Rakshasa. That last stretch of the journey was a daunting experience, even for Rama, but he got through the forest and confronted Ravana with his bow and arrows. It was a gruesome battle, with a good deal of bloodshed and a lot of disorienting and frightening shapeshifting. Rama's arrows struck, but were pushed back out by Ravana's indestructible body. Finally, Rama used an arrow that had been crafted by the god Vishnu and carried his power, thus fulfilling a prophecy that Ravana would be defeated by a mortal.

Of course, that wasn't the end of Ravana. Nobody ever just died in Hindu mythology; they came back again and again.

"So what're the Rakshasa doing in Sunnydale?" Willow mumbled to herself. She clicked on a link to an illustration of the Rakshasa.

The confused, dreamlike illustration looked as if the artist had been unable to decide exactly how to draw the creature. It was short and squat, dwarflike, and wore a long cloak that concealed its limbs and body. A lizardlike face peered out from the cloak's hood. Small but elephantlike earflaps hung from the sides of its overlarge head. Just above each slanted, bloodred eye was a small nub that came to a rounded point; it took a moment for Willow to realize they were horns, like cow horns just beginning to sprout. It almost looked as if the creature were smiling, with the tips of razorlike fangs visible over the lower lip.

Something about the illustration gave Willow an icy chill. She stared at it intensely. She felt almost as if the creature were . . . familiar. That was ridiculous, of course. She knew nothing of Hindu mythology and was sure she had never seen anything like the Rakshasa on the screen before her. But still . . .

The Rakshasa were the minions of Ravana, feverishly devoted to his every whim. They did his bidding without question or hesitation, killed for him, sometimes died for him—and apparently they still managed to find the time to eat a few dogs or a horse now and then.

So, if the Rakshasa are Ravana's posse, Willow thought, *then why isn't he here with them now?*

"Maybe he is," she replied to herself with a chill down her back.

Willow read through more text, more stories of curses and conquests, and found a list of links to other Ravana-related Web sites. She clicked on one called Abyss. The link took her directly to a page within the site, rather than going to the main page first. In ornate gold letters at the top of the light-blue page were the words "Resurrecting Ravana." The black text below was about that very thing—bringing the demon back to life.

Willow felt the slight nervous tremble she felt whenever she found something important. This felt very important. She started the printer, then read from the screen. Her shoulders drooped and she sighed heavily a moment later, when she read that the most important element in raising the Hindu god had been lost.

Nothing could be done without the Ravana statuette. No one knew how old it was or where it had come from, but for something so enigmatic, quite a bit was known about it. The statuette stood a little over two feet tall and was said to be carved from the bones of some of Ravana's countless victims. It allegedly contained the essence of Ravana, a living force waiting to be reborn. But that rebirth could not be accomplished without the Rakshasa.

Six smaller pieces symbolizing the Rakshasa had to

accompany the Ravana statuette. For the resurrection to be completely successful, the Rakshasa had to be summoned first. They moved ahead of their lord and master and prepared for his arrival by sewing seeds of paranoia and suspicion in the immediate area. It was said that their very presence, known or unknown, could have a powerful negative effect on the emotions and behavior of people in the surrounding area. They stirred anger and turned hearts cold. They turned people against one another, turning love into anger, anger into hatred, and finally hatred into murder.

"Yeah!" Willow exclaimed at her laptop. "That's what we've got! They're here already!"

What started out small after the arrival of the Rakshasa grew into chaos, which was precisely the goal. Ravana stepped with ease into that environment of hatred and murder, and in his presence, it grew. Ravana's new rule spread out around him with the help of the Rakshasa, and before long, Ravana's new kingdom would be complete, built on the blood and bones of the human race.

"But what's the point of ruling if you're just gonna trash the place?" Willow asked herself at a whisper. The next line she read served as somewhat of an answer to her question:

"Ravana rules in chaos, but it is his own chaos."

Willow waited for the printer to finish. Her hands were trembling again. She'd been right the first time; the information she'd found was important. It meant—at least, to Willow—that someone was trying to resurrect Ravana . . . if they hadn't already. They'd gotten at least halfway through the process, because the Rakshasa were active in the town already.

Was it possible that Mila had something to do with

it? That she was involved? She understood why Buffy was so certain that Mila was the source of the problem. It was so obvious, such a natural conclusion to reach, but Willow couldn't believe it. Even when she tried, she could not buy it. Giles had said it was only a possibility, but even that was too much for Willow to accept. She tried to see their side, and she could see it, but it didn't alter the gut-level trust she had in Mila.

Willow pulled the chain out from beneath her shirt and looked at the tiny figure of Rama that Mila had given her. Was her blind certainty a sign that Buffy was right? Had Mila done something to her? Cast some kind of spell on her? And did it have anything to do with the little stone Rama? If so, then why Rama? He was benevolent, beloved, a hero, a godlike man, the guy who got all the prettiest and most popular girls. If Mila were going to do something bad to her, why would she use the star quarterback of Hinduism to accomplish it? It didn't make sense.

There was always the chance, of course, that Mila knew absolutely nothing about the whole thing, and would laugh hysterically if Willow told her.

The Ravana statuette and accompanying six Rakshasa pieces had passed from hand to hand over the centuries. They had been owned by royalty and stolen by common thieves; people had killed and died for them, and they left a path of blood and madness wherever they were. There were periods of decades when no account could be made of the Ravanna statuette's whereabouts, and then it would turn up in a prestigious museum or in the hands of some prominent collector. It was last seen in a museum in London, from which it had been stolen, around the turn of the century. It had not been seen since.

Someone had found it, though. And for some reason, they had brought it to Sunnydale. Willow clicked on a link to a picture of the statuette. It was a copy of an old black-and-white photo that had yellowed and creased and lost a corner. Little detail could be made out, but what was obviously the statuette stood with three Rakshasa on each side, all seven figures dark and grainy, as if hiding in the shadows.

As if waiting.

She felt a chill on her neck and shoulders and broke out in gooseflesh.

Willow needed to take what she'd found to Giles. But she couldn't do that until she'd put her own mind at ease about Mila. If Willow was able to stumble over some doubts, then she would be irresponsible not to consider it a possibility, at least. But she felt confident enough to ask Mila to her face. Even though it was late, Willow decided to get a telephone directory and find Promila Daruwalla's address, then go knock on her door.

If her new friend was trying to resurrect an ancient Hindu demon that was going to spread mayhem and chaos from Sunnydale to the four corners of the globe, Willow wanted to find it out for herself.

Chapter 13

BUFFY AND ANGEL APPROACHED A CONVENIENCE STORE. Angel waited outside while Buffy went in. Inside, the store was like a flourescent bath with awful music. A boombox behind the counter played the deafening white noise of some skater band that probably had a sick name. The clerk sat slumped on a stool, head hanging forward over an open magazine on the counter. There was a dark-haired guy wearing a long black coat in the corner hunched over a pinball machine, his whole body jerking as he hit the bumpers. The machine's backboard was entirely made up of a demon's red, horned, grinning face. Each time a player lost a ball, the demon's eyes glowed green and the mouth opened and closed repeatedly as a deep, hellish laugh made the whole pinball machine tremble.

Buffy hated the machine instantly. It gave her the creeps. Of course, all convenience stores gave Buffy the creeps. The unnatural light with its grating, gnatlike hum, and the shelves of junk food . . . fake food, filled with all kinds of chemicals and preservatives, stuff that would survive a nuclear war without even glowing. Buffy saw something sinister in their cases of fake drinks with fake sweeteners and fruit slooshies in cups the size of milk buckets.

Maybe it was just so normal she found it jarring. Buffy hadn't been on very good terms with "normal" in a long time.

She grabbed a bottle of diet cola, a package of Twinkies, despite all their accompanying chemicals and carcinogens, and went to the counter.

The pinball demon in the corner roared with laughter.

The clerk did not move when Buffy put the soda and Twinkies on the counter. He remained staring down at the magazine, the top of his head covered by a red uniform cap with a yellow bill. His hands were palm-down on the magazine.

Buffy reached over and nudged his arm.

The clerk slowly slumped forward and Buffy pulled her hand back just before his head clunked onto the counter. The red cap came off, tumbled over the counter and dropped to Buffy's feet. The clerk landed facedown, and when Buffy leaned forward slightly, she could see the ragged fang marks in his neck.

The demonic laughter stopped. The pinball machine did not ring or buzz or play any explosive sound effects.

Buffy turned just as the vampire in the long black coat reached her, clamped a hand on to her neck and pressed his thumb into her throat. He smelled of mud and decay. She crushed his nose with the soda bottle in her hand; it hit the vampire's face so hard that the glass, thick as it was, shattered and cola sprayed in all directions. With a sharp movement of her forearm, Buffy fractured his elbow with a loud crack and bent it backward. The vampire did not make a sound, but it loosened its grip on her throat.

Her fists closed over the lapels of the black coat and she swung the vampire around hard. He crashed into the counter and she pushed him onto his back. The clerk's body slid backward and dropped to the floor in a heap on the other side of the counter. Buffy reached under her jacket for a stake.

There were no stakes.

She punched the vampire in the face a few times when he tried to sit up, setting off his broken nose. It just pissed him off.

There was a cup by the cash register stuffed with pens and pencils and a couple fat magic markers. She pressed her right hand to the vampire's chest and reached for the cup with her left.

The vampire knocked her right arm away and clutched her left elbow.

Buffy closed her hand on something—a pen, a pencil, she couldn't tell—just as the vampire bent a knee back to his chest and slammed his foot into Buffy's chest and kicked outward. Her feet left the floor for an instant and she crashed into a lottery scratcher machine. She grabbed the magazine rack to keep from falling, but he was on her before she could recover fully.

He hauled Buffy up by her jacket and slammed her hard against the scratcher machine, pressing his body against hers. Her left hand was pinned between them, so even if she was lucky enough to have grabbed a wooden pencil, she couldn't use it.

Buffy did two things almost simultaneously. She

smacked her forehead into the vampire's forehead, shot a knee between his, curled her leg around his, and twisted powerfully. When his head dropped back in response to her headbutt, and his body started to twist away from her, Buffy raised her left arm and brought it down fast, without even looking to see what she held in her fist.

The tip of the Number 2 pencil snapped at first when it hit his shirt, but the rest of the pencil went in, anyway.

The vampire collapsed in a cloud of dust and disappeared just before landing on the *Weekly World News* rack, where headlines warned New York City of a coming ratboy invasion.

How did I lose track of the number of stakes I had? Buffy wondered, angry at herself. She pushed the glass door open hard as she hurried out of the store, thinking out loud. "Shit! How could I not have any stakes?"

"What took you so long?" Angel asked. He was standing by the ice freezer, swallowed in shadows.

"Vampire," she said, picking up her pace. He joined her and they started across the small parking lot. "They're getting their food at convenience stores now. If this keeps up, they'll be running for political office by Monday. And I can't believe I'm out of stakes! What kind of brain-freeze was that?"

They were on the sidewalk, putting the store behind them.

"You're bound to use them up faster than usual with all this activity," Angel said. "And with all this activity, it's not a good idea to be without stakes."

Before Buffy could respond, she saw headlights up ahead, growing closer, and heard an engine get louder. It was the same gleaming white limousine she'd seen the night before.

The back window on the passenger's side lowered slowly. The black glass peeled back over a long dead-white face wearing silver-rimmed reflective sunglasses. The face seemed to hover there without a body, or even a full skull . . . just the face, held up by the thick darkness inside the car. Hidden eyes latched onto them and the face turned to watch them as the limousine passed.

Then it was gone. But Buffy and Angel stared after it.

"You seen that limo around here before?" Buffy asked.

"No. You?"

"Yeah. That guy, did he look at all suspicious to you?"

"He looked dead."

"That's suspicious in my book." Buffy started walking again, but stopped abruptly. "Wait, where are we? What's closer, my place or the school?"

"We're closer to the school," Angel said. "You think Giles will be there this late?"

"What, you think he goes out dancing, or has a social life or something?" She turned around, took Angel's hand, and started walking. "C'mon, let's go see."

By the time Buffy and Angel headed for the school library, Giles had already left.

Even Watchers had to eat, and that meant an occasional trip to the grocery store. Giles shopped when it occurred to him or whenever the refrigerator yawned emptily at him like a cold, white coffin, whichever came first. Sometimes that meant shopping late at night, while most people were home watching the local news. Fortunately, there was a twenty-four-hour supersize grocery store in town that fit his erratic schedule perfectly. The only thing Giles didn't like about the store was the way the clerks asked you if you had a club card. They pushed it aggressively and were always trying to get him to sign up for one. Giles never did. He'd have to show his card each time he bought groceries and it would be a nuisance, like some kind of ridiculous scene from an old World War II movie, with Nazis asking to see his papers.

Ven ve see zat your pay-pers are in order, Mr. Giles, ve vill release you. Or . . . mebbe not! Heh-heh.

Giles sighed and shook his head. He was doing a German accent in his head. He decided he was tired.

The right front wheel of Giles's grocery cart kept trying to lead him in the wrong direction as he pushed it up one aisle and down the next. He had no list, although he knew he was out of milk and bread, which usually meant he'd be needing everything else, too.

Giles rounded a corner a little too fast and collided with another cart.

"I beg your pardon!" he exclaimed, pulling his cart back.

The other cart was being pushed by a beautiful redhaired woman, tall, about Giles's age. She pushed the cart around his and came up beside him in the opposite direction. She paused as she smiled and looked directly into his eyes. "No problem at all," she said, and he could hear the smile echoing in her voice.

Giles did a double take as he pushed his cart forward, because she was still looking at him, still smiling. He almost flinched, but then took a moment to return the look and the smile before moving on. He kept smiling for a while, though; it felt good to know he still had a bit of . . . something in him.

He was openly flirting with total strangers. Giles decided he was much more tired than he'd thought.

Although he did all his grocery shopping at that particular store, Giles was never able to find everything he wanted. Each time he came, he couldn't be more lost if the store changed its layout daily. His mind was always on other things, in other places. Worrying about Buffy, more often than not.

Giles turned down an aisle and spotted the back of a man leaving the aisle at the other end. Something about the figure, or perhaps the movement, had looked familiar enough to make Giles frown. It looked like the man was wearing a very expensive Italian suit. Giles took a can of coffee from the shelf, put it in his cart, and followed the faceless man.

He turned right at the end of the aisle. The man was up ahead, a couple aisles along. He passed the meats and seafood before turning down another aisle. The walk, the rigid posture . . . it was too familiar.

He stopped in his tracks and shivered involuntarily. What was Ethan Rayne doing in Sunnydale? Nothing good, no doubt, but what?

Giles turned down the same aisle. Rayne was up ahead, perusing the shelves of bottled water. Was he stocking up for something?

Giles had found in his line of work that there were moments when he wanted to claw at his hair and scream at the top of his lungs, "Everybody freeze and nobody move until I've figured out what the hell is going on here!"

This was one of those moments. First mutant hellhounds and slain cattle eaten to the bone, then people killing each other and getting eaten, the Rakshasa, not to mention some rather odd behavior from Buffy and

Willow, who had always been such close friends, and now Ethan Rayne, dressed to kill and buying bottled water shortly before midnight. And that suit—it must have had a formidable price tag. Rayne was a sharp dresser, but certainly not rich. At least he hadn't been the last time Giles had seen him.

Rayne turned to him and smiled, as if he'd known Giles was there all along. "How very domestic of you, Ripper. Shopping for groceries."

Giles did not return the smile; his lips remained a straight, tense line until he spoke. "What brings you to Sunnydale, Ethan?" he asked very quietly, using his deadly serious tone of voice to cover his underlying concern. The two men had known each other long enough for Ethan to respond to the tone as well as the words.

"Nothing. Just passing through," Ethan replied smugly. He went on scanning the shelves of bottled water, almost as if Giles had walked away. "This just happened to be a convenient place to stop." He chose two bottles, turned to Giles with one in each hand, and smiled again. "You know how I feel about tap water. Especially in roadside motels."

"I would think you could afford the very best of accommodations," Giles said. "From the looks of you." Giles sounded a bit distracted, because he was; there was something wrong with things, something more than Rayne's mere presence. He looked at the plastic bottles Rayne held. His fingers were hooked through the handles and the label was tilted downward, so Giles couldn't make out the brand name, but he could see it was distilled water.

Rayne tilted his head back a bit, evened his shoulders and said, "Yes, Giles, I've done quite well for myself, thank you."

Giles's eyes narrowed slowly. "And how have you managed that?"

Their eyes remained locked for a silent moment. Rayne was unsmiling, serious. "Love, Giles. That's how." A grin exploded on his face. "I fell in love."

Giles stared at Rayne's back as he walked away without another word. *Ethan Rayne? In love?* It was almost enough to make him laugh out loud. But he didn't laugh because he was too busy wondering why Rayne had told him that. It didn't make sense. And of course he wasn't just passing through—Rayne didn't just pass through anywhere.

He tried to conceive of a connection between Rayne and the Rakshasa, but reminded himself that he and the others did not know everything about the Rakshasa themselves yet. He needed to go home and start absorbing some of the information in his books.

Giles dumped the can of coffee and other items into a nearby pretzel display and headed for the door.

"Willow, what are you doing out so late?" Mila asked. Her apartment door was open a crack and she peered out between two chain locks. She had to raise her voice to be heard above the rain, which had started coming down in great sweeping sheets just a few minutes before.

"Oh, it's not that late," Willow said quietly. "Is it?" She stood on the covered, second-story concrete walkway, but it was too late for shelter from the rain to do any good because she was already wet from head to toe. The umbrella Willow carried had worked at first, but when the wind came along, it couldn't protect her from the blowing downpour.

"I'm watching *Politically Incorrect* That's late for

a school night." She closed the door and the chains rattled inside before the door opened again. "Come in, come in." As she closed and locked the door behind Willow, she asked, "Is anything wrong?" She took Willow's closed umbrella and leaned it beside the door.

"I just had to . . . I'm sorry for coming so late, but I . . . I just had to talk to someone. No, to you."

"Come sit down." Mila led her across the small living room to the sofa. "I was just having some tea. Can I get you some?"

"Oh, yes, please."

"Did you walk here? You're all wet."

"It's not that far from my house, really. It was only drizzly out when I left the house, but a couple minutes ago, I don't know, a cloud ruptured, I guess, and it started to pour."

"Go into the bathroom and get a towel, dry yourself off. First door on the left down the hall."

It was a small apartment, but felt roomy in spite of its dimensions. A bar separated most of the kitchen from the living room, and as Mila went around it to get Willow's tea, she gestured toward the hall to her left.

In the bathroom, Willow found a towel in the cupboard and scrubbed her hair dry. She dried her neck and arms and dabbed uselessly at her clothes. She took the towel with her when she left the bathroom . . . and she froze in the hall.

The door to the room across from the bathroom was wide open and a lamp glowed on a nightstand beside a queen-size bed. In the corner, on a stand all its own, stood a statue, four feet tall, maybe taller, but made to look even taller by the height of the stand beneath it.

Willow couldn't make sense of the statue's shape at first, and went to the open doorway to get a better look, then stepped inside the bedroom. The lamp didn't give much light and the shadows in the corner were deep, but the statue appeared to be of some kind of tree, with branches oddly placed and curving in all directions. But the top part didn't look right. She moved closer, squinting to make out details, to pull the shape together.

She stumbled to a halt when she made out the face, and straightened up with a quiet gasp. There was another face . . . and another . . .

Willow didn't have to count them to know how many there were. It was no tree, and those weren't branches.

A click from behind her bathed the room, and the ten-headed creature before her, in light, and the face looking directly at her with needle-fangs bared, looked about to stretch out and bite off a chunk of flesh from her body.

Willow screamed at the large statue of Ravana, and spun around.

"What's wrong, Willow?" Mila asked with surprise, concern, and a little fear in her voice.

It felt as if somebody had dumped a bucket of icewater into Willow's stomach, and the chill spread outward through her body. The statue didn't mean anything, not a thing, but just the same, Willow wanted to jump out a window as fast as her mind jumped to conclusions.

"Are you all right?" Mila asked as she rushed toward Willow and reached out to put a hand on her shoulder.

Willow pulled her shoulder away as she took a step back. "Don't touch me," she breathed. She was surprised she'd said it out loud, but she was so frightened that she'd been unable to keep the thought to herself.

Mila looked very worried. "Please tell me what's wrong, Willow. What can I do? Should I call your parents?"

"Oh, no, that's okay, I was just startled by the, um, statue." She pointed a thumb over her shoulder. "I wasn't snooping, or anything, I just—"

"Of course you weren't," Mila said with a little laugh. She was more at ease now. "Most people who pass my bedroom feel the need to come inside and inspect the statue."

"Ravana," Willow whispered as she turned around and looked at the monster.

"Yes, that's right! How did you know?"

"I've been doing some reading."

"It took my brother almost two years to complete it. He's made many since then, most with far more intricate details. But this was his first, and he gave it to me. He likes to experiment on me," she said, chuckling.

Willow turned to her again. "Have you ever heard of something called the Ravana statuette? It's centuries old and comes with six smaller figures, the Rakshasa."

Mila went to her bed and sat on the edge of the mattress. "Such statues are very common in India. You could probably find dozens like them in the markets. They're everywhere."

"Not this one." Willow sighed and looked around the room. There were small statues on every shelf, even in the bookcase headboard.

"Tell me about it."

She stopped pacing and faced Mila. "It's supposed to be made of the bones of some of Ravana's victims and it contains his essence."

Mila frowned. "Are you serious?"

Willow bit her lower lip nervously. Either Mila was going to think she was crazy or she was going to want to get rid of her. She nodded.

An uncomfortable silence rose between them for a moment.

Then Mila laughed. The laugh burst out of her explosively, as if she'd been trying to hold it in. "I'm sorry, Willow, I'm not laughing at you. I just . . . I am surprised to find that you believe in Hindu mythology."

"But I . . . I thought it was a religion."

"It is a religion. It just doesn't happen to be my religion."

"You're not Hindu?"

"Much to the chagrin of my parents, no, I am not. I have all these statues of Hindu gods and demons only because my brother made them and gave them to me. He is a devout believer, and I think the things he carves are beautiful, but I do not believe in any of the gods or demons they represent. I suppose you could call me an atheist with a Hindu background." She smiled, but her smile melted when she saw the way Willow was staring at her.

Willow's eyes were wide and her jaw slack. "You mean you don't believe in any of it?"

"No."

"So, if I told you that the Ravana statuette is supposed to be able to resurrect Ravana, you wouldn't believe in that, either?"

Mila laughed. "No, of course not."

"And you don't believe that the Rakshasa could be revived, either?"

"No. Why?"

Willow sat beside Mila on the bed. "So you'd never try to resurrect Ravana and the Rakshasa, because you don't believe in them?"

Mila laughed so hard she fell back on her bed, and so long that tears rolled from her eyes. "Of course not!"

she said, her words coming sporadically through her laughter. "I would do no such thing!"

Relief rushed through Willow. Mila couldn't possibly be involved in the killings if she didn't even believe in the very creatures doing the killing. Unless, of course, she was lying. But Willow couldn't believe that. Mila could not have faked so much genuine, teary-eyed laughter.

So Mila was okay, but now she thought Willow was a lunatic.

"I hope I haven't offended you by laughing so hard at your questions," Mila said as she wiped leftover tears from her eyes. "But you caught me off guard, Willow. What on earth would make you ask such things?"

Willow ignored the question and stood, saying, "I've really gotta go." She headed for the door.

"Wait, wait!" Mila called, getting off the bed and following Willow. She laughed a little more as she followed Willow through the hall and to the front door. Still smiling, Mila asked, "Aren't you going to tell me why you asked those questions?"

"Well, as a story, Mila, it's a bit longish."

"You're not going to go back out there, are you? Let me put on some clothes and drive you home."

"No, I'll be all right," Willow said. She opened the door and looked outside. "See? It's stopped." She smiled. "I'm really sorry for bothering you so late."

As Willow started down the walkway, Mila leaned out the door and called after her. "But what about those questions you—"

"It's really not important, and I'm late already. I'll see you at school tomorrow."

Willow hurried down the concrete stairs and to the sidewalk in front of the building. She stopped and looked in both directions, trying to work out the shortest route to the closest telephone, which was in front of the Handi-Spot Market. She would have used Mila's, but Willow wanted to be able to speak freely to Giles.

The rain that had fallen so violently earlier had been reduced to a weak but chilling sprinkle; the moisture formed a thin mist that floated through the glow of streetlights like a ghost. But lightning flashed in the distance, followed by a muted crack of thunder. It could start pouring again any second. That didn't matter.

Willow turned right, and at the corner of the block, she made another right.

She didn't want to wait until tomorrow to show Giles everything she'd found on the Internet, especially now that she could tell him Mila was not a part of their problem.

At least two blocks ahead of her was a group of people walking in her direction in the middle of the road. Caught between the streetlight overhead and its reflection on the wet pavement, they were black figures that melded into one single shadow.

Just to be safe, Willow crossed to the other side of the street.

Giles's mind was preoccupied, but he was paying enough attention to his driving to notice the group of pedestrians that suddenly stepped into the intersection from nowhere as he passed through a green light. He slammed on his brakes and the Citroen DS wobbled, nearly going into a swerve.

The pedestrians were dark figures that stood motionless, living shadows in the intersection, faces shrouded by darkness until the last instant, when Giles's headlights flared in their faces.

The sudden light glistened on their saliva-slick fangs and created shadowy lines where their batlike faces creased.

There were five of them, two males and three females, but Giles's car struck only one of the males. He flew over the hood and slammed face-first through the windshield, which broke into a million tiny sparkling pebbles, and landed on Giles. The vampire's clawed hands clutched Giles's shoulders and pressed him hard against the back of the seat. The car jerked to a sudden uncomfortable halt as Giles put all his weight on the brake pedal, and the engine died.

The vampires outside closed in on the small car in a semicircle while the one inside grinned at Giles.

"You should watch where you're going," he said, his breath like warm, rotting meat in Giles's nostrils. He slapped a hand over Giles's forehead and pushed his head back as far as he could, then opened his mouth and leaned toward Giles's exposed throat.

Chapter 14

No SELF-RESPECTING WATCHER WOULD LEAVE THE house without at least one stake on his or her person. Giles was no different. He usually kept a stake or two in each of the side pockets of whatever tweed jacket he was wearing, and there were always a few in his briefcase. As the vampire pressed Giles's head back to expose his throat, Giles calmly removed one of the stakes from his pocket.

The creature opened its mouth, bared its fangs to bite, and Giles stabbed the stake upward, into the vampire's chest. Into its heart. The vampire vaporized just a couple inches from Giles's face, causing a stir in the air that he felt on his cheeks.

Giles sat up, but the back of the seat remained where it was. A male and female grinned at him through his side window. The other two females stood in front of the car, giggling.

"Car trouble?" the male vampire asked with a deep, stupid-sounding laugh.

Giles jerked his head back reflexively when the vampire put a fist through the window, then pulled it back out. Giles turned the ignition key and gave the old machine a couple pumps of the gas pedal. The engine started, and Giles was about to run over the two vampires in front of the car. It wouldn't kill them, but it would mess them up for a little while, long enough for Giles to drive on, because he just didn't have time for them. But before stepping on the accelerator, he heard a familiar voice.

"Giles!" Willow called.

He looked out the broken window, and he could see Willow up the street, running toward him. He could see her because the vampire that had been standing at the window an instant ago had turned to look at Willow as well. The vampire released a low growl of pleasure as it watched Willow get closer.

Giles moved quickly, stake still in hand. He pushed the car door open and swung both legs out, about to get up and out of the car.

"You just stay where you are," the vampire said. He stabbed an elbow backward, directly into Giles's face.

Giles was unconscious before his back hit the seat.

"What's going on?" Angel asked, as they walked toward the school.

"Exams are next week. I'm not ready for 'em. Nothin' new there."

"How's your mom?"

"Oh, she's got some weird woman driving her crazy to exhibit some collection she's got." Buffy frowned and stopped walking.

They'd encountered several vampires on their way to the school. If Buffy hadn't climbed a tree and come down with several thick, broken branches with sharp ends, they would've had no weapons. She was tired and hungry and just wanted to go home, eat something, and go straight to bed.

"What's the matter?" Angel asked.

"That's Giles's car up there!" she said. She broke into a run and Angel followed her.

Giles's car was parked in the middle of the intersection, headlights on, driver's door open. Two figures were moving toward the door while two others struggled several feet away. A scream cut through the quiet night, and Buffy recognized it immediately: Willow

Buffy's teeth clenched as she picked up her pace and thought angrily, *Just what am I supposed to do now?*

Willow was fighting her assailant's embrace, screaming, jerking her body back and forth. Finally, she brought her knee up hard between the vampire's legs and broke away from him when he doubled up in pain. Willow backed away several steps, but turned and ran when the vampire recovered and lunged after her.

"Hey, fangboy!" Buffy snapped.

The vampire stopped and looked at her, then smiled and turned his whole body toward her as she quickly closed the gap between them. He smiled lewdly.

Buffy drove the broken branch into his heart without even a few seconds of violent preamble, and pulled it out to use again. She was already on her way to the Citroen, branch still clutched in her fist, when the vampire disappeared into fading dust.

Holding the branch between her teeth, Buffy grabbed the heads of two of the vampires and pulled hard. Caught off guard, they both flew backward and landed roughly on the pavement.

Giles's legs dropped out of the open door where they

were standing and his feet hit the road, while his torso was still propped up on the car's seat. He was unconscious. At least, Buffy hoped he was unconscious . . . and not dead.

She saw the stake in his hand, leaned down, and snatched it up. She spun around and sent it home into one of the female vampires, who was just about to pounce on her. The vampire was gone in the blink of an eye and Buffy looked around for the others, whom Angel had already taken care of. The only other person she saw was Willow, jogging toward her.

Angel was already on one knee beside Giles as Buffy came over and knelt at her Watcher's side.

"He's just unconscious," Angel said.

Giles's eyes snapped open wide for a moment, then narrowed to a wince as he tried to get up. Angel helped him to his feet, then Giles leaned against the car and covered his face with a hand.

"Good Lord, my face hurts," Giles rasped in a rough, dry voice.

"Giles, I'm out of stakes," Buffy said. "Can you believe that? I mean, it's like vampire rush hour in this town. I've gotta go to the library to get some more."

"I . . . I still feel dizzy," Giles said. "I don't think I should drive."

"I can drive," Willow offered as she joined them. "If there's room for me?"

Buffy didn't answer, nor did she look at Willow. She suddenly felt tense.

"Of course, Willow," Giles said, walking slowly and cautiously around the car.

Willow hurried to Giles's side. "What happened?"

"Well, if I remember correctly, I assaulted a vampire's elbow with my face."

Buffy leaned into the car and pulled the seat back into its upright position, then scrambled in to the back and looked up at Angel. "You coming?"

"No, you go ahead. I'll see you later."

"Okay."

Willow started the car.

"I'll be back out in just a few," Buffy said.

No one spoke during the short drive to the school. The small car felt smaller and more uncomfortably close than usual. Buffy was overly aware of Willow sitting in the front seat and it made her tense. It made the air tense.

"What's that you said about a statuette?" Giles asked. He was seated at a table with them in the library, three large, fat books stacked in front of him. He still had not recovered thoroughly from his encounter with the vampire.

Willow had called Oz as soon as they got to the library and told him to come over. He'd arrived minutes later with Xander.

"It's needed to resurrect Ravana," Willow said. She walked slowly around the table, where she'd put her bag upon arriving. She was too nervous to sit still, too suspicious of Buffy to stop watching her carefully. Willow didn't know why she felt that way, but it wouldn't go away. The only light was provided by the table lamps. The rest of the library was dark.

Willow told them all about the statuette and the six smaller Rakshasa figures.

"Wait," Giles said, gently rubbing the side of his face. "The Rakshasa are already here."

"That means someone has already started summoning the demon," Xander said uncertainly. "Um . . . right?"

"Somewhere here in Sunnydale," Giles whispered. "But where? And who?"

Buffy pushed her chair back and stood as she said, "Well, I'm drawing a big blank on the where part. But I don't think the who is such a big mystery." She looked at Willow for a brief, cold moment. "Is it?"

"Hey, Buffy," Xander said quietly, cautiously.

"Buffy!" Giles started. "I think you're both being affected by the Rakshasa. It's—"

"That's the other thing I wanted to tell you," Willow addressed her friend, ignoring Giles. She stopped walking and leaned her hands on the tabletop, glaring at Buffy. "Promila Daruwalla is not involved in this. She's not even Hindu! She's an atheist. She doesn't believe in gods, singular, plural, or otherwise. Mila couldn't possibly be doing this."

"That's what she told you?" Buffy asked. Her voice trembled with anger and she could feel her heartbeat in her throat. It was unnerving, completely out of her control, and growing worse. "And you believe her, of course."

"I'd be an idiot not to believe her," Willow said. "And if you'd been there, you would've believed her, too."

At that moment, Buffy stopped noticing her building anger, and instead fell into it. It swallowed her. Suddenly, there was nothing other than the anger . . . and Willow across the table from her. Her vision blurred slightly as the whispering voices from her dream hissed in her mind, but clearly now, not muddied by memory, but as clearly as if she were having the dream while wide awake . . .

She's the part of your life that doesn't work . . . a draining force, taking and taking from you . . . never giving back . . . a stone around your neck . . . sucking your energy, your goodness, your life force from you like a vampire sucks blood . . . emptying you . . .

Willow heard the voices, in her head and her heart.

The shadow that darkens your life and stunts your emotional and social growth . . . the source of all your problems . . . the cause of all your trouble . . . you never got in trouble in your life before you met her . . . your life was calm and ordered . . . then she came . . . and brought trouble, problems, chaos, evil . . . she is what is wrong with your life. So kill her. Kill her. Kill her. Kill her.

Willow found herself mouthing the words silently, along with the suddenly clear voices reciting them in her mind. *Kill her.*

Adrenaline hummed beneath her skin, and a feeling of great excitement swelled in her chest. It was not a bad feeling. Not at all.

Willow picked up a chair and lifted it over her head, where it collapsed into its folded position.

Buffy was already on her way across the table when Willow threw the chair. The rounded metal edge of the chair's back hit Buffy in the forehead. It knocked her off the table, and skittered over onto the floor.

Willow saw nothing but Buffy on the floor, trying to get up. She heard nothing but Buffy's groans of pain. To Willow, there was nothing, and no one, else in the room. Just Buffy, and those two words.

Kill her. Kill her.

Kill her. Kill her.

The hissing voices remained unfazed by the pain in Buffy's head. But the pain did not go away, either. For a moment, the library darkened and Buffy thought she was going to lose consciousness, but that passed. The pain remained. It swirled in her head, pressed on the backs of her eyeballs, oozed into her ears and made them ring like cathedral bells. She struggled up onto her side, then onto her feet, but swayed with a fit of dizziness. When the dizziness subsided, Buffy lifted her head just in time to see Willow diving at her from the table.

Xander and Oz had already shot to their feet as Giles shouted, "Girls! Stop this!"

Buffy stretched out both arms, caught Willow, and threw her aside. She slammed into a couple of empty chairs, but was back on her feet in a heartbeat, coming for Buffy with teeth bared.

Giles still felt a bit dizzy when he stood, but his pain was forgotten as he watched Buffy and Willow fight. His heart thundered in his chest and his throat tightened with fear, because he knew Buffy would kill her and he was beginning to understand why.

Buffy punched Willow in the face so hard, Willow collapsed to the floor like a sack of laundry. Buffy pounced on her like a cat on an old, tired mouse. Straddling Willow, she raised her fist, and brought it down fast and hard on Willow's face once, then again. She put both hands on Willow's neck and pressed hard with her thumbs on her throat. Willow moved slowly, but raised her hands and clamped them on to Buffy's throat, doing the same to her. Gurgling sounds came from their blocked airways, but they did not stop, or even weaken their grasp on each other.

Xander and Oz closed in on Buffy, one on each side, grabbed her arms and tried to pull her off Willow. With a sweep of her arms, she knocked them off her like a couple of pesky flies. Xander slid across the table and knocked over a chair on his way to the floor, and Oz slammed his back against a large shelf of books with a pained grunt.

On the floor beneath Buffy, Willow gagged as she tried to fill her lungs with air as she continued to choke Buffy.

Her face turning red, Buffy grasped Willow's wrists and jerked her hands away from her throat. Gasping for breath, she raised her fist to continue beating Willow, whose lower lip and left cheek were already swollen and bleeding.

"Buffy!" Giles shouted. He lifted one of the fat, heavy books on the table before him and threw it down hard on the tabletop. It made a thunderous sound that was followed by Giles's angry cry: "Buffy, stop it!"

Buffy froze. Her fist was over her head, ready to strike again. She slowly lifted her head and looked up at Giles, her face a mask of pure murderous hatred. Her fist lowered very slowly and Giles went to her, pulled her to her feet, and led her around the table and away from Willow.

Oz knelt beside Willow, who was coughing and gagging as she gulped in deep breaths, dazed but conscious, bleeding but not seriously injured. After a moment of staring up at him with wide, confused eyes, Willow's face pulled together in an angry sneer as she sat up and growled, "Where is she?"

"Hey, hey, why don't you leave the wrestling to the professional fakers, huh?" Oz said as he pushed her back down to the floor.

Giles took Buffy to a chair and pushed down on her shoulders until she finally lowered herself into it. Her eyes looked at nothing in particular, as if she didn't even notice him there, and she whispered something to herself repeatedly, something Giles couldn't quite make out. At first, it sounded like she was saying, "killer . . . killer . . . killer," but when he leaned forward, Giles heard her words clearly:

". . . her . . . kill her . . . kill her . . . kill . . ."

"Buffy," Giles said, kneeling in front of her. He clutched her shoulders and shook her hard. "Buffy, listen to me, look at me, Buffy!" Her eyes slowly made their way to his. "Buffy, it's the Rakshasa. It has to be. They've done this to you, they've gotten to you." He continued shaking her, making her head flop forward and back. "Whatever's going through your head right now, you must fight it! Reject it, Buffy! Do you hear me? Buffy? Do you hear me?"

Confusion and anger bled from her face and her eyes widened slowly, darted around frantically, until settling on Giles.

"Giles, I . . ." She winced and touched her forehead gingerly with four fingertips. A sizable lump was developing.

"One of my books claims that the very presence of the Rakshasa can adversely effect people in the surrounding area. Their personalities, their behavior," Giles said.

Buffy covered her forehead with her whole hand and closed her eyes.

Giles continued: "I'm certain that is what happened to you and Willow. It was the—"

"Oh, my God," she interrupted, speaking the words in a breath.

"What?"

"The nightmares."

Giles frowned. "What nightmares?"

"I've been having nightmares. Except . . ." She shook her head slowly, wincing again at the pain in her head. "I don't think they were nightmares at all."

"Willow mentioned something about having nightmares." His frown deepened as he turned his head away and muttered to himself, "Why didn't I listen?"

"Willow." Buffy stood, unsteady at first, then stepped forward.

Giles put a hand on her shoulder to stop her. "Are you all right now, Buffy?"

"I can still feel it," she whispered. "Not as strong as before, now that I know what it is, but . . . it's still there." She made her way quickly around the table.

Oz and Xander were kneeling on either side of Willow, holding her down. She was struggling and saying something through clenched teeth. Buffy knelt down next to Xander. Willow's right eye was wide, almost crazed, but her left eye was puffy with swelling and turning the color of a banana going bad. She was growling hatefully, "Kill 'er, kill 'er," over and over, condensing it into one word.

Buffy leaned over Willow and said, "I'm sorry, Willow, I—"

Willow became even more enraged and spittle flew from her mouth as she repeated the two words louder, spitting them at Buffy. Xander and Oz were finding it difficult to hold her down as her body bucked and her legs kicked.

"Willow, listen to me," Buffy said, leaning closer. "This is not you! It's the Rakshasa, they've . . . they've . . ." She stood suddenly and looked around at the surrounding darkness in the library. Stepping away from Willow, Buffy listened closely to the darkness.

Something . . . movement? The quiet, coarse sound of something being dragged over the carpet?

"Buffy, what is it?" Giles asked.

Her posture stiffened and both fists clenched at her side as she recognized another sound: the sibilant, whispering voices she'd heard in her nightmares. Staring into the darkness she said, "The Rakshasa. They're here with us. Right now."

Buffy walked to the edge of the light, paused, and continued into the darkness. She passed an aisle of books, and another, a third. Buffy stopped. Peered into the deepening darkness of the fourth aisle. Something was at the other end of the aisle, deep in the darkness where she couldn't see. It moved.

"Somebody turn on the far lights!" Buffy called as she reached beneath her coat and removed the stake she'd taken earlier, in the street, from Giles.

The movement grew closer, louder. Something was running through the dark toward her, something that made a wet, panting sound, almost like forced laughter.

"The lights, over in the far corner!" Buffy shouted.

Fluorescent lights flickered on as a dwarf-size creature with red eyes, razor fangs in a lizard's snout, and a fleshy pink tail released an earsplitting shriek as it jumped for Buffy's throat.

Chapter 15

BUFFY PLUNGED THE STAKE INTO THE CREATURE'S small, round, gray-skinned belly. Its small red eyes bulged as its snout opened wide. A black, narrow, forked tongue fluttered between two curved rows of small shiny fangs as it screamed in pain. Its breath was a foul mixture of fecal matter and rotting meat.

She shook the thing off the stake and it fell to the floor facedown, its pink, ratlike tail swiping back and forth furiously.

Buffy looked around for more, but turned her attention back to the floor when the creature rolled over and hopped to its feet. A viscous, yellowish-green substance dribbled from the hole made by the stake, but not for long. The hole made a sucking sound, pulling the slime back in, then closed up and disappeared, as if it had never been there.

She didn't wait for it to make another move; she kicked it in the belly and watched it roll clumsily back down the aisle. Buffy followed it, caught up with it, and stomped a foot on it.

Vampires have spoiled me, she thought as she got down on one knee, took her foot off the creature, held it down with one hand, and stabbed it repeatedly. The Rakshasa did not disappear in an explosion of dust, which was what Buffy had grown accustomed to in dealing with vampires. She wasn't even sure if they died, but she didn't stop to find out. She continued stabbing the small, vile creature with the stake until it stopped squirming and kicking its short, stubby legs. With the stake poised to strike again if necessary, Buffy watched the creature.

It decomposed rapidly, seeming to melt into a thick puddle of yellowish-green goo that made wet, sticky sounds as it spread over the floor. Before it was finished settling, the substance began to evaporate, as if it were being sucked into the floor. In a moment, it was gone, leaving only a faint, vaguely unpleasant-smelling stain on the carpet.

Giles shouted, "Buffy, above you!"

She tilted her head back and saw one of the red-eyed creatures glaring down at her from atop a bookshelf. It jumped.

Buffy tucked in her chin and rolled forward over the floor and shot to her feet as the Rakshasa landed behind her. Clutching the stake, she spun around, ready to stab the creature as many times as it took to kill it. But it was not one of the dwarfish, lizard-faced things she saw when she turned.

"Hello, Buffy," Angel said. He wore black jeans and no shirt, and he smiled at her warmly.

"That's not Angel, Buffy," Giles said. He stood several feet behind the thing. "I saw it change in mid-air."

"I know," Buffy said quietly, still looking into those beautiful deep-brown eyes. "You've been coming to my bedroom at night, haven't you?" she whispered to the creature. "Whispering to me in the dark. Telling me to kill my best friend. Haven't you?"

"I . . . I don't know what you're talking about, Buff," he said, frowning.

It was a perfect duplicate of Angel; the hair, the muscles, the eyes. There was probably a tattoo on his back. She knew if she touched the skin, it would feel exactly like Angel. It might even smell like Angel. But it wasn't—and she had to keep telling herself that inside, again and again—as she pounded the stake into his flat stomach.

Angel's body shimmered like the surface of a pond and quickly melted into what it really was: a short, fanged Rakshasa. Buffy pounced on it and began stabbing it repeatedly with rapid swings of her right arm as she held it down with her left.

The Rakshasa's snout closed on her left forearm, burying its small fangs into her flesh. Buffy screamed in pain, but didn't miss a beat with the stake; she just changed the location of her stabs and drove it into the creature's left eye, and kept driving it in there.

The creature squealed as its viscous fluids splashed over the floor and onto Buffy with each strike. Its squeal became a gurgle as its body liquefied and spread over the floor, then seemed to be sucked up into nothingness.

The second the Rakshasa dissolved, Willow stopped struggling with Oz and Xander. Her brow furrowed above wide eyes that darted back and forth between the two faces hovering over her. Her stiff body slowly relaxed, and in return, the boys relaxed their hold on her.

"Willow?" Oz asked cautiously.

"What happened?" she asked in a coarse whisper.

Oz and Xander looked at one another, then back at Willow.

Xander said, "Um, you, uh . . . tripped over the ottoman?"

"We're not quite sure," Oz said, ignoring Xander's response.

Willow sat up and gently touched her face, then looked at her fingertips. "I'm bleeding!" she exclaimed. She looked at Oz and asked, "Why am I bleeding?"

"Also unclear," Oz stammered, glancing at Xander for help.

Before Xander could speak up to help Oz, Buffy joined them.

"Are you all right, Willow?" she asked, wincing as she looked at her friend's bruises. She hunkered down in front of Willow, and without taking her eyes from the wounds on her friend's face, she said, "Xander, or Giles, or somebody . . . get some alcohol and some ice."

"Get enough for both of them," Giles added. "You're bleeding, Buffy. That should be dressed immediately."

As Xander headed for the office, Buffy said, "I am so sorry, Willow."

"You're sorry?" Willow asked. "For what?"

"You don't remember what happened?"

"Last I can remember, we were talking about Ravana and the Rakshasa. Next thing I know, I'm on the floor with a headache, and I'm bleeding. Is my lip cut?"

"Willow, have you been having nightmares?" Buffy asked.

Willow frowned. "Well, yeah. One nightmare over and over. Why?"

"Do you hear voices whispering to you in the nightmare? And when you wake up, you feel angry and tense but at the same time really, really good, like all the problems in your life have been solved, but you can't remember exactly what the voices were telling you?"

She frowned even more, sat up straighter. "Yeah. But how do you know?"

"I've been having the same nightmare. But they aren't nightmares."

Xander returned with some ice in a plastic bag and a white tin box with a red cross on the lid. He handed them to Buffy, then turned to Oz, who was standing nearby with the fingers of both hands stuffed into his back pockets.

"Do you know what they're talking about?" Xander whispered.

Oz said nothing, didn't even glance at Xander.

"Do you see red eyes in your nightmares?"

Willow nodded, looking very concerned now.

"Me, too. The Rakshasa. They come to our rooms at night and whisper to us. Maybe they put us in some kind of trance or something, I don't know, but it's not a nightmare. They've been telling us to kill each other."

"What?" Willow breathed.

Buffy opened the tin box, put some alcohol on a cottonball, and dabbed Willow's face with it. Willow hissed at the stinging pain, then gently held the bag of ice to her cheek. "Oh, my God," she said.

"What?" Buffy asked.

Willow shook her head, closed her eyes a moment. "It . . . it just came back to me. What happened. In here, I mean. Just now, between us."

"It wasn't us, though," Buffy said. "It was them. They wanted one of us to kill the other. Then the survivor would be dinner. Their dinner."

"But, how could we not know?" Willow asked.

Giles said, "We all have dreams that we forget upon waking, but those dreams are still with us, in our subconscious. They come from the subconscious. I suspect it was to your subconscious that these creatures were speaking, so that you would have no conscious memory of their visitations. Just a cloudy, dreamlike recollection."

Willow turned to Buffy. "Um . . . thank you for not taking my head off and pulling my spleen out through my neck-stump. I know you could have if you'd wanted."

"I probably would have if Giles hadn't stopped me." When finished treating Willow's wounds, Buffy sat in a chair and Giles started cleaning and bandaging her injured forearm.

"This is precisely what the Rakshasa have been doing all over town," Giles said. "They have been working people up into a hateful frenzy, inspiring people to kill their friends. For all we know, it's happening somewhere right now."

Buffy said, "Giles, you mentioned something you read in one of your books. You said the presence of the Rakshasa alone affects the personalities and behavior of people in the surrounding area."

"Yes," Giles said with a nod.

"Well, it's not just people. All the vampires in town have their panties in a bunch, and I bet that's why. It's worse than a Marilyn Manson concert out there."

"Yet another reason for us to stop this before it goes any farther," Giles said. "Willow, I need more details from you. We must get to work on stopping this now before more people are killed."

"And eaten," Buffy muttered, her arm wrapped neatly in crisp gauze.

Willow stood slowly, made her way carefully to the table, and took a seat. The others joined her as she reached for her bag and pulled out several sheets of paper that had been folded over once. "Here," Willow said, handing the papers to Giles. Her voice was still hoarse. "I printed them up off the Internet." She turned to Oz, who sat beside her. "Could you please get me a glass of water?"

Oz was gone immediately and returned seconds later with a paper cup of water.

Willow took a few sips, cleared her throat, winced, then drank some more. "Why would anyone want to raise something like that? I mean, there doesn't seem to be anything to gain from Ravana coming back and turning the whole world into his own personal hellhole. Who would do such a thing?"

"I'm afraid I might have some idea," Giles said as his eyes scanned the pages for a moment. He set them down and looked at the others. "I ran into Ethan Rayne in the grocery store tonight."

"Rayne?" Buffy asked. "What's he doing in Sunnydale?" She picked up the sheets Willow had printed and flipped through them, stopping on the grainy photograph of the Ravana statuette and the six Rakshasa.

"The very question I asked him. He said he was just passing through. I don't believe him, of course. But neither can I imagine any reason he would have for resurrecting an ancient Hindu demon. He does nothing that doesn't benefit him directly."

"That's an odd image," Xander said, frowning. "Ethan Rayne in a grocery store. He was actually shopping for groceries?"

"Yes, it was odd. For one thing, he told me he'd fallen in love just before walking away. As for groceries . . . he seemed interested in nothing more than bottled water. He took two bottles of distilled water from the shelf. As far as I know, that was all."

Willow covered her mouth as she yawned, and groaned at the pain the motion caused her. A couple seconds later, Xander yawned as well.

"It's much too late for this," Giles said. "I'll take you all home and we can continue tomorrow. We all need our sleep."

"What about the nightmare?" Willow asked. "I mean, we know that it's not a nightmare now, but that doesn't mean those things won't be back again tonight."

"I wish I could tell you some way to hold them off," he said, shrugging helplessly. "If such a thing exists, I don't know what it is. Yet."

"We're on to them now, Willow," Buffy said. "We'll just have to be prepared. Lock your bedroom door and windows. Sleep with all the lights on so they can't hide in the dark. And if they do show up . . ." she trailed off. She had nothing left to offer.

Giles stood with a sigh. "It's very late. Shall we go?"

When Buffy got home, her mother was in bed and the house was dark and silent. Buffy hadn't eaten any dinner and was famished, but by the time she entered the house, she was much too tired to even think of eating. After going through the house to make sure every door and window was locked, she went to her bedroom.

Buffy closed and locked her bedroom door, then checked the locks on both windows. Out of her clothes in seconds, she slipped on a long nightshirt that had the kids from *South Park* on the front. With the overhead light still on, she got into bed, turned on the bedside lamp, and made sure her alarm was set. She snuggled under the covers and rolled onto her side, away from the light. But she knew even the light wouldn't keep her awake.

If anything could keep her from surrendering to her fatigue, it would be tightening knot in her stomach. It had relaxed somewhat once things had settled down in the library, but it was back now, bigger and harder, deep in the middle of her gut, a hardening lump of worry and anger and fear.

Buffy closed her eyes. The sound of rainfall outside was soothing, comforting. In spite of the lump in her hungry stomach, Buffy felt herself gliding down toward sleep almost immediately. It was the slippery sliding feeling that always came just before she lost all awareness of the room around her and the bed she was in, just before sleep embraced her and carried her off . . . to dreams or nightmares, or that one particular nightmare . . .

Something jarred her out of her almost-sleep. Buffy opened her eyes and lifted her head slightly from the pillow. She heard nothing. The bedroom's doors and windows were locked, the whole house was sealed up tight. She was as safe as she could be, given the nature of what she was, and there was no reason not to sleep.

Her eyes closed again and her head settled back on the pillow.

The bed moved.

Buffy's eyes snapped open wide and all thoughts of

sleep disappeared. She rolled onto her back and sat up halfway, propped up by both arms with locked elbows.

She felt movement beneath her. Under the bed.

A shiver passed through Buffy as realization flooded her mind. While she was going through the house locking all the doors and windows, and while she was locking the door and windows in her bedroom, the Rakshasa had already arrived and were waiting for her under the bed.

Buffy thought fast. The wooden stake had taken too long to finally kill the two creatures in the library. She guessed there were several of them huddling under the bed. A sharp knife would do much more damage in less time.

She turned her head slowly to look over at her dresser. There was a knife with a very sharp nine-inch blade in her equipment drawer.

Something moved under her bed again. Just slightly.

Buffy carefully peeled the covers back and turned on the bed so she was facing the dresser. She took in a deep breath, let it out slowly, then jumped off the bed to dive toward the dresser.

The second her feet hit the floor, a rough-skinned, clammy hand jabbed out from under the bed and grabbed her left ankle in an iron grip.

Chapter 16

THE BEDROOM FLOOR SWEPT UPWARD IN A BLUR AND slammed into Buffy. A second hand clutched her right ankle, and this time, she felt sharp claws press against her skin, coming very close to breaking it. The creature began to pull on Buffy's legs to drag her under the bed. Its clawed hands had a powerful grip, and in spite of its small size, the creature was very strong.

Buffy clutched at the carpet and tried to pull herself forward, but without something to get a firm hold on, she could not do it. Instead, she rolled over onto her back and sat up. The creature was beneath her legs suddenly, caught off guard, and its grip loosened. She spread her knees, grabbed the creature's ears, and pulled its head up between her thighs, then closed her legs on its neck.

The creature made a strangled gurgle and began to struggle.

The bed jostled as the other creatures beneath it scrambled to get out.

Buffy reached up, took a pen from her desk, and stabbed it into the creature's right eye, then the left. The Rakshasa released a horrible mewling cry of pain, but she did not stop. She stabbed the creature's face and neck repeatedly, holding the head by the left ear to keep it as still as she could. The familiar yellowish-green slime splashed onto her legs and hand until the creature collapsed into a viscous mass. As Buffy got to her feet, the thick substance evaporated instantly.

More small, clawed hands swept out from under the bed, reaching for Buffy's feet but grasping only air. A reptilian snout appeared as one crawled out from under the bed, then another.

Buffy opened her dresser drawer, snatched up the knife, and spun around to face the Rakshasa.

Four had come out and were getting to their feet, with a fifth right behind them.

"Buffy?" her mother called out in the hall. "Buffy, what's wrong?" The doorknob rattled, but the locked door didn't open. "Buffy, open this door!"

"Hang on, Mom, I'll be with you in a sec." She turned to the drawer again and dropped the knife back in before rustling around for something else. She took out a small machete and removed the leather scabbard. "Okay," she said as she faced them again, all five now, "batter up." Holding the machete like a baseball bat, she stepped foward and swung low.

Her first strike lopped the head off the closest Rakshasa. The head thunked to the floor as the body dropped and convulsed. Both melted away in seconds.

Buffy swung the machete low and indiscriminately. She felt the impact of the blade on the creatures with each swing, but wasn't sure what kind of damage she was doing; her eyes squinted and sometimes even closed against the splash and spatter of warm viscous fluids that came from the wounded creatures. Their cries of pain blended into one single shrieking squeal.

"Buffy!" Joyce screamed outside the bedroom. She pounded on the door frantically. "What's happening? What's going on?"

"Hang on, Mom!"

One of the creatures latched on to her leg and tried to climb up her body. Buffy bent down and grabbed the pink, fleshy tail with her left hand and jerked the Rakshasa off her leg. She lifted her arm high and let the creature dangle for a second, then swung the machete hard. It cut through the creature diagonally, and the top half of the body dropped to the floor with a thunk.

The room fell silent. Buffy looked around but only saw yellowish-green goo evaporating rapidly on the floor, bed, nightstand, and wall.

"Buffy, open this door!" There was more anger than fear in Joyce's voice this time.

Buffy unlocked and opened the bedroom door. Joyce was in a nightgown, hair splayed, eyes puffy. She put a hand on each side of the doorway and leaned into the room, looked around cautiously, settled her eyes on the machete in Buffy's hand for a moment. When she looked at Buffy, it was with an expression that said she wasn't sure she wanted to know what had just happened. She embraced Buffy and said, "My God, what was all that noise, what was happening in here?"

"I'm fine, Mom." The yellowish-green substance was gone, leaving no sign it had ever been anywhere in the room or on Buffy.

Joyce pulled back with her hands on Buffy's shoulders. "I'm fine, Mom? That answers neither of my questions, Buffy. And why do you have that—" Her attention was caught by something behind Buffy. Her eyes widened, and she stumbled backward as she screamed.

With her heart still hammering from her experience just ended, Buffy turned, ready for anything.

One last Rakshasa had just crawled from under the bed and was running toward her on stubby legs. Buffy bent her knees and leveled the machete's blade with the creature's abdomen an instant before it reached her. The Rakshasa's eyes widened as it realized it was running too fast . . . and it impaled itself on the sharp blade.

Buffy clutched the machete's handle with both hands, raised it over her head with the small creature still skewered on the blade, and brought it down hard like a club. The creature's feet hit the floor first, and the machete cut downward, coming out between its legs to hit the carpet. A second after the Rakshasa's life fluids began to gush from the deep wound, it decayed swiftly, spreading in a puddle. A moment later, it too was gone.

"Good Lord, Buffy, what was that?" Unspilled tears glistened in Joyce's eyes and her face was drained of color.

"C'mon, Mom, let's get out of here." Buffy set the machete on top of her dresser, then put a hand on Joyce's shoulder, gently turned her around, and eased her out into the hall, then pulled the bedroom door closed. "Now, wait right here, I'll be back in a second."

"B-but what are you—"

"Just a second." Buffy went into her mother's bedroom and checked under the bed and in the closet. She made sure the windows were locked, then went back into the hall, still unsure of how much to tell her mother of her ugly, disturbing story. She smiled and said, "Okay, Mom, you can go back to bed if you want."

"Back to bed?" Joyce put her hands on her hips. "Buffy, with the sounds I heard coming out of your room, it's a wonder I didn't wet my bed."

"I know, and I'm sorry. That won't happen again."

"At the risk of sounding glib, did you bring your work home with you tonight?"

Buffy closed her eyes and nodded. "Yes, a Slayer-related problem that came in under the radar. But it's all gone now."

Joyce's eyes widened as she frowned and gently touched Buffy's forehead. "Where did you get that bump?" she asked breathily.

"Oh, that. I fell. In the library. Hit a chair."

"Mmm, well . . ." Her arm dropped to her side, she took a deep breath and let it out slowly through puffed cheeks. "There's no way I can sleep," Joyce said with a sigh. "My heart feels like a disco band."

Laughter blurted unexpectedly from Buffy, surprising even herself. "Hey, that's a good one, Mom."

Joyce leaned against the wall. "Yeah, well, I show signs of wit every now and then." Her hand moved down to her stomach. "Fear makes me hungry. I'm starving."

Hunger was grumbling in Buffy's stomach as well, even louder than when she had gone to bed. She nodded and said, "Me, too. I didn't have any dinner."

"Would you like me to fix you something?"

"No, that's okay. I'll just—"

"Don't be silly. I'll put on my robe and . . ." She

frowned a moment, thinking. "No, wait, I've got a better idea. Let's go out."

"To eat? Do you know what time it is?"

"We can go to Denny's and have a nice breakfast." Joyce grinned as she playfully poked Buffy in the ribs. "Come on, it'll be fun."

"I have to go to school tomorrow."

"Well, I don't know about you, but there's no way I'll be getting back to sleep for a while."

Buffy looked back at her room and nodded slowly. "Yeah . . . me, neither."

"Let's put our clothes on before we start feeling tired again and change our minds."

Buffy changed into overalls and a sweatshirt. While her mother was still changing, she went to the phone. She had to call Willow and warn her.

Denny's was busier than Buffy had expected at that hour in a town as small as Sunnydale. She and her mom had a booth at the front window, looking out on the rainy street.

"Mmm, an omelet sounds good," Joyce said, perusing the menu. "What are you going to have?"

Buffy frowned as she looked over the breakfast selections. "I don't know. Maybe a muffin."

"A muffin? For goodness' sake, Buffy, you haven't eaten since lunch. Have a real breakfast. Tell you what, I'll order for you."

"Sounds good. I'll abdicate responsibility for my cholesterol and weight." Buffy closed her menu and put it on the table.

Before leaving the house, she had called Willow and told her to get out of her bedroom and sleep on the couch or something, that the Rakshasa were under her bed.

Willow had told her to hold on, then returned a couple minutes later and said she'd swung a yardstick back and forth under her bed and there was nothing there.

"Are you crazy?" Buffy had exclaimed. "They could have been there!"

"Well, they aren't now."

Buffy wondered if they had been warned somehow. Were the Rakshasa able to communicate with one another telepathically? It was possible. Once she had discovered their hiding place under her bed, maybe the creatures under Willow's bed had been warned that the cat was out of the bag. Or maybe they'd sensed the deaths of the ones Buffy had killed and had decided not to take the same risk. Whatever the case, it was another detail she would have to pass on to Giles.

The waitress came and Joyce ordered a Denver omelet for herself, and eggs, two slices of bacon, two sausages, hash browns, and sourdough toast for Buffy. And hot chocolate for both of them.

"There's no way I'm leaving this restaurant without having a stroke," Buffy said, putting her face in her hands, elbows on the edge of the table.

"Oh, stop. It won't kill you."

"I guess not. Not tonight, anyway."

"Now, are you ever going to tell me what happened in your room tonight, Buffy?"

"It's a long story, Mom. Some . . . unsavory creatures were hiding under my bed, and I killed them."

Joyce smiled. "You used to think that when you were a little girl. That there was some kind of monster under your bed. Do you remember?"

Buffy nodded, smirking. "I couldn't sleep with the closet door open, either, because I thought the closet monster was watching me." Buffy knew the longer she kept her mother off the subject of what had happened in her bedroom, the more likely she was to stay off the subject. "What's up at the gallery these days?"

Joyce's eyes widened. "You heard?"

Buffy frowned. "Heard what? I was just wondering."

She released a long, weary sigh and closed her eyes for a moment. "The gallery has been closed all day. When we got there this morning, we found that someone had broken in and ransacked the place."

Buffy's mouth dropped open and she gasped. "Oh, no! What was stolen?"

"That's the weird part. Nothing. The place was just trashed. We spent the whole day cleaning up, tallying our losses."

"Do you know who did it?" Buffy asked. Before her mother could answer, she added, "What about that crazy woman? What's her name?"

"Lovecraft, Phyllis Lovecraft."

Buffy chided herself for not running the name by Giles, and made a note to do so the next time she saw him. She knew she'd heard the name before, and something told her it was either from, or in connection to, Giles.

"Yes, I'd thought of her," Joyce continued. "But the others seemed convinced it was that strange man who'd come into the gallery the day before."

Frowning, Buffy asked, "What strange man?"

"I don't know who he was. He came in, looked around for a few minutes, said something to Beth, then left. But he was the center of attention while he was there."

"Why? What was so strange about him?"

Joyce laughed quietly. "Everything."

The waitress came with their food.

Buffy looked at the plate before her. "If I knew there was gonna be this much grease, I would've brought some Easy-Off."

"Oh, stop it."

"So, what about this man?"

"He was very tall. Six-five, I'd say. Maybe taller. He wore a black trenchcoat and a black wide-brimmed hat . . . the kind of hat the Shadow wore in that movie."

"What movie?"

"The Shadow."

Buffy shrugged and gestured for her to go on.

"Well, aside from being all black—even his pants and boots were black—his clothes really weren't the strange part. He was white. Not white as in Caucasian, but white as in . . . well, flour. I don't know about his hands because he wore gloves, but his face was white as a ghost." She winced suddenly. "Oh, I suppose that was an unfair thing to say. I mean, you'd know better than I, but I imagine there are Asian ghosts and black ghosts and—"

"Mother." Buffy closed her eyes so her mother couldn't see her roll them. "I know what you mean. What about his eyes?"

"He was wearing black reflective sunglasses."

The face in the limousine? Buffy wondered. She tried to remember if he'd been wearing a black wide-brimmed hat.

"But I saw a little of his hair," Joyce said, frowning, "and believe it or not, it looked white, too. Platinum, maybe. I don't know."

"So you think he might have trashed the gallery?"

"I don't think so, no. Why would he do something like that? Nothing at all was stolen, let alone anything of value. And he rode up to the gallery in a limousine."

Buffy's eyes widened. "A white limousine?"

"Yes. How did you know?"

"I've seen a white limo prowling around town recently. Late at night. And one night I saw a very pale face wearing sunglasses looking out the back window."

"Do you know who he is?"

Buffy shook her head.

"When I saw him get out of the limousine, I figured he had to be from out of town. Los Angeles, or maybe Santa Barbara."

"Could be. Or maybe even farther than that."

"Our breakfasts are getting cold," Joyce said.

They began to eat and were silent for a few minutes, except for the sounds of their chewing and the utensils clacking gently against the plates.

"You know," Buffy said, "even though I can actually feel my arteries hardening as I eat this . . . it's way delicious."

"See?" Joyce said with a smile.

After another minute of silent eating, Buffy asked, "Did the guy in the hat happen to ask about a statuette of some kind?"

"Statuette? No, not that I know of. Of course, Beth never told me what he said. Why? What statuette?"

Buffy shook her head as she took a bite of bacon. "It's nothing."

Joyce sighed, frustrated. "I wish you wouldn't do that, Buffy. It's not like I'm going to write down everything you tell me and fax it to the *Los Angeles Times*." She continued eating her food and neither of them said anything for a while. Then: "Does it have something to do with those horrible killings?"

"Killings?" Buffy asked, looking up from her food. "What killings?"

"How could you not hear about them? They're all over the news. Those two teachers at your school. The old man who killed his friend with the lawnmower, and then . . . well, what happened to him. And that woman who stabbed her friend before . . . well, it was the same thing as the old man. They were both eaten."

"Oh, yeah. *Those* killings." Buffy nodded slowly. "Yes. It is related to that. There's something . . . well, new in town. Something we've never dealt with before. And it involves a statuette. I just wondered if the guy from the limo had something to do with it. Probably not."

Joyce smiled. "See? Was that so hard?"

Buffy returned the smile and took a bite of toast.

"Distilled water," Giles muttered to himself. He sat at his desk in his apartment, books open in front of him. But instead of reading the books, he was combing through the pages Willow had printed up from the Internet.

Giles took a mug of coffee from the desk, leaned back in his chair, and sipped it. The information found by Willow did not tell how to resurrect the ancient Hindu demon, but it listed some of the things needed in order for the procedure to work. And one of them was distilled water.

That left no doubt in Giles's mind that Ethan Rayne was behind the attempt to raise Ravana. But it didn't explain why he would do such a thing.

Giles agreed with what Willow had said earlier that night. If Ravana's reign spread from Sunnydale to cover the globe, and if his reign meant nothing but chaos and bloodshed, what could Rayne, or anyone else, profit from it?

His question was answered on the very next page. He read it aloud in a hoarse, weary voice: " 'Once revived, Ravana will reward the mortal who aided in establishing his new reign. That mortal shall sit at the right hand of Ravana and be given his own rule, and he shall live as a prince in Ravana's kingdom.' "

Giles read it again, and again, as dread rose in his throat like bile. He sighed and buried his face in his hands.

There was a long list of things Giles did not like about Ethan Rayne. His voracious hunger for power was near the top.

As he sat there with his face in his hands, Giles found himself dropping off to sleep. He sat up abruptly and scrubbed his face with his palms. He'd been drinking coffee all night, but it wasn't helping. His weariness was cutting through the caffeine and pulling him down with its weight. There was no way he could absorb any more information without sleep.

Giles stood and stretched his arms high over his head as he yawned. He turned off the desk lamp and headed for bed.

As Joyce drove home through the rain, Buffy turned on the radio and tuned in to the news station to see if there had been any more murders. Sure enough, the Rakshasa had not slowed down in their work.

A Sunnydale man had killed his wife and their eight-year-old twin boys with an ax. Police had found the man dead in a crawlspace over his garage. No details were given about how the man had died or in what condition his body had been found, but Buffy didn't need them. She knew the condition of the dead murderer— she could see it in her mind.

At the house, Buffy and her mother walked to the front door beneath her mother's large umbrella. Joyce fumbled with her keys, unlocked the door, and they went inside.

"Oh, no!" Joyce cried as Buffy closed the door.

Buffy spun around to see what was wrong.

The living room looked like a tornado had hit the house. The coffee table had been knocked over and everything on it was scattered over the carpet. The sofa cushions had been tossed across the room, and the sofa itself had been turned upside down, the dustcover underneath sliced open from one end to the other. The walls were bare, and everything that had been hanging on them was on the floor.

"Just like the gallery," Joyce whispered tremulously.

Buffy's stomach, full from the breakfast she'd eaten, felt sick as she looked over the mess. She walked between the toppled coffee table and overturned sofa and went upstairs to her room. She paused before opening the door, not sure she wanted to look.

Her room had been violated, too. At its absolute messiest, it had never come close to the condition in which Buffy found it now. The mattress had been taken off the bed, the closet had been emptied, drawers had been pulled out and dropped to the floor, including her equipment drawer; knives and stakes and all her other weapons were scattered over the floor.

Joyce brushed by on her way down the hall to her own bedroom. A moment later: "They went through every room in the house!" She sounded near tears.

Buffy felt sick to her stomach. Someone had gone through their house, throwing furniture this way and that, emptying drawers, breaking things . . . and that someone had gone into her bedroom, touching her belongings—private things, things only she had touched—violating her privacy, soiling the very air in the house. All those things still belonged to her, but Buffy wasn't sure she wanted to touch anything after it had been smeared with the intrusion of some faceless stranger.

She left her room and headed for the kitchen, wondering if indeed every room in the house had been torn up. She flipped on the light as she went in.

All the cupboard doors were open and broken bits of china, shards of glass, and silverware covered the floor. Drawers had been pulled out, sponges and brushes and bottles of cleaners had been scattered over the floor, and the cupboard under the sink was open and empty. Even the crisper drawer had been removed from the refrigerator and placed on the counter, where its contents had been set aside.

"Somebody's looking for something," Buffy whispered. "And I bet I know what they're looking for."

First, somebody turns over the gallery. Then the home of one of the employees of the gallery. Whoever it was, they were looking for the Ravana statuette.

Giles said Ethan Rayne was in town, and that he suspected Rayne of being behind everything that was happening. But he didn't know for sure. What if Rayne was just looking for the Ravana statuette? What if someone else had it and was using it to bring the Hindu demon back, and Rayne was trying to find it for himself? Something else she would have to remember to tell Giles.

She wondered if she should start making a list.

Buffy could hear the faint sound of her mother crying down the hall. She decided to sweep up the mess on the floor before she or her mother took a piece of glass in the foot. She made her way slowly and carefully across the kitchen, trying to avoid glass and bits of china but crunching some of it under her feet nonetheless. When she reached the narrow closet where the broom was kept, she pulled the door open—

And a face as pale as death, with red eyes and shiny metal teeth, came out of the rectangle of darkness toward her.

Chapter 17

THE MAN IN THE CLOSET WAS FASTER THAN BUFFY'S reflexes. A gloved hand covered her whole face and pushed hard. She stumbled backward, trying to keep her balance, but fell anyway. Pain made her cry out as the jagged edges of broken glass and china pierced her back.

Heavy foosteps ran out of the kitchen, crunching the pieces of dinnerware.

Buffy started to get up, but froze. She would have to be careful not to slice up her palms. She reached up with one hand and grabbed the lip of the counter behind her and pulled herself into a sitting position, brought her knees up to her chest and awkwardly got to her feet.

Joyce screamed. The front door slammed shut.

"Buffy!" Joyce cried, terrified.

Buffy moved fast, but gingerly, over the kitchen floor and found her mother in the living room, standing at the entrance to the hall.

"Who was that man?"

Buffy didn't stop to answer. She clicked on the porch light on her way out the front door, ran across the lawn, and stopped on the sidewalk. Eyes squinting against the rain, she looked to her right, her left, across the street.

A car door slammed and the engine started nearby, to Buffy's left and across the street. Headlights came on.

Buffy spotted the white limousine and ran toward it. She was ready to kick the windows in, if necessary.

Moving surprisingly fast for its size, the limousine pulled away from the curb and sped by before Buffy reached it. Angry, frustrated, she could do nothing more than stand in the street and watch its taillights grow smaller and dimmer with distance, until the car completely disappeared.

"Oh, Buffy, that was the man from the gallery!" Joyce said when Buffy came back inside. Her voice trembled almost as much as her hands. She paced frantically between the coffee table and sofa.

"I know," Buffy said distractedly. "He was still in the kitchen."

"His eyes—"

"He's an albino." During the split-second in which Buffy had looked into the man's face, his pink irises made her think of the Rakshasa, and she'd thought, at first, that he was one, or was perhaps some giant human-Rakshasa hybrid. The silvery glint of his teeth confused her further, and she thought perhaps he was some kind of robot. But the instant she recognized the metal on his teeth to be braces, it all came together, and she realized he was an albino man, most likely the one her mother had mentioned at Denny's. "And he's got braces on his teeth. Like an eleven-year-old."

"Well, he's certainly the biggest eleven-year-old I've ever seen." Joyce stopped pacing, fists clenched at her sides, eyes tightly shut, and shouted, "What does he want?"

"He was looking for the Ravana statuette," Buffy muttered, to herself as much as her mother. "He tried the gallery first. He'll probably be hitting the houses of the other gallery employees, if he hasn't already."

"I'm calling the police," Joyce said, already on her way to the telephone.

"No, wait," Buffy called. "I don't know, maybe we shouldn't." She wondered if it was a good idea to bring the police into it. In her line of work, they only made things more difficult. "I just thought—"

"Thought what? Buffy, our insurance won't cover this if there's no police report."

Buffy shook her head slowly and sighed. "I don't know what I thought."

Joyce went to Buffy's side and put an arm around her. "You should go to bed. You've got school tomorrow. Today."

"My bed's on the floor."

"So, we'll put it back where it belongs and make it up."

"As long as I'm up, I should probably patrol—"

"You'll do no such thing. You're going to bed right now. Go brush your teeth while I call the police and the other employees to warn them. Then I'll help you make up your bed."

Buffy knew she was right. Her bones ached with weariness and she felt as if her skull had been stuffed with wet cotton. She went into the bathroom, swept some broken glass into a corner with her sneakered foot, and brushed her teeth. In the bedroom, she changed back into her nightshirt, then pulled the mattress toward her bed. She stumbled and fell on it with a grunt.

Seconds later, she was sound asleep.

It was sprinkling lightly when Willow left early for school the next morning, and the sky was still dark with clouds. But there was a large gap to the east that revealed bright blue sky and through which shined corrugated shafts of sunlight. A misty, unfragmented rainbow arced in front of the diamond-shaped opening in the clouds.

A sight like that normally cheered Willow, but she had too much on her mind to pay much attention to it. That morning, she'd heard about the latest murder, which had taken place early the previous evening, and she wondered how many more were going to take place before they found out how to stop them. That was why she'd left early that morning. She planned to spend some time on a computer in the library before classes, looking for more information about Ravana and the Rakshasa. But that wasn't the only thing on her mind.

Willow still couldn't shake what had happened the night before. If they had been alone, if there had been no one else around or in earshot, both Willow and Buffy would be dead. Of course, Willow would have been dead first, but it hardly mattered. It was either that, or kill Buffy and become the all-you-can-eat buffet for the Rakshasa.

The whole thing still creeped her out; if she thought about it long enough, it made her want to crawl out of her skin. But disturbing as it was, something good had come with it. She no longer had to wonder what had happened to her friendship with Buffy. That it was nothing she had done—or hadn't done—was an enormous relief to Willow; she felt like she'd lost twenty-five ugly pounds overnight.

Before leaving Giles's car last night, Willow had turned to Buffy and asked, "So, we're cool?"

Buffy had grinned and given her a big, tight hug.

The grin had been contagious, because Willow wore it into her house. On the way up the front walk, Willow had chanted to herself quietly, "Cool at last, cool at last!"

There was a bruise beneath Willow's left eye that a little makeup managed to cover, for the most part. Her lower lip was still swollen, but the cut didn't look nearly as bad as she had expected. Although she'd come up with an explanation—she was going to say she'd run into the edge of a door—she wasn't looking forward to being asked about it all day. She took some consolation in the fact that she was able to *walk* to school. Buffy could have put her in a hospital bed in the space of a few seconds.

At school, the halls were still quiet; it was too early for much activity. In the library, Giles's office was dark and the door was closed, so she assumed he hadn't arrived yet.

Willow went to her usual computer and booted up.

There was a sound somewhere in the library, so soft it could not be identified immediately—a wet sound . . . squishing? sucking?

Standing slowly and without a sound, Willow left her computer and crept toward the sound. It was just on the other side of the bookshelf in front of her. She walked along the rows of books, listening carefully to the strange, moist sound. She slowly rounded the end of the bookcase . . . and rolled her eyes.

"You guys make out louder than anyone I've ever known," Willow said.

Xander and Cordelia bounded from the sofa and away from one another, straightening their clothes and hair on the way. They spun around almost simultaneously and faced Willow.

"Don't you make any noise when you come into a room?" Xander asked.

Willow laughed. "Over all that racket? You sounded like hippopotami frolicking in the mud." Smiling, she turned and went back to her computer.

Xander and Cordelia followed her.

"Hey, uh, did you hear about the murder?"

"Yep. Another Rakshasa banquet."

"Have you seen Giles?" he asked.

"Not yet."

"How about Buffy?"

"No. But it's early and she had some Rak activity at home last night. I came to do some more searching on the 'Net. I don't know what you and Cordy are doing here." She was still smirking as she sat down at the computer again.

Xander ignored the remark. He stood beside her. "So, what do you think?"

"What do I think about what?"

He lowered his voice almost to a whisper. "About the current weirdage we're dealing with."

Willow glanced up with him, then did a double take when she saw the dead-serious look on his face. It wasn't an expression Xander wore often, and it startled her a little.

"Well, I haven't thought about it long enough to form an opinion. Between defending Mila and looking for information about—"

"I think it's scary. And serious."

She pushed her chair back from the computer and turned to him fully.

"You know," Xander continued quietly, "I'm the first one to admit I'm about as brave as a turkey on Thanksgiving. That's why, y'know, I usually lay low. I hate pain, and I'm not into, y'know, suspense . . . especially when the suspense is over whether I'm gonna live or die. But this thing . . ." He shook his head and wrinkled his nose distastefully. "What happened last night—between you and Buffy, I mean—that scared the hell outta me. I couldn't sleep last night because I was afraid I'd have that nightmare and what if I suddenly wanted to open a can of whup-ass on you? I mean, what if, God, what if I felt that way about Cordy? And just the thought of those ugly little boogers hanging out in my room at night, watching me sleep makes me wanna move into a bank vault for a few weeks."

"They wait for you under your bed," Willow said.

Xander's face fell. "They . . . what?"

"Well, see, after I went to bed last night, Buffy called me with a heads-up about the lizard-rats. She'd locked all her windows and her door, just like she told us to, but it didn't work because they were already there. They were waiting under her bed for her to go to sleep."

"Under . . . her bed." He lost some of the color in his face. "Well . . . thanks. That's just great." He stepped away from her and walked nervously in a small circle. "I'm just now getting over my childhood fear of the monster under the bed, and now you tell me the monster under the bed is for real. You're like that Rod Serling guy stepping out from behind the refrigerator to say the next stop's the Twilight Zone."

Willow stood and went to him, put a hand on his shoulder and got him to stop walking in a circle, like a dog chasing his tail. "Look, Xander, we're gonna find a way to stop those things. I wouldn't be surprised if we came up with something today." She sounded far more certain than she felt.

"You think?" he asked, giving her sidelong glance.

She couldn't lie to him, not when he seemed so vulnerable. He looked like a little boy waiting for his turn to see the dentist. "I'm hoping. Okay?"

"Well, hoping's not as good as thinking, and thinking's not nearly as good as knowing . . . but I'll take it."

Willow went back to her seat and started clicking her mouse.

Xander muttered, "But I'm not goin' near my freakin' bed till this is over."

Giles entered the library looking older than his years. He carried his briefcase as if it were full of bricks. His face seemed to have physically lengthened and there were crescent moons of puffy flesh under his eyes. Even his clothes looked weary.

"Ah, hello, Willow, Xander," he said hoarsely.

Cordelia joined them and stood next to Xander. "Too late, Giles. We've taken over your library," she said, smiling.

"The way I feel today, I'm quite tempted to give it to you." He went into his office and returned a moment later with a Thermos cup of tea.

"Are you sick?" Willow asked.

He shook his head. "Just exhausted. I was up quite late going over the material you gave me, Willow. And it proved to be quite fruitful. I simply didn't get enough sleep."

"What did you find in those pages?"

"A lot, and I'd like to discuss it. But not without Buffy. Have you seen her?"

"Not yet."

"Could you call her, Willow? I'd like her to get here as soon as possible."

"Sure." Willow got up from the computer as Giles went behind the front desk, took a seat, and sipped his tea. "Did you find, you know, a way to stop these lizard-rat thingies?"

"I'm afraid not," Giles said. "But I think I found out the reason behind all this."

"Really?" Willow frowned. She didn't remember anything like that in what she'd read of the information she'd printed up. "How'd you find it?"

"Actually, I found it . . . quite mortifying."

Buffy rose from the black swamp of sleep gradually, finally breaking the surface to hear the muffled sound of her mother talking to someone down the hall, probably in the living room. When she realized she was on her mattress, but her mattress was on the floor, she became momentarily disoriented, until she sat up wearily and looked at the mess around her. It came back to her, and she groaned, wishing only to go on sleeping. But she needed to check the time.

Her legs were tangled in a comforter; she peeled it off and got to her feet, looked around for her clock radio. She found it on the floor, broken, its bright numbers gone. She stretched. It was light out . . . as light as it could be with the unseasonal rain they'd been getting. Her mother was up. Had she gone to bed? Or had she been up all night cleaning up the mess and forgotten to wake Buffy?

She groaned again as she left her room and went down the hall.

"The police didn't seem too concerned," Joyce was saying into the phone. She was sitting on the sofa, which was upright once again with cushions in place. In front of it, the coffee table was back in place. The living room looked a little better, although the walls were still bare. She didn't notice Buffy come in. "My house looks like it's been through a major earthquake, but they just sort of shrug it off while they take a few notes. I probably interrupted one of their doughnut breaks. Maybe because there was no sign of a break-in. I think he probably picked the lock. Though why anyone would go to that trouble to get in here is—no, nothing was stolen."

The clock wasn't in its usual place on the wall, and Buffy didn't see it anywhere in the room.

"Mom? What time is it?" Her voice cracked with unshed sleep.

Joyce started. "Hang on," she said, and pulled the cordless phone from her ear. "I didn't hear you come in, Buff. I completely lost track of the time." She looked at her watch. "It's almost twenty after eight."

"What?" Buffy's eyes widened. "I've gotta get dressed!" She hurried back to her room.

"I'll call you right back, Beth," Joyce said, standing. After she hung up, she followed Buffy. "You've still got time. And I'll drive you to school." She stood in the bedroom doorway as Buffy searched for her clothes.

"I need to see Giles." She made a growling sound. "It looks like somebody's garage sale blew up in here."

"Want some breakfast?"

"We had breakfast earlier, remember?"

"You should eat something before you go. I'll fix

you a couple of Pop Tarts. If the toaster still works." On her way to the kitchen, she hit the redial button on the telephone.

Buffy finally found a blue long-sleeved top and a pair of pants that hadn't been too wrinkled by spending the night in a pile on the floor. She dug her books out of the mess and put on a black jacket. In the bathroom, she quickly washed up, brushed her teeth, and ran a brush through her hair a few times. There was no time for makeup; that bruised lump on her forehead would just have to stand out for all to see.

In the kitchen, Buffy found that her mother had swept up all the broken glass and china. Some of it remained piled in the corner, out of the way, but the floor was clean and safe.

Two Pop Tarts popped up in the toaster on the counter. Still talking on the phone, Joyce put them on a small plate and handed them to Buffy.

"I'll eat them in the car," Buffy said. "Let's go."

"I've gotta go, Beth," she said, nodding to Buffy. "I have to take Buffy to school, then I've got to finish with this mess, which will probably take all day. Okay, that's fine, thanks. And let me know if you hear any more from that crazy woman and her ugly Indian art. 'Bye-bye." She put the phone on the counter and said, "All right, let me get my keys."

Buffy had already taken a couple bites of one of the Pop Tarts and was chewing. It was delicious and made her realize how hungry she was in spite of the big meal she'd eaten in the earliest hours of the morning.

She stopped chewing abruptly, staring intently at nothing in particular.

What had her mother said on the phone? Had it been something about Indian art? Native American, most likely. Yes, that was probably what she'd meant. Buffy had seen some Native American art the last time she'd visited the gallery.

"You ready?" Joyce asked, keys jangling from her hand.

Buffy tried to speak, but her mouth was full. She chewed quickly, then swallowed. "Did I hear you say something about ugly Indian art on the telephone?" Buffy asked.

"Yes."

"As in Native American, right?"

"No, as in India. That kind of Indian. I thought you were going to eat those in the—"

Buffy dropped her Pop Tart onto the plate and put the plate on the counter. "What Indian art?"

Joyce looked at her reproachfully. "Buffy, I'm standing right here, there's no need to shout."

"What. Indian. Art?"

"Phyllis Lovecraft's collection of Indian art. At least, she says it's Indian. But it's so ugly, I'm not sure if—"

"Her art? You never said it was *Indian* art!" Buffy's voice had risen again and her eyes were suddenly frantic.

"I-I didn't realize it mattered, and . . . and . . . you never asked."

"What kind of art?"

"Indian, you know . . . elephants and Hindu gods and—"

"What did they look like?"

"Why is this so important to you, Buffy?"

"It just is, Mother, now please, tell me, what did they look like?"

"I don't know, she had a lot of different pieces. I thought you were in a hurry to get to school."

"Please, Mom, you've got to remember . . . was there a small statue of a thing with ten heads and twenty arms?"

Flustered, Joyce sighed as she looked quickly around the kitchen. "She gave me some Polaroids, but I can't remember where—"

"You have *pictures?*" Buffy asked, clutching her mother's upper arms.

"Buffy, would you please calm down? You're scaring me!"

"Listen, Mom, please listen. That statuette I told you about at Denny's last night? It's very old, and it's Indian, and it's somewhere here in Sunnydale. We have to find it, or more people are going to be killed, more people are going to be eaten. So, please, Mom, tell me—"

"Eaten?"

"The photos, Mom. Do you have the photos?"

"The photos," Joyce muttered, going to the junk drawer at the end of the counter. She opened it and shuffled through the contents. "I put them in here, but that was before I cleaned up this mess, and . . . I don't remember seeing them—"

"He didn't take them, did he?" Buffy asked. She felt a sudden tightening in her chest.

"Here they are," Joyce said, taking an overstuffed business-size envelope from the cluttered drawer. Before she could hand the envelope over, Buffy reached around and snatched it from Joyce's hand.

Buffy took the Polaroid snapshots from the envelope so fast she almost dropped them. The first one was of a woman with several arms, and Buffy quickly transferred it to the bottom of the stack, doing the same with the next few. Elephants, more unfamiliar gods, some kind of palace carved in stone.

She stopped shuffling the pictures abruptly and gasped, stared open-mouthed at one in particular.

"Oh, my God," she breathed.

Glaring at her from the Polaroid snapshot was the Ravana statuette, surrounded by six small Rakshasa.

"She has it," Buffy said, her whispered voice trembling. "Lovecraft."

Chapter 18

"YES, THE NAME IS FAMILIAR," GILES SAID TO BUFFY. He was seated behind the front desk, and the others—including Oz, who had arrived shortly before Buffy ran in, wide-eyed and breathless—were standing around, leaning against it. Xander was sitting on it, rubbing Cordelia's shoulders as she stood between his knees with her back to him. "Not only is the name Lovecraft familiar, but Phyllis Lovecraft, as well. But I'm not certain why."

Giles stood and went into his office. There were shuffling sounds as he looked for something.

Willow turned to Buffy, who stood beside her. "How's your owie?"

Buffy touched the large, discolored lump gently with her fingertips. "Ugly, but painless. Unless I touch it."

"Don't," Oz advised.

"You look better than I thought you would," Buffy said, smiling at her.

Willow shrugged one shoulder. "A little makeup."

"I didn't have time for makeup," Buffy said. Her smile was gone and she frowned, suddenly distracted again, as she had been since arriving.

"You okay?" Willow asked.

Buffy nodded but said nothing.

"Benson Lovecraft was an art collector," Giles said as he came out of the office. He was paging through a book that was, for him, surprisingly normal-looking. It was an average-size hardcover, and while it was worn and far from new, it was not ancient, like most of the books he used as a Watcher. "But he was actually much more than that," Giles continued. "He collected only art that was, in one way or another, connected to the occult, which was his true interest." Giles returned to his seat and continued looking for something in the book.

"Yeah, but how long ago was that?" Buffy asked. "This woman is, oh, I don't know . . . maybe in her mid-forties, something like that."

"That was some time ago," Giles said. "If he were alive today, Lovecraft would be well over a hundred years old. But there is no record of his death. Over the years, it has been rumored that he is still alive on his private island off the Washington coast. Ah, here," he whispered to himself. He placed the open book on the desk before him and scanned a page as he continued distractedly. "Lovecraft was born into great wealth and was known as a notorious—and obsessively reclusive—practitioner of the black arts. He was a contemporary and friend of the infamous occultist Aleister Crowley, as well as the author of several journals said to contain some of the most powerful and dangerous incantations ever written." He fell silent and concentrated on the book for a moment. "There is no record of Lovecraft beyond his ninety-fifth birthday. According to this biography, he had many children, most of them illegitimate. Ah, yes, here it is. Lovecraft's youngest son had a daughter named Phyllis."

"What does it say about her?" Buffy asked.

"Nothing other than listing her name and identifying her as Lovecraft's granddaughter."

"Well, she's a lot more than that," Buffy said. She removed a Polaroid snapshot from her jacket pocket and slapped it onto the countertop.

Giles stood and leaned forward as the others moved in to see.

Willow gasped. "That's it!"

Giles picked up the photograph and his eyes narrowed as he studied it. "Where did you get this, Buffy?"

"From my mother."

They stared at her, waiting for her to continue. But she said nothing as a smile grew on her face.

"Buffy," Giles said, "I do hope you intend to explain further."

Buffy did explain. She told them about Phyllis Lovecraft and her determination to display her collection of Indian art.

"Why didn't you tell us sooner, Buffy?"

"Because I didn't know! My mom's been complaining about it all week, but I didn't find out the art was from India until this morning."

She told them about the albino, as well. The limousine intrigued Giles.

"A white limousine," he muttered. "Ethan was wearing a very expensive suit when I saw him, and he seemed quite proud of the fact that he was doing rather well for himself."

"You think it's his?" Buffy asked.

An explosive breath came from Giles as he shook his head. "I don't know. Quite frankly, I don't have the foggiest idea what most of this means. Someone is using the statuette right now, or we wouldn't be dealing with the Rakshasa."

Willow said, "If this Lovecraft woman is using the statue to summon Ravana, why would she be worked up about exhibiting it in the gallery?"

"Maybe she's not the one summoning Ravana," Oz suggested.

"Then who is?" Willow asked.

"And, if Phyllis Lovecraft has the statuette," Buffy said, "what are they using to summon Ravana?"

"Could there be more than one of these statuettes?" Xander asked.

"If there are others, they're fakes," Giles replied. He stood and leaned forward on the countertop. "According to the information Willow pulled off the Internet, there is only one, and it was last seen in a London museum around the turn of the century. It is, however, quite possible that Benson Lovecraft obtained it for his collection. The statuette is precisely the kind of thing that would interest him. In my younger days, I read everything I could find on Lovecraft. I remember coming across a partial list of his acquisitions, and being astonished by the pieces he was able to find, some of them thousands of years old, some thought to be lost forever. If this woman is, indeed, Benson Lovecraft's granddaughter, it's possible she has access to his collection. That might be where she got it. But that doesn't explain why she would want it to be exhibited in the gallery."

"The last time I saw her," Buffy said, "she was pretty

desperate about that. I mean, it almost sounded like she was afraid of *not* getting her collection into the gallery."

A silence settled over them as they all stared at the picture of the Ravana statuette. The door opened and a small group of students came into the library, talking and laughing as they went toward the stacks.

Giles sighed as he stood up straight, and the others followed his lead. "Buffy, is it possible to contact Miss Lovecraft?"

Buffy reached into her pocket again and removed a page torn from the small spiral-bound notebook her mother kept in her purse. She placed it on the counter and the others leaned forward again to read it.

"She's at the Rocking R Motel?" Xander asked, squinting his eyes and pulling his upper lip back. "I think it's pretty safe to say the white limousine isn't hers."

"Before we go any farther," Giles said, "we need to talk with her."

"Let's go now," Buffy said.

"No, Buffy," Giles said firmly. "I don't want you to miss any more classes this week. I'll have to—"

Just then Miss Beakman's junior Lit class swarmed in to the library, armed with books and highlighters.

Buffy said nothing. But she looked over at Willow to find that Willow was looking at her. They exchanged small smiles. Without a word, they both knew they were going together to see Phyllis Lovecraft.

Now.

"What can they do?" Oz asked as he drove his van through town. "Hold me back *again?*"

"Buffy's the one taking the biggest risk," Willow

said. "If Principal Snyder found out about this, he'd squash her like a bug."

"And then my mom would squash my squashed remains," Buffy said quietly, seriously. "Especially if she found out I was going to talk to Phyllis Lovecraft."

After they left the library earlier that morning, Xander and Cordelia had wandered off together promising to cover for Buffy and the others if asked.

It was raining again, and the windshield wipers on Oz's van made pigletlike squeals with each sweep. The radio was tuned to the news station, because Buffy wanted to see if the Sunnydale body count had gone up.

"Direct me," Oz said.

"Keep going until you get to Cobblestone, then turn right," Buffy said. She turned to Willow. "You know, once we find this statuette, we won't be able to just take it and go. I mean, not if it's being used to summon Ravana."

"Yeah, and it's probably, like, all, all leaky with his essence."

"We're gonna have to destroy it where it is," Buffy said. "I mean, if it's not . . . too late. That's where you come in, Willow."

"I come in?" Willow's eyes widened with uncertainty. "Where do I come in? And what do I do when I get there?"

"Do you think you can come up with something that will destroy the statuette and the essence of Ravana?"

"Essence of Ravana," Oz muttered with a chuckle. "Sounds like perfume."

"I don't know," Willow said. She frowned and chewed on a thumbnail, thinking. "What if it's not really made of the bones of his victims?"

"I think we're gonna have to assume it is," Buffy said. Then, to Oz, "Turn right."

"Yeah, I guess so," Willow said, nodding. "When in India, do as the Hindu."

"Well, what do you think?" Buffy asked. "Doable? Undoable? What?"

"I think I can find something."

"I'd prefer a definite yes, but I guess we can't be too picky on such short notice." Buffy sighed.

When they arrived at the Rocking R Motel, Buffy told Oz to park at the curb on the street rather than in the parking lot, which was enclosed on three sides by the old two-story U-shaped building. The motel looked rundown and was in need of a paint job. The rectangular sign over the front office looked like something out of the 1950s. There was a large, crooked red R in the middle of it mounted on a curved rocker. The bottom of the sign was a marquee and read Cable Free BO; apparently the H had fallen off the HBO. The word Vacancy was lit up in red with a dead-looking No in front of it.

Buffy and Willow got out of the van, then Buffy leaned in and said, "If you see anything that looks like trouble, honk, okay?"

As the girls walked away, Oz muttered to himself, *"Looks* like trouble."

Buffy and Willow hurried for the covered sidewalk that went all the way around the motel's parking lot. Buffy took the piece of paper from her jacket pocket and looked at it.

"Room 207," Buffy said, speaking up to be heard above the rain. She nodded toward the covered balcony that covered the sidewalk. "Up there somewhere."

They climbed the concrete stairs, walked along the balcony, and passed the orange doors until they came to 207.

"Let me do the talking," Buffy said, "and just go along with whatever I say."

Willow nodded as Buffy knocked on the door. When there was no response, Buffy knocked again, harder.

"I don't think she's here," Willow said quietly.

"Maybe she's in the shower." Buffy pounded on the door with the side of her fist, so hard it made the door rattle in its frame.

"I guess we'll have to come back later with Giles," Willow said.

Buffy looked around quickly. There was no one on the balcony or below; no one in the front office could see them where they stood. She gripped the doorknob and tried to turn it. It wouldn't move. "Darn," she whispered. "I'd sure like to see what Miss Lovecraft's got in that motel room."

"Hey!" Willow exclaimed. "There's something I've been wanting to try, and now would be like the perfect time for it!"

"What's that?"

"S'cuse me." Willow gently pushed Buffy away from the door. "Cover me," she said with mock drama. She got down on one knee and cupped a hand over each side of the doorknob. Leaning forward, she whispered into the keyhole.

Frowning, Buffy tried to make out what she was saying, but the rain was too loud.

Something within the doorknob clicked. Willow stood and said, "Drumroll, please." She turned the knob and pushed the door open.

"Quick, get inside!" Buffy said, pushing her. She

closed the door behind them. "Cool!" she said, grinning at Willow.

Willow cocked her head cheerily. "With each passing day, I get better and better."

"Have you shown that to Giles?"

Willow's smile broke. "Uh, no. And don't mention it to him. Okay?"

"Gotcha."

The looked around the room. It was a mess. The bed was not only unmade, the blankets were on the floor. That probably meant Lovecraft had left instructions with housekeeping to stay out. There were several empty beer bottles on one of the nightstands and more on the desk by the television. Clothes and underwear had been thrown over the backs of the two chairs by the table as well as one end of the desk and the foot of the bed. More clothes hung in the open closet.

"Wait a second," Buffy said, looking at the clothes. She picked up a shirt from the bed. "What's wrong with this picture?"

Willow looked at the shirt Buffy held, at the pairs of pants on the bed, over at the undershorts and ties on the desk. "Men's clothes," she said.

"Congratulations. You get to go on to the bonus round." Buffy tossed the shirt back onto the bed. "Either we've got the wrong room, or she's staying here with someone."

"Maybe we do have the wrong room."

Buffy checked the paper again, put it back in her jacket pocket. "Nope. It says 207 here, and I don't think she would have given Mom the wrong room. She was too anxious for Mom to say yes to her collection." She went to the desk and opened a drawer. "If you were staying in this room, where would you put something if you didn't want anyone to find it?" The drawer was empty.

"Well, if I had to go out, I wouldn't leave it here."

"Tell her what she's won, Johnny." All the desk drawers were empty except one, which held a Gideon Bible. "But the statue is being used. How much did you learn about the process of bringing Ravana back?"

"Not much. But it didn't sound quick, and I don't think it's portable."

Buffy nodded. "That's what I thought. So the statuette's not here, and she's not carrying it with her." She turned to the bed. "He sleeps on that side," she said, pointing to the side of the bed with the beer bottles on the nightstand.

Willow went to the other nightstand, which had only a clock on it. She opened the drawer and removed a thick, dog-eared paperback book. On the cover, a shirtless, Fabio-like man held a beautiful, scantily clad woman in his arms. The title was written in shiny red embossed letters: *Savage Passion*. "She's got four more in here," Willow said.

"Now that I can believe. But a man . . ." Buffy shook her head slowly. "You should see this woman. I mean, she's a born spinster. No wedding ring. No jewelry at all, in fact. She was so . . . I don't know, awkward. Like she wasn't comfortable in her own skin, not to mention that awful green dress she was wearing. I would've bet money she'd never been on a date. So who's sleeping with her here?"

Willow put the romance novel back and closed the drawer. "Maybe that's all they're doing together. Sleeping, I mean."

"But why not get two rooms?"

"Couldn't afford it?"

"Giles said Benson Lovecraft was rich."

"That doesn't mean she is."

"Let's check out their luggage," Buffy said. She went to the long open closet where six suitcases of various sizes were lined up against the wall. "They've got enough." She got down on her knees and put one of the suitcases flat on the floor in front of her.

"Wait," Willow said, standing beside her and looking pensively at the luggage. "It just kind of occurred to me that we're, um . . . we're sneaking around here and, you know, poking through people's things, and it's not like we know them, we weren't even invited here, and, and I-I'm feeling kind of, um, kinda . . . guilty."

"Oh. Yeah." Buffy sat on the floor with her legs crossed. "Well, we both know we're not the kind of people who going around doing this, right? I mean, not unless it's absolutely necessary. But this is necessary, because if we don't find that statuette and destroy it, more people are going to do to each other what we tried to do to each other, except they'll succeed. And more people will be eaten. And Ravana will turn the whole world into his own perverted, evil playground."

Willow stared down at Buffy for a long moment, undecided. Then she dropped to the floor and grabbed a suitcase, saying, "You take that one, I'll take this one."

Two of the suitcases were empty. In the other two, they found shoes, a stack of road maps, lots of breath mints of various brands and flavors, several scarves, some gloves.

"Oh, look," Willow said. "More romance novels with Fabioids on the cover. She must be a big reader."

Buffy shook her head. "Books like that don't really count as reading." She found a stack of opened envelopes bound tightly together by a fat rubber band.

She thumbed through them and saw they each sported a canceled stamp in the top right corner. They were all addressed to Phyllis Lovecraft at a post office box in Mossrock, Washington. Buffy went through them again, but slowly, and found that not a single envelope carried a return address.

She slid one out of the rubber band, removed the letter, and unfolded it. There was only a single page of plain gray stationery, and the letter didn't take up all of one side. The handwriting was very neat, but not at all feminine.

Dearest Phyl,

Seeing you again revived me. But our time together is so *short.* I look forward to seeing you again soon. In the meantime, I shall see your face in every crowd and feel your touch in every dream.

Have you started gathering together your grandfather's Hindu collection yet? The pieces you showed me were exquisite. I am especially enamored of the Ravana statuette and the six accompanying pieces. The placement of the heads and arms on the Hindu demon is quite beautiful. I have no doubt that the gallery I have in mind will share my enthusiasm for that particular piece. But first you must pack it up so you'll be ready to go when I finish my business in New York.

I shall see you in two weeks, my love. We will take to the road together with your grandfather's art. But the *real* art will be when we're together, my sweet.

The letter was signed, "With all my love, Lloyd."

"I think I'm going to hurl," Buffy said.

"You feel sick?"

"No, I read this letter. It's postmarked the nineteenth of last month. From a guy named Lloyd." She put the first letter back in its envelope, then slid another out of the stack and opened it. Her eyes darted back and forth over the page for a while, then she took out another.

"And?" Willow asked, waiting for her to continue.

"He brings up the Ravana statuette," Buffy said, scanning a fourth letter. "Her grandfather's whole Hindu collection, really, but he brings up the statuette specifically."

"And that makes you want to hurl?"

"No, all of his schmaltz is what makes me want to hurl. They're all love letters with a little statuette talk thrown in. They sound like one of those books she reads." She handed one of the letters to Willow.

"Eewww," Willow said after reading it, wrinkling her nose. "Bring on the insulin."

"He doesn't mention Sunnydale in any of these letters, but he keeps talking about the gallery," Buffy said. "It's gotta be my mom's." She frowned as she quickly scanned one letter after another, carefully returning each to its envelope when she was done. "It looks like it was Lloyd's idea to exhibit that collection in the gallery. And each time he mentions it, he specifically brings up the Ravana statuette."

"Okay, that's the part I still don't understand," Willow said. "What's the deal with putting it on display if they're gonna use it to resurrect Ravana?"

Buffy read silently for a moment, then said, "Listen to this: 'Your grandfather's collection is so vast, I am certain he would not miss something as comparatively insignificant as the Hindu collection, in spite of the value and significance of the Ravana statuette. Once we arrive, I promise to . . .' Oh, um . . . oh." She grimaced. "He goes on to promise he'll suck on her toes."

"Hmm. Actually, that's kind of romantic."

"Not if you've seen her, Willow, trust me." She read the passage again silently. "The way Lloyd writes about him, Benson Lovecraft is still alive. 'I am certain he would not miss something.' Remember what Giles said about Lovecraft? That if he was still alive, he'd be well over a hundred years old?"

"Maybe Lloyd is referring to him figuratively," Willow suggested. "You know, the way some people refer to the dead. Like, 'I'm sure Grandpa would like that,' that kinda thing. You think?"

Buffy shook her head. "I don't think so. I think this guy's still alive and living on that island."

"He can't be too alive at that age, you know? I mean, he's gotta be, like, hooked up to a bunch of stuff. IVs, tubes, like that."

"You'd think." She read another letter and frowned. "Who is this Lloyd guy? Whoever he is, I just can't imagine what he'd see in someone like Phyllis Lovecraft." As her words grew farther apart, Buffy's eyes widened, and she looked over at Willow.

Willow said, "I'm guessing some kind of realization has just dawned on you."

"He doesn't see anything in her," Buffy said breathily. "There's nothing to see in Phyllis Lovecraft. I don't want to sound mean, Will, but she . . . well, this poor woman's uglier than a jar of warts. And I really think there's something wrong with her, you know, like she's not hauling all her kids in one minivan, if you know what I mean. Lloyd's just using her to get to the Ravana statuette! He, he . . . I don't know, maybe he knows Benson

Lovecraft has it, but there's no way for Lloyd to get it from him. Until he finds out Lovecraft has a granddaughter and she's not too bright and maybe she's lonely and looking for love—"

"The kind of sappy love she reads about in those books."

"Yes!" Buffy agreed enthusiastically. She began putting all the letters back together in their stack. "Lloyd wants to summon Ravana, but he can't come right out and say that to Phyllis. So instead, he tells her all those Hindu pieces should be exhibited so people can see them and appreciate them."

"But why would he want to bring them here? To Sunnydale? I-I mean, there are bigger museums in bigger cities."

"If you were going to revive an ancient demon, you'd want to do it in a place where it would most likely work, wouldn't you?"

Willow thought about that a moment, then her face brightened. "A Hellmouth!"

Buffy nodded. "This place is the supernatural demonic equivalent of Lourdes, so of course he'd want to do it here."

"Okay, so . . . if they're here, why is this woman still so desperate to get the stuff in the gallery? You said she's still bothering your mom about it, right?"

"I . . . I don't know," she said with a shrug. She looked over at the messy bed. "I wonder if Lloyd is the one who gave her the black eye she had when she came to our door."

"So much for romance," Willow said.

Buffy put the rubber band around the letters and the letters back in the suitcase. She and Willow closed the suitcases they'd been looking through.

Willow started to say something more about the romance novels, but she swallowed her words when keys jangled outside the door. They stared at one another with expressions of shock frozen on their faces.

"What do we do?" Willow breathed.

Before she was finished asking the question, a key slid into the lock of the motel room door.

Chapter 19

Aᴄᴛɪᴠɪᴛʏ ʜᴀᴅ ɪɴᴄʀᴇᴀsᴇᴅ ɪɴ ᴛʜᴇ ʟɪʙʀᴀʀʏ. Sᴛᴜᴅᴇɴᴛs were coming and going, some looking for books, others returning them. A few students were gathered around the computer. The quiet clatter of fingers on keyboards blended with the sound of whispered voices to create the library's usual sound.

Giles sat at the front desk with books open before him, rapidly taking notes. They would have to talk to Phyllis Lovecraft later that day. With any luck, she would lead them to the Ravana statuette. But it had not occurred to Giles until about twenty minutes ago that once they found it, they hadn't the first clue what to do with it. It would have to be destroyed, of course, along with the demon's essence inside. But how? He was searching for answers to that question. When he next saw Willow, he planned to discuss it with her, as well; she had been doing some extensive reading lately in the area of spells, incantations, and potions, and perhaps she had come across something that might work.

A voice was speaking nearby, but in the intensity of Giles's concentration, it sounded like it was coming from the bottom of a lake.

". . . iles? Um . . . Giles? Giles?"

Giles jerked his eyed up and saw Xander leaning his folded arms on the countertop.

"Are you there?" Xander asked.

"Yes, I beg your pardon. I was rather involved in my reading. What can I do for you, Xander?"

"I was just wondering if you've seen Buffy. Or Willow."

Giles shook his head. "No, why?"

Xander suddenly looked sheepish. "We were all going to meet back here and . . . uh . . . meet, study. You know, the book thing. And . . . they're late."

"Late? Xander," Giles glanced at the clock, "the bell just rang." Then his Watcher sense—or rather prolonged exposure to this group of Slayerettes—kicked in and he glared at Xander. "Good Lord, what have they done now?"

Buffy and Willow lay facedown under the bed in Phyllis Lovecraft's motel room. The instant Buffy had heard the key slip into the lock, she'd used her foot to push the last suitcase back into place, then she'd crawled quickly over the floor and slid under the bed, with Willow right behind her.

The first thing Buffy noticed about Phyllis Lovecraft was her shoes; they were ugly. She also noticed that Phyllis was limping and crying. As she walked around the bed, she favored her right side and cried quietly, sniffling occasionally, a small hitch of breath catching in her throat now and then.

Where's Lloyd? Buffy wondered. *Was she just with*

him? Maybe that's why she's crying. She remembered the black eye Phyllis had the day Buffy had come home to find her on the porch talking with her mom. *Had Lloyd hit her?* Buffy wouldn't be surprised. He was, after all, just using her to get to a statuette that would allow him to rule over chaos at the right hand of an ancient demon. A guy like that was liable to do anything.

Although she could only see Phyllis's feet, Buffy could tell what she was doing from the sounds she heard.

Phyllis slipped off her shoes and walked away from the bed. She ran water in the sink just outside the bathroom door, washed her hands. Still sniffling, she returned to the bed and sat on the edge. The sound of the telephone receiver being lifted, buttons on the base of the phone being pushed. Buffy could faintly hear the tone of each number being pushed and then the purring of a phone ringing at the other end of the line . . . a tiny, pinched voice.

"Hello, Seth. It's Phyllis." Her voice sounded thick from crying, as well as a little hoarse from weariness. "Oh, no, I'm fine, fine. Actually, I-I . . . yes, well, I was calling to see how Grandpa is doing." She stretched out onto the bed, but only for a moment. She jumped up. "What? How did he—" She paced as far as the coiled cord would allow. "But I closed that. I put everything back just *exactly* as I found it. Seth, did you tell him?" Insistent chatter from the earpiece. When Phyllis spoke again, her voice was low and whispery. "Oh, Seth, you're not serious." She dropped onto the bed again, making Willow wince for fear of being crushed. "But he doesn't know where I am! You didn't tell him that, did you? Of course you didn't, you don't even know where I am." She sounded like more tears were coming, as if she might break down soon. "Oh, his supernatural hoo-ha! Where did he say he was going? Sunnydale? Oh . . . oh." She sniffled. "When did he leave? Oh . . . oh."

She sounds pathetic, Buffy thought.

Phyllis released a long sigh, then said, "I have to go, Seth. I've got things to do. Yes, you do the same, Seth. 'Bye-bye."

The receiver clattered back in its cradle and Phyllis groaned. She didn't move for about a minute, then stood. She muttered to herself under her breath as she went into the bathroom. The shower door snapped open and she turned on the shower.

Buffy and Willow turned to each other instantly, smiled, and nodded.

Phyllis came out of the bathroom and undressed at the foot of the bed, tossing her clothes onto all the others scattered over the bed, fat, big-toed feet moving back and forth. When she went back into the bathroom, she absently swung the door closed behind her, but not hard enough; the door stopped about an inch short of closing. The shower door opened again . . . and a moment later, it closed again. There was a change in the sound of the shower's stream as Phyllis stepped under it.

"Okay, she's in," Buffy whispered as she crawled forward. Willow moved beside her. Once on their feet, they ran before they were standing up straight. Buffy opened the door slowly, careful not to make a sound; she pulled the door closed once they were both outside.

"That was close," Willow said as they went down the stairs. "Too close."

Buffy laughed.

Enough adrenaline was still pumping through the two that they hardly noticed the rain at all, and walked through it without a blink.

"Who do you think she called?" Willow asked.

Buffy replied, "I don't know, but it's someone she trusts, someone back home in Washington. Someone who knew she'd taken the Indian pieces from her grandfather's collection."

"It sounded like he used something supernatural to find out where she was once he realized she'd run off with his stuff."

"Yep. Giles says he's an expert. And it worked, too, because he headed for Sunnydale. He's here in town somewhere, or will be soon."

"You think a guy that old travels well?"

"A guy that rich does, no matter how old he is."

The got into the van and Buffy closed the door, thinking about the limo she'd seen. *Bingo!*

"What'd you do?" Oz asked. "Order pay-per-view?"

"We got held up," Buffy said.

"Yeah," Willow said excitedly, smiling. "She showed up while we were going through her stuff, and we had to hide under the bed. It was total *Mission: Impossible.*"

"Better than the movie," Buffy said.

"Are you upset because we kept you away from school?" Willow asked Oz. She leaned over and kissed his cheek.

Oz started the van and drove away from the curb. "I'd like to be ready for exams, just in case we all survive."

"Then take us back to school, Jeeves," Willow said. "And make it snappy."

* * *

Giles sat at the desk in his office listening to Buffy, while Willow stood beside her silently. He spent most of his time with his face in his hands. The more he listened and learned how much information she had gathered, the more certain he was that he would not get angry, even though she had done something he'd specifically told her not to do.

"I can't believe you went through her things, Buffy," he said.

"How could I not?" she asked, spreading her arms wide. "I mean, look at all I found out. This Lloyd guy? He wooed this homely woman—who might even be suffering from some kind of mental illness, I'm not sure—and he got her to care for and trust him enough to steal her grandfather's collection of Hindu art and run away with him. And according to those letters, he told her he wanted to do it so that collection could be exhibited in a gallery where people could appreciate it and enjoy it, instead of being packed away in some storeroom. At least, that's what he told her. And now that he's hidden away with that statuette, now that he's started the summoning, I think he's gotten tired of Phyllis. I think he's beating her. She had a black eye the first time I saw her and when Mom asked her about it, she got really nervous. And today, she was limping. Look, what I'm saying, Giles, is she might be in danger. If this Lloyd dude succeeds in calling up Ravana before we can stop him, then we're all up the creek. But if something goes wrong, he might take it out on Phyllis."

Giles shook his head slowly, took in a deep breath, and let it out in a long sigh. *If she weren't a Slayer,* he thought, *she could be a detective.*

"She may be weird," Willow chimed in, "but she's

also pretty sad. She doesn't deserve that. Nobody does."

"How did you get into the room?" he asked.

Buffy and Willow glanced at one another.

"Oh, um . . . that. We, um . . . we managed. And we didn't have to break anything, either."

He narrowed his eyes slightly. "Buffy—"

"Okay, we . . . we kind of, um, picked the lock."

"Yeah," Willow said, nodding. "We picked it."

"I see."

"Oh, and Benson Lovecraft is probably somewhere in Sunnydale right now. Or at least on his way."

Giles's eyes widened. "What are you talking about?"

"The rumors are true. He's still alive. He found out she took the—"

"Are you quite serious?"

Buffy nodded. "Yes."

"That . . . that is extraordinary!"

"Yeah. Anyway, he found out Phyllis took his collection of Hindu art, and apparently, he left Washington to come looking for her."

Giles said, "I'm not sure I want to know how you learned that."

"We overheard a telephone conversation while we were hiding under the bed."

"Hiding under the bed?" He looked at her, appalled. "You mean, you were in the room with her? Hiding?"

"She didn't see us. Didn't even suspect we were there. And as soon as she got in the shower, we got out of there."

Giles stood, walked around in a U-turn, and faced her. "That's not the point, Buffy . . . Willow. Do you realize the kind of trouble you were flirting with? We can't afford that. Mistakes are far too easy to make when you're prowling through someone's personal belongings like a common cat burglar. Let alone if you'd been caught. How would you explain—"

"She didn't even have a cat," Buffy said. She didn't give Giles a chance to continue. "Look, Giles, waiting until after school today to go talk to Phyllis Lovecraft? Bad idea. I think we should go right now. She's upset, crying . . . I think she might be on the verge of turning on Lloyd, especially now that she knows her grandfather is coming. If we go now and you talk to her, you might be able to get something out of her. Like where that statuette is. But if you wait, Lloyd might get to her again and sweet-talk her some more."

"I'm having serious thoughts about this Lloyd fellow. He's probably—"

"There've been more murders."

Giles stared at her a moment, stroked his chin. "Plural?"

Buffy nodded. "Just heard it on the radio on the way in. At the Sunnydale police station. Several cops went nuts and started shooting each other. There are a dozen dead, and the shooters have disappeared."

Giles sighed and stood up. "I'll ask Mrs. Tucker from the front office to come in and mind the library for a little while."

Buffy smiled. "That's a major idea, Giles."

He turned to Willow. "We need something to destroy that statuette and its contents. Have you—"

Willow grinned. "Are you kidding?" She grabbed for her bag—which Buffy knew sometimes doubled as a spell kit.

"There are a couple books on my desk. I've marked a few places in them and made some notes. Look over them and add any suggestions you think are relevant.

But don't actually go through with anything until I return. I won't be long."

"You got it, Chief," Willow said. She went behind the desk to the office.

"You mean *we* won't be long," Buffy corrected.

"No, Buffy, you'll be staying here," he said. "You've done enough right now." He tried to look stern.

"But you don't know where to find Phyllis Lovecraft." She wore a self-satisfied smile.

"She's at the . . ." He closed his eyes a moment, then opened them and smiled. "The Rocking R Motel."

"And her room number?"

"I don't remember the room. What's the number?"

"Uh-uh. Not gonna tell."

Another sigh as Giles lowered his head and massaged a temple. He stood again, reached into his pocket, and handed her his keys. "Go wait for me in my car. I'll be there as soon as I talk to Mrs. Tucker."

"Buffy," Willow said from the office doorway. "We'll do some concentrated, industrial-strength studying together once this is over. Right?"

"You're the best, Will," Buffy said over her shoulder as she hurried out of the library. She left her umbrella behind again.

In the parking lot, she jogged through the rain to Giles's car and unlocked the door. Before getting in, she stopped to watch an ambulance drive into the school parking lot, followed by two police cars.

"Uh-oh," Buffy muttered. She got into the car.

When Giles arrived, he slid behind the wheel.

"What's happening?" Buffy asked.

"Apparently, the janitor stabbed a sales rep from a cleaning supplies company to death," he replied, a pained expression on his face.

"Do you think it was Rakshasa? Or do you think he was just tired of the salesman?"

"The janitor has disappeared."

"Ah. Rakshasa."

After giving Giles Phyllis's room number, Buffy walked a step behind him as they went to the door of Phyllis Lovecraft's motel room. She hoped to keep Phyllis from recognizing her from their one brief meeting at Buffy's home.

Giles knocked on the floor.

"Lloyd?" Phyllis called inside.

Giles glanced at Buffy, then knocked again.

A moment later, the door opened and Phyllis faced them in a light blue terrycloth robe in need of washing and enormous furry pink slippers. The bruise beneath her eye was still there, but had grown smaller, lighter. She looked at them cautiously, paying more attention to Giles, and asked, "What do you want?"

"Miss Lovecraft?" Giles asked.

"That depends. Who are you?"

He smiled. "My name is Rupert Giles. I'm quite an admirer of your grandfather's work."

Phyllis's eyes darkened as she took a step back and closed the door, leaving only an opening of a foot or so. "You work for my grandfather?"

"Oh, no, not at all. I've come to ask you a few questions. May we come in?"

She eyed them suspiciously for a long moment, then stood back and opened the door. As they walked in, she looked at Buffy and said, "I recognize you. You're the gallery woman's daughter."

Buffy smiled, but it was an effort. "Nice to see you again."

The bed had been cleaned off, and the rest of the room wasn't quite as messy as it had been when Buffy and Willow were there.

"But I don't know you," Phyllis said to Giles. After closing the door, she walked past them, deeper into the room. She was still favoring her right leg.

"Well, I am a librarian. I have quite a collection of your grandfather's books."

"He doesn't sign books anymore, so if that's what you—"

"No, no, that's not it. Miss Lovecraft, I have, um, very good reason to believe that you are in a considerable amount of danger."

She frowned. "What are you . . . a gun salesman or something?"

"A gun sales . . . ? Oh, no, not at all. Could you tell me, by the way, where is Lloyd?"

She was surprised by the question, and not very happy about it. "You're a friend of Lloyd's?"

"Well, I do need to find him."

"Then you know him?"

"Uh, well no, I do not. But I know what he's doing. And it's putting all of us in danger, Miss Lovecraft, yourself included. So, tell me, please, where is he? Where has he taken the Ravana statuette?"

Phyllis clenched her fleshy fists at her sides and her mouth curled up as if she'd just bitten into a lemon. "You *are* working for my grandfather!" she exclaimed, and there was a slight growl in her voice. "Well, you tell him I'm not going back. You tell him I've found someone who cares about me, who *loves* me!"

"No, Miss Lovecraft," Buffy said, "Lloyd doesn't love you. He's been using you to get to the Ravana statuette. He knew he would never be able to get it from your grandfather's collection unless he had an insider help him. Like you. He never intended that collection to be exhibited in a gallery, and he—"

"How do you know all this?" Her pasty face became splotchy with bright red fury. "Who are you that you know all these things?"

"He's got what he wants now, Miss Lovecraft," Buffy went on, louder now. "He doesn't need you anymore. That's why he's been hitting you lately. Beating you. You're just in the way now, and if you don't tell us what we need to know, he'll—"

Phyllis stepped forward and raised a trembling hand high to slap Buffy, but Giles reached out and grabbed her thick wrist.

"No, Miss Lovecraft," he said firmly. "Your anger is misplaced. Do you know what your friend Lloyd is doing with the Ravana statuette and its six accompanying pieces?"

She lowered her arm slowly and averted her eyes, but said nothing.

"You know . . . or you've got some idea," Giles said. "Do you actually think you will survive what he's doing?"

Still not looking at them, head bowed, she said, "He . . . he loves me."

"This resurrection will plunge the entire planet into darkness, Miss Lovecraft," he went on. "Do you really think you are any more important to Lloyd than anyone else?"

She mumbled something.

"What's that?" Giles asked.

When she looked at them, she was baring narrow, crooked teeth and the angry red splotches had returned to her face, brighter, more vivid. "I said . . . *get out!*" she shouted.

Buffy and Giles flinched as Phyllis spun around and disappeared into the bathroom. There were shuffling sounds, as if she were going through a bag.

Buffy turned to Giles and said, "I've got a feeling we're not gonna get a whole lot of valuable information out of her. Know what I mean?"

"I quite agree. We should—"

Phyllis returned. In her right hand, she held a large knife with shiny blade that extended about nine inches.

"You go tell my grandfather to leave me alone!" she roared.

Buffy and Giles backed away as she approached them.

"You tell him I'm not a little girl anymore!"

Giles quickly opened the door and gestured for Buffy to exit. "Shall we go?"

"You tell him Lloyd Kaufman is a good and decent man who loves me!" Phyllis screamed as they left. She stepped outside the door onto the balcony walkway. "You tell him he *loves* me!"

Buffy and Giles hurried down the stairs and across the street without looking back. In the car, they sat unmoving for a long moment. Finally, Giles took off his glasses and rubbed his eyes, exhaling explosively, cheeks bulging.

"See, Giles? That didn't take very long," Buffy said sarcastically.

"You were right about one thing. Miss Lovecraft is quite unstable. If Lloyd is actually hitting her . . . well, do you think it's possible he's done so in self-defense?"

"Are you kidding? You heard the way she talked about him. She seems to know something about what he's doing, and still she says he's 'a good and decent man.' " Buffy shook her head. "She's got it bad."

"He is most likely the first man who has ever paid her any attention . . . shown her any affection."

"That's the sad part. I feel sorry for her. Even if she did pull a knife on us."

"But who is he?" Giles asked. "For a while, I was certain Ethan was behind this. He has an appetite for power exceeded by no one, and sitting on the right hand of Ravana, ruling like a god . . . that is precisely his cup of tea." He slipped the key into the ignition. "We should get back to—" He didn't start the car or finish his sentence.

Buffy saw him staring across the street and followed his gaze to the motel parking lot.

Phyllis had come downstairs wearing a long green coat over her robe. Her feet were still swallowed by the large fluffy slippers. She got into a white Ford Taurus and started the engine. The car shot backward from the parking slot and nearly slammed into a pickup truck parked on the other side of the lot.

"Follow her," Buffy said as Giles started the engine.

"That is precisely my intention," Giles replied.

Phyllis's tires squealed as she gunned the engine and sped out of the parking lot without pausing to check for traffic from either direction. She turned left, and the car swerved back and forth from one lane to the other for a moment before she regained control.

Giles waited for a car to pass them in his lane before pulling into the street. He followed her at a distance, with a Toyota between them and Phyllis's car.

"Let's hope she's going to see Lloyd."

Buffy replied, "Dressed like that, I doubt she's going out for bread and milk."

Phyllis's driving was erratic and reckless. She sped up, swerved a lot, and went through stop signs without even slowing. Giles followed her at a distance because he didn't want her to recognize them . . . and also because he wanted to stay the hell away from her.

She led them to the edge of Sunnydale, to a part of town were many of the buildings were unoccupied and boarded up. Buffy and Giles and the others had driven through that very part of town earlier in the week when they were looking for seedy bars and motorcycle-driving hellhounds. Phyllis's wild driving slowed a bit as she rounded a corner up ahead.

Giles turned the corner just in time to see Phyllis getting out of the Taurus. She was parked in the potholed, muddy area in front of the dark, empty, burned-out bus station.

"I'm afraid if I stop, she'll notice us," Giles said. "Keep an eye on her as I drive by."

Buffy watched as Phyllis slogged through the mud toward the building. She stepped into a pothole so deep, it nearly tripped her, but seemed to not notice it at all and just walked on. She went along the front of the building, then down the narrow alley between the bus station and a dilapidated building with a barely readable sign that read, Billiards. In a moment, she was out of sight.

"She's gone," Buffy said.

"Did she go inside?" Giles asked.

"I didn't see her go in, but I think that's where she was headed."

"I believe we've found the location of our statuette."

"Yeah, me, too. But that place looks about as stable as she is."

"But it is no doubt large and roomy inside. With this ritual producing who knows how many Rakshasa, as well such a large, unwieldy demon, it is probably an ideal location. He's hidden from view and I doubt anyone pokes around that place much, except for an occasional homeless person, perhaps, and there aren't too many of those in Sunnydale these days."

"No, we don't have a homeless problem," Buffy said. "Just vampires, demons, werewolves, and other assorted monsters."

Buffy turned on the radio and they listened to a report on the killing at Sunnydale High. The janitor still had not been found.

"We're going to go in there today, aren't we?" Buffy asked. "Into the bus station?"

"The material I've been reading gives very few details on the process of summoning Ravana," Giles said. "But it says that process takes up to seven days. Never more, but sometimes less. We aren't certain when he began, but even so . . . that leaves us little time. We don't even know how little. So, yes, we'll go in there today."

"Probably gonna be a whooole lotta Rakshasa in there, huh?"

"I suspect so."

Buffy leaned her head on the window. "Great. I won't wear my good clothes, then."

"Your encounter with them in your bedroom . . . did you learn anything helpful?"

"Only that it's a good idea to have something long and sharp. The machete worked well, but something longer would have worked better. Something like . . ." She turned to him. "You wouldn't happen to have any swords lying around, would you?"

"As a matter of fact, I would. They're in my apartment."

"Let's go get them now," she said enthusiastically.

"I want to go back to school first. I suspect everyone will be sent home after what's happened." He looked over at her. "We're going to need backup."

Chapter 20

Except for the arrival and departure of the EMTs and police, which took place during classes, there was no sign within the school building that anyone had been murdered on campus. Two police officers entered Principal Snyder's office through the side door to avoid going through the main building. In the office, the only witness to the murder, an assistant janitor, was interviewed. The killing took place in the basement, so the scene of the crime and the police officers tending to it disrupted none of the traffic between classes.

The biggest concern of the police was the fact that the janitor had not yet been found. A killer on the loose at the high school put the students and faculty in danger. It was decided to get everyone off the campus and close the school for the day. Again. But before the decision could be implemented, Principal Snyder's telephone rang. What appeared to be human remains had been found in the basement of the gymnasium . . . freshly eaten.

The two police officers looked at one another knowingly. It was nothing new to them, not anymore. They told Principal Snyder it would not be necessary to close the school, because they were certain the remains were those of the janitor. They left to go to the gymnasium basement.

For Buffy, time moved along as slowly and tediously as a line at the Department of Motor Vehicles. She waited for the end of the next period, wanting to round up the gang before they headed in different directions. Or were questioned by the police.

She watched the day darken through a hall window. Clouds that started out a light gray became bloated and developed charcoal-shaded undersides. Rain that fell straight down to the ground slanted more and more as a strong wind grew. She wondered if it was just unseasonably bad weather these last few days, or something else.

With Ravana so close, she thought, *and Rakshasa all over the place, maybe even the weather's upset.*

When the bell rang, Buffy was waiting in the hall for the others. As they each came out of their classrooms, she took them aside, and once they were all together, they headed for the library.

"You guys ready to kick some Rakshasa butt?" Buffy asked.

"Those little guys that look like they came out of Steven Spielberg's nightmare?" Xander asked.

"Yep," Buffy replied.

"Well, uh . . . will we be armed?" he asked, more cautious this time.

"Oh, yeah, we'll be *armed.*"

"And where is this going to take place?" Cordelia asked suspiciously.

"Well . . . let's wait till we get to the library." Buffy remembered how easily she had been fooled by the shapeshifting Rakshasa before, and wasn't comfortable talking about anything important there in the hall.

The library was empty except for Willow, who was already working diligently in Giles's office. She was seated at his desk with a mortar and pestle, grinding something into a fine powder. When Buffy and the others came in, she stopped and shook her right hand, wincing.

"This gets a little hard on the wrist after a while," she said.

"Did Giles tell you about our visit with Miss Lovecraft?" Buffy asked her.

Willow nodded. "And about the old bus station."

"Bus station?" Xander asked. "If the current one is any indication, the old one must be spectacular!"

Buffy told them all about the experience she and Giles had with Phyllis Lovecraft, and about where she had led them afterward.

"She pulled a knife on you?" Xander asked, amazed. "She sounds crazy."

"Tragic," Oz added quietly.

"Yeah," Buffy said. "That's what I thought. Tragic."

Xander nodded as he backpedaled. "Well, yeah, of course . . . *tragic*. But also crazy."

"You'd know," Cordelia muttered.

Buffy said, "We don't know anything about this Lloyd Kaufman."

Xander chuckled. "Sounds like a geek."

"Again," Cordelia said, "you'd know."

Xander turned to her, frowning. "Hey. I'm trying to listen to Buffy here, okay?"

They heard a clatter by the doors, and a moment

later, Giles entered the library carrying a long bundle wrapped in blankets under his right arm. He put it on the counter and it clunked heavily. He was wet from the rain and droplets of water clung to the lenses of his glasses. He removed a handkerchief from his pocket, took the glasses off, and dried them.

"This storm is getting worse," he muttered. He put his glasses back on, returned the handkerchief to his pocket, and asked, "Have you filled them in, Buffy?"

"Pretty much," she replied, as the others filed out of the office behind her.

He looked down at the powder in the mortar, then at Willow. "How is it coming?"

"Almost done," she said with a smile.

"Good. I brought the alcohol and the ground owl's bones. They're out in the car."

"Owl's bones," Xander muttered, nodding his head slowly, thoughtfully. "Where, um . . . where do you get something like that?"

"Fortunately, I happened to have some at home," Giles replied.

"Ah. Sure. Of course. Who doesn't?"

Giles turned to Willow again. "Have you memorized the incantation?"

"Yeah, it's pretty short. But are you sure it's okay if I do it in English?"

He patted her shoulder reassuringly. "It will either work or not, Willow. We don't have time to translate." He turned to the others, his eyes moving from face to face. "I'm afraid we have quite a dangerous task ahead of us. Buffy and I are obligated to confront it. That is our job. You, on the other hand, are obligated in no way whatsoever, and I want you to know you are free to—"

"You haven't told us what we're doing yet," Willow said. "How can we know if we're uncomfortable with it if we don't know exactly what it is?"

"I'm uncomfortable with it already," Cordelia said. "I mean, I don't like the sound of it. And besides, I . . ." She looked around at the others self-consciously. "Okay, so I have a hair appointment this afternoon. And I'm proud of it. I know that sort of thing means nothing to you people, but it's important to me."

Xander tilted his head back and rolled his eyes. "Can't you reschedule with Froi?"

"Are you kidding?" Cordelia asked, turning to him. "He has a waiting list as long as the 405 freeway! And besides . . ." She fluffed a hand through her hair. "I don't want to die with my hair looking like this!"

"Look, nobody's going to die," Buffy said. Her words didn't sound as confident as she'd meant them to. "I mean . . . well, you've all done this kind of stuff before. It's just that this time, we're going to be in unfamiliar territory."

"We don't know the layout of the building inside," Giles said. "And from the outside, it doesn't look structurally sound, so the building alone could be a threat. A weak floor or beam could potentially do us more harm than the Rakshasa."

"I don't know," Willow said. "I think I'd take a concussion or a broken bone over being eaten."

Buffy frowned and turned to Giles. "Is there a chance they'll do that? I mean, I thought they, you know, set people against each other, waited till one killed the other and then ate the survivor."

"That's strictly for entertainment," Giles repied. "You might say it's like . . . like the difference between going to a movie theater or watching a movie at home on television. One is more expensive and more trouble, but far more enjoyable. The other is convenient."

"So, uh . . . which one are we?" Xander asked. "The cineplex or Cinemax?"

Giles continued: "The Rakshasa enjoy manipulating people, making them turn on one another. The setup, the anticipation . . . it helps get the digestive juices flowing for the upcoming meal. But they will eat at any time, whether it's to satisfy hunger or simply in the act of defending themselves. They will eat anything they kill . . . and they will kill anything that threatens or offends Ravana."

Buffy suddenly felt a little nauseated. "You mean," she said, "when they were in my . . . my bedroom—"

"Had you not acted quickly," Giles said, "or not been a Slayer . . . yes, Buffy, that might have been your fate." He looked at the others. "That's why I warned you all earlier. We have no way of knowing how many Rakshasa we'll be facing inside that bus station, but I suspect quite a crowd."

"Then you'll need all the help you can get, right?" Xander asked.

Giles nodded ever so slightly and said, "Well, that may be true, but, uh, I can't ask you to—"

"So why is this any different than all the other times we've helped you?" Willow asked, smiling. "The more the merrier. Count me in." She went back to work with the mortar and pestle.

"I'll play," Oz said with a nod.

"Me, too," Xander said. He turned to Cordelia.

She stared at him a moment, then snapped, "I'm thinking, I'm thinking!"

"I expect it to be quite dark in there," Giles said, "so I stopped by the hardware store and got each of us a long, heavy Mag-Lite flashlight. Not only will they provide light if we need it—although it might be a good idea to use them only if absolutely necessary to avoid being seen—they're sturdy enough to serve as weapons."

"Whoa-ho-ho, swing back sweet chariot," Xander said, holding up a hand. "You mean . . . we're gonna go in there armed with . . . with flashlights? Are we gonna . . . I don't know, what . . . shine those things to death?"

Giles turned to the desk and said, "Excuse me, Willow."

She stood and took the mortar and pestle over to a table.

Leaning forward, Giles slowly unwrapped the blankets from the bundle he'd carried into the library. The others moved in close around the desk to watch. Even Willow stopped what she was doing and joined them. Within the blankets were seven long objects individually wrapped in towels.

"There are seven here," Giles said. "I brought an extra in case—"

"Am I interrupting anything?" a quiet voice asked.

Everyone turned to the doorway. Buffy smiled warmly when she saw Angel leaning into the office. She'd lost track of time. It might not've been dark out yet, but with the sewers between school and his mansion, and the blacked-out windows in Oz's van, Angel could get around—carefully—before sunset.

Giles's eyebrows rose high above his glasses. "In case Angel shows up." He handed each one of them a towel-wrapped object, and they began unwrapping them.

"Holy silverware, Batman!" Xander blurted with genuine awe and surprise.

"Wow!" Willow said.

Oz smiled and muttered, "Cool."

Frowning, Cordelia said, "I'm gonna get a hernia."

Each of them unwrapped a long sword in a leather sheath, some black, some brown, and a couple the deep black-red color of dried blood.

"All but one are scimitars that differ slightly in design and length," Giles said, "but weigh no more than three pounds. They all have grips designed to accommodate two-handed use, but are balanced enough to be swung with just one hand, if you so choose."

Xander removed the sheath from his sword, put it on the counter, and marveled at the gracefully curved, gleaming steel blade. He moved it slowly through the air, this way and that, and with each sweep, he made a humming-buzzing sound with his mouth. He turned to Cordelia, held the sword as if he were about to strike her down, and made a muffled, heavy breathing sound, as if he were breathing through a tube. Then, in a voice as deep as he could manage, he said, "I . . . am . . . your father, Luke . . . now go clean your room."

Cordelia gave him a withering look. "Aren't you late for a convention, Trekkie-boy?"

He lowered the sword and shook his head. "Oh, no, no, that's 'Star Trek.' I was doing Darth Vader, from *Star Wars.*"

"Sounded more like Ed McMahon from 'Star Search,' " Cordelia sneered.

"Hey, there's a big difference between—"

Angel cleared his throat loudly as he went to Buffy's side. "I think I came in the middle of this movie."

"Don't worry," Buffy said, still unwrapping her sword. "I'll catch you up on the plot on the way over there."

"Over where?"

"I'll tell you that, too, I promise," she said, smiling up at him. As usual, Buffy's voice lowered in his presence, became almost secretive, as if everything she said to him was meant to stay just between them. It happened automatically; she couldn't help it.

Giles approached Buffy as she inspected her sword.

"It's a little different than the others," he said. "I thought it was more . . . you. It will do more damage because it's heavier, and I knew you could handle that, and it has a double-edged blade."

A bloodred groove ran down the center of the silver thirty-six-inch blade. The blade itself ended in an arrowhead-shaped tip with a diamond cutout in the center. The crossbar was formed by a down-turned steel horn that came out each side of a flat, brushed steel skull. The dark, wooden grip extended from the top of that skull and ended in a smaller, but three-dimensional, solid steel skull pommel with red eyes and an up-turned horn growing from each side.

"This is incredible, Giles," Buffy said.

Giles nodded. "Isn't it? It was a gift from a friend. Specially made for me."

"Really? Then it's . . . important to you. What if something happens to it?"

"In your hands, Buffy, I have great faith that nothing will. Except, of course, for the slaying of Rakshasa."

Still trying out his sword in slow motion, Xander asked, "So, do we get to keep these things?"

"You most certainly do not," Giles answered abruptly without missing a beat. "These swords come from my personal collection."

"You collect these things?" Cordelia asked. Her arms were stretched out, elbows locked, and the scimitar lay across her open palms. She looked at it as if it were a dead snake.

Giles shrugged absently, looking a bit sheepish. "Swords have been an interest of mine since boyhood. But an expensive hobby, I'm afraid, which is why my collection is a small one."

"Why swords now, in particular?" Angel asked Giles.

Buffy said, "I'll tell you on the way."

Angel sighed, frustrated. "This better be a long trip."

"Before we go," Giles said, his voice raised slightly so all of them could hear, "I think it would be a good idea for you to spread out here where you'll have more room and get used to the feel of your weapon. This will require you to think and act quickly, so let's prepare as much as we can."

"I've got work to do first," Willow said, returning to the mortar and pestle on the table.

Xander went to Cordelia's side and put a hand on her back. "C'mon, I'll help you get acquainted with that thing."

Cordelia pulled away from him and met his eyes. "Is that supposed to be some kind of joke? Because if it—"

Xander raised his free hand in surrender and said, "No, no, I swear, I was being serious! I meant it just like it sounded! Really!"

She eyed him for a moment, looking for any sign of insincerity. "All right," she said hesitantly. "But that doesn't mean I'm going along with this thing."

"Hey, you don't need Froi," Xander said as they moved away with Oz. "As sharp as these things are, I could do your hair right here."

Buffy and Giles joined Willow at the table. Angel

followed a step behind Buffy, looking impatient and uncomfortable.

"What's cooking, Betty Crocker?" Buffy asked.

"Ravana cream pie," Willow replied. "I hope."

"You hope?

"While there seems to be plenty of material available on Ravana and how to resurrect him," Giles said, "we were unable to find anything on stopping or undoing that resurrection. I found a melting potion that seemed vaguely appropriate, but still very uncertain at best. Then Willow made a few suggestions."

"And he actually liked them," Willow said, smiling at Buffy over her shoulder.

"She suggested we add an active ingredient from another potion," Giles explained, "and a catalyst from still another. Of course, there is no way to be certain until the moment of truth, but I think the resulting dissolving potion will be quite effective."

"So she's turning into quite a witch, huh, Giles?" Buffy asked.

Giles put a hand on Willow's shoulder. "Willow is an excellent *student* of magic, Buffy. There's a tremendous difference." Willow didn't smile.

The piercing clang of blades clashing sounded from the library.

"Good God!" Giles exclaimed before rushing out of the office. "No contact! No contact!" he shouted. "Just get comfortable with their weight, so you can swing them."

Buffy leaned closer to Willow and whispered, "Sounds like you impressed Giles. Maybe he'll back off about the magic, you think?"

"I don't know." Willow's voice was suddenly tremulous. "I'm really not sure if this is gonna work."

"Don't worry, Will. If it doesn't work, it won't matter, because we'll all be dead."

Willow stopped grinding with the pestle and looked over her shoulder and up at Buffy with big, frightened eyes.

Alarmed by the expression on her friend's face, Buffy said, "I was only kidding!"

"I know, I know. But I feel like I'm under a lot of pressure now, and if it doesn't work, then it'll be my fault that we'll all be dead."

"Willow, you can't think that way! Jeez, if I did, all my teeth would turn around in my head and eat my brain."

"Then how am I supposed to think?"

"That you've done your best. And if it doesn't work, then we'll do something else that will!"

Thunder cracked in the sky, and Buffy, Willow, and Angel looked up at the ceiling, as if they might be able to see it.

"Great night for it," Buffy muttered.

"You think you could clue me in on this?" Angel asked quietly. "Or, if you'd rather, I could always just leave."

"No, no, Angel," Buffy said. She went to his side and put a hand on his arm. "We need you, believe me." She led him aside as she began to explain everything, leaving Willow alone with her work.

Beneath her sweater, Willow felt the tiny hand-carved Rama resting against her chest. She was relieved that Mila had never found out what Buffy had suspected her of, what she had accused her of doing. Mila probably would have had a good laugh over it, but even so, Willow preferred that she not find out at all.

As she worked, Willow thought about Mila's brother.

She wondered what he looked like, how many hours a day he spent carving the gods and devils of his religion out of stone. Mila had said that, unlike herself, her brother was a devout Hindu. To him, the carved figures Willow found merely pleasing to the eye and touch were images of beings he believed really exist, or existed at one time; they were a part of his deeply felt spiritual beliefs, not just wildly imaginative monsters and superheroes.

Willow supposed that the miniature carving of Rama she wore around her neck was just as important to Mila's brother as a crucifix would be to a Christian, or a Star of David to her father. When Mila had told her about the many gods of Hinduism, and of the many other identities each god had, it had sounded so completely foreign to anything Willow knew, it was hard to not to think it was silly. But it was a legitimate religion that had been around longer than many, perhaps even most.

No wonder so many wars are fought over religion, she thought.

She wished Mila's brother were there with them. He would have a much better idea of what they were going up against, and he'd probably know of a way to vanquish Ravana, a prayer, or some sort of scripture, maybe. It would be better than the alleged dissolving potion she was whipping up. Even if it didn't work, it would be his fault . . . not Willow's.

The bus station stood in the rainy night like the dark ghost of a building once bright and full of life. Its boarded up windows were multiple blinded eyes, the cracks and holes in its blackened walls bloodless open wounds that had never healed. The muddy, pocked ground around it was littered with chunks of what had once been a paved sidewalk; in the rain, the ground seemed to bubble and churn like a poison swamp. In the dark, the building seemed to be still and hunkering, waiting patiently for something—or someone—to happen by so it could pounce and feed. But in those strobelike moments when lightning flashed, it became a monstrous face in great pain: window-eyes clenched shut, portal-mouth—deeply shadowed beneath its tall archway—yawning open in a silent, tortured shriek.

They sat in Oz's van, looking at the bus station through the front window, none of them moving to get out.

"Looks hungry," Oz muttered.

They had decided to take Oz's van because Giles's cozier Citroen would not hold all of them and the swords as well.

Willow had finished preparing the potion. In a nylon bag that hung from a shoulder strap, she carried two containers: one metal with a plastic lid containing the fine powder she'd ground by hand, and another of plastic containing a milky liquid that was to be poured in with the powder at the last possible moment before the potion was to be used. As she poured the liquid, she was to recite a brief incantation. The potion would become active the instant the liquid met the powder and had to be used immediately.

Giles had warned them that once inside the bus station, they would very likely encounter rats and stray cats. "Don't let them startle or distract you," he'd said. "If you hear them moving in the dark, that means they're just trying to get away from you." He'd explained to them, as well, that the Rakshasa did not regenerate very fast, and could be killed by repeated stabbing, cutting, or dismemberment. "The swords are ideal weapons, as Buffy suggested to me today. They allow you distance from the creatures to avoid being bitten, and you can hit several at once with broad sweeps."

Back in the library, Xander had continued trying to convince Cordelia to come with them. Giles told him to stop trying to coerce her into doing something she didn't want to do, and Xander pointed out that Cordelia had a reputation for needing no coercion whatsoever, at which point she swung a foot up, kicked him in the butt, and told him to beam himself up, adding, "And you know what I mean, Spaceboy." She'd decided, in the end, to join them because she said she could always make another appointment with Froi. Even if she had to wait for it, that would be better than never having another hair appointment ever again, which was exactly what would happen if her friends failed to defeat Ravana because they didn't have enough help.

"Reminds me of the fair," Xander said absently, mostly to himself.

"The fair?" Cordelia asked. "Your syntaxes are misfiring again."

"Synapses," Xander corrected.

"Whatever."

"It reminds me of the fair," Xander explained, "because when I was a little kid, I'd go every year with my parents, and I'd always want to go through the spook house. So my dad would buy two tickets, while I stood there and looked at all the scary pictures painted on the side of the spook house. I'd get myself so worked up that, the second he handed over the money and got the tickets, I'd tell him I was too scared to go in. He'd pick me up under his arm and carry me through the thing. It was never as scary as it looked outside ... wasn't really scary at all. But it happened that way every year." He frowned and scratched his head. "Maybe that's why I like hanging around with you, Buffy. My dad traumatized me outside the spook house so many times that now I'm warped and I think I actually like being scared."

Cordelia said, "I'm not carrying you in there, so don't even ask."

"I suggest," Giles suggested, "that we not sit out here and get ourselves all worked up. Shall we gather our things and go inside?"

They got out, removed the sheaths from their swords and tossed them inside the van, and checked their flashlights.

"Everything's boarded up," Giles said to Buffy. "But Miss Lovecraft got in here somehow. Where did she go as we drove by today?"

Buffy pointed. "Down that little alleyway. To the right of the building." She led the way, getting soaked in the process, and the others followed closely in the dark.

"Your swords are going to rust, Giles," Xander warned.

"I doubt it. But even if they do ... if they get us through this, they shall take on greater significance in my collection simply for having done so, and not for their appearance alone."

They had agreed to not use their flashlights unless absolutely necessary; they did not want to be seen approaching the building. The long, heavy, black metal lights remained dark and clipped to their belts.

Their feet sloshed in puddles and squished in mud, Xander whispered to Cordelia to be quiet, because she kept saying, "Eewww!" over and over again.

The alleyway was narrow and littered with concrete rubble, blackened boards, and garbage that had been carelessly dumped around the building and would probably stink on a hot day.

Concealed between the two buildings, Angel led the way so no flashlights lit the dark alley. He stopped in front of a door set back a foot or so in the side of the building. It was a metal door covered with obscene graffiti, and it had a handle instead of a doorknob. Angel tried the handle. It moved, and the door opened inward a couple of inches.

"Here," Buffy whispered to the others behind her. Angel pushed the door open farther and he and Buffy stepped inside. She stopped, giving her eyes a moment to grow accustomed to the deeper darkness.

Behind her, Giles knew exactly what she was doing, and whispered, "Let me know when you can see something."

A moment later, Buffy said, "It's a corridor. I think . . ." Angel nodded. She led the way and moved forward, then turned to the left. An open doorway with viscous darkness beyond it. She turned on the light. The beam slid over shattered tile floors, broken sinks and urinals, some of which lay on the floor, and the remains of stalls. "Restrooms," she whispered. "We're by the restrooms." The beam of light disappeared with a click.

Their feet crunched on dirty floors as they moved along cautiously. The sound of rainfall outside faded, as other sounds grew up ahead. Similar sounds. Water running.

Buffy passed another restroom. Ahead, she could make out the open end of the corridor. Beyond it, there appeared to be . . . light? If so, it was impossibly soft in the vast darkness that lay beyond the corridor's entry. As she drew nearer, the light seemed to move within the oppressive darkness . . . to dance.

Over her shoulder, Buffy whispered, "Okay, keep the flashlights off. Looks like there's light up ahead."

"I see it, too," Giles said.

The sound of water was much louder, as if it were right in front of Buffy. Another step, and cold water doused her. She gasped and backed up, running into Giles.

"The roof is leaking," he whispered. Over his shoulder, he whispered to the others, "It may get worse farther on, so don't let it startle you."

As their eyes adjusted, they made out the faded graffiti spray-painted on walls darkened by fire long ago; some of the graffiti had faded, and more had been painted over it. Amid the large spray-painted gang signs and crude pictures were smaller drawings and writings made with brightly colored, metallic ink: limericks, telephone numbers, meeting times.

As Buffy reached the doorway, Angel pointed to the light and whispered, "Candlelight." When she stepped out of the corridor and looked to the right, she saw that he was correct.

She guessed there were a hundred candles, maybe two hundred. They fanned out from the rear left corner of the building. A path was cleared down the center of the mass of candles. In the corner itself, more light came from two sources: a pulsating blob about the size of a microwave oven that glowed a sickly green, and behind it, something that shimmered a dark, undulating red.

They stopped in a group, just outside the corridor, all of them looking at the strange lights beyond the candles.

"That's what we came for," Buffy whispered. She looked all around the cavernous blackness. Water spattered everywhere. There were piles of rubble here and there, and she saw what looked like two old pinball games lying on their sides. Other than the candles and the glowing objects beyond them, there was no sign of life.

Buffy moved forward, her boots crackling over the floor. She walked through another cold shower of rainwater. When it was behind her, she stopped and looked up.

There was no ceiling. No roof. At least, there appeared to be none. Overhead, Buffy could see the night sky. On the other side of the station, she could see a patch of dark clouds that, after a moment, flashed with lightning. Everywhere else, Buffy could see stars. Tiny, twinkling red stars.

Wait a second, Buffy thought. *Stars? During a rainstorm? Red stars?*

They were everywhere above them. Among the exposed rafters. Everywhere. Her upturned head moved back and forth slowly as she scanned the station's ceiling. She now realized that, except for the hole through which she could see clouds, there was a ceiling high up there, however leaky. And she wasn't looking at stars.

They were the red, watchful eyes of scores and scores of Rakshasa.

Chapter 21

"WE'RE BEING WATCHED," ANGEL WHISPERED TO BUFFY.

"But not attacked," she replied suspiciously. Buffy turned to face the others. "Walk very slowly. Don't do anything that might look threatening, like arm movements. Don't talk unless you absolutely have to, and then only whisper."

"How do I whisper a scream?" Cordelia asked in an unsteady breath.

Buffy turned around and moved on very slowly, the rest of them moved with her.

Along with the leaks, there were the faintest of shufflings overhead, constant, waving across the station and back again slowly: the clicking of little fangs . . . the soft belching of well-fed stomachs, and the impatient gurgle of others that hungered . . . the shuffle of squat bodies . . . the slither of rat-pink tails sliding along rafters. Each sound spread a blanket of icy gooseflesh over Buffy. To her, it felt suddenly—now that she knew they were there—as if the creatures were much lower than they were, low enough to reach down and run claws through her hair, or curl a fleshy tail around her neck. For a moment, she wanted to slap them away and start swinging her sword. But she pushed it away like the flimsy mental obstacle it was, and moved on.

Up ahead, the glowing green object continued to pulsate, and a shimmer of red came from behind it. As Buffy drew slowly nearer to the corner, objects became clearer. The red shimmer was emanating from the Ravana statuette in front of it, a swirling funnel that was bigger than Buffy had first thought. It snaked and wobbled like a glowing Silly Straw, then widened and grew steady. It spun in place around a dark hulking object forming inside the funnel.

Buffy looked at the bottom and saw the enormous, powerful legs; dark, muscled, and glistening, crossed in the lotus style. The rest of the body formed before her. Gold and brown shorts covered the tops of the thighs and the waist, above which a matching, low-cut vest displayed developing abdominal and chest muscles that seemed to have been carved out of dark stone. Twenty arms quickly grew out from all the way around the top of the upper body, hands resting on the body, elbows jutting outwardly sternly. Ten heads faced all directions in a carousel of open mouths that talked rapidly, teeth flashing, tongues working, but made no sounds. The spinning funnel ended at the eyes. The thing continued to form.

The eyes were finishing up, the brow about to begin, leaving only the top of the head to go.

Buffy looked down at the pulsating green blob. It was attached to the six pieces accompanying the Ravana statuette; a green tentacle of the same glowing substance extended from the open mouth of each of the small Rakshasa and came together to form the blob.

There was a sudden tremble in the shapeless green glow, and lips formed in the gelatinous substance, opened with a wet peeling sound. A Rakshasa came out of the opening, as if it had been kicked out. Beads of the green goo were attached to its small body. It hit the floor running, and as it ran down the aisle down the center of all the candles, it expanded and lengthened rapidly until it was the same size as the other Rakshasa Buffy had seen.

With the creature running toward her, Buffy stopped, took a couple steps back. But it seemed not to notice her. Once past the candles, it turned right and climbed up out of the way as another Rakshasa came from the green blob. It did the same thing.

Buffy looked at the hole open to the rainy sky above. They were shadows as they crawled like flies up the wall and over the ceiling to the hole. For an instant, she saw one silhouetted blackly against a bluish-silver flash of lightning. Then it was gone.

She didn't know how often they came out, or if it was always two at a time, but Buffy was certain there would be more. She didn't understand why the two new Rakshasa had ignored them. Maybe their senses were weak at first . . . or maybe they were in too big of a rush to get outside and start spreading big bundles of vicious hatred and bloody slaughter like the eager elves of some twisted Santa Claus.

There was a click somewhere in the dark, and Buffy was blinded by light pointed directly at her face. Her feet made abrupt *chitch* sounds as she stopped suddenly, squinted, and turned her head away. Footsteps came toward her hard and fast.

"You kids mind telling me just what you're doing here?" a deep male voice said.

The light lowered and Buffy blinked her eyes several times. A uniformed police officer with a flashlight stood in front of her.

Giles put a hand on Buffy's shoulder and stepped forward.

"Excuse me, officer," he said, "but I can explain this, I assure you."

The police officer put the light on Giles's face for a moment. He passed it over the faces of the others, then returned to Buffy. He smiled and his head bobbed a few times.

"That's quite a blade you got there, young lady," the police officer said. He held out a hand. "Why don't you hand it over before you hurt somebody? C'mon, you first."

Buffy looked to the right of him, into the corner, and focused her eyes carefully on Ravana's face. The twenty eyes were finished and glowed a dull red, but it seemed the red glow was getting stronger, brighter. The mouths were still yammering, but as she watched them, she realized suddenly they were no longer entirely silent.

She heard a distant, ghostly sound, voices, speaking rapidly, even wildly, in an unfamiliar language. The faint sound was synchronous with the movements of Ravana's mouths. Buffy turned to Giles.

"It's almost done," she said.

"Hey!" the officer barked. He sounded angry, but his eyes twinkled mischeivous, and the spirit of a smirk darted around the corner of one corner of his mouth. "I thought I told you to give me that sword!"

When Buffy looked at the cop again, she noticed his badge for the first time. Something about it didn't look right; without moving her arm, she flicked on her flashlight and aimed it at the cop. His badge reflected a flash of light. There was nothing engraved or embossed on the badge . . . it was a shiny, star-shaped piece of perfectly smooth metal.

"Give it to me, dammit!" the cop snapped again.

"Okay, take it." Buffy drove the long blade straight through the middle of his upper body.

The cop's mouth fell open and he made a groaning, gurgling sound. Willow and Cordelia stifled screams, and Giles gasped.

She pulled it out just as fast as she'd put it in, and dropped her flashlight to the floor as she clutched the handle with both hands. Stepping clear of Giles and the others, she spun around as she moved toward the cop.

The blood-streaked blade caught and reflected a strobe of lightning as it flashed first through air, then through the cop, just above the waist. He shrieked as he hit the floor in two pieces.

Giles was the first to be splashed with green goo.

Both pieces of the cop fluttered, dreamlike . . . shifted and warped as the horrible scream continued. The cop's appearance broke down, liquefied, became taut, then reformed. The Rakshasa abruptly stopped shrieking and used its arms to crawl toward the stubby, kicking legs.

Buffy didn't let it.

She brought the blade down on the head rapidly, repeatedly. It melted into a mound of the green gelatinous substance. Buffy stepped back from it and watched as it disappeared.

But the legs did not.

All of them stared down at the hairy, scabrous legs, which continued to kick wildly. At the top of the legs, though, from just above the waist, something was growing.

The rest of the Rakshasa's severed body was being replaced.

"Evil flatworms," Xander whispered. "Are we done yet?"

Buffy swung her sword like an ax until the growing, kicking legs were gone.

As she stood up straight, wet strands of hair stuck to her face. The babbling voices were louder, their words more distinct, though foreign. She bent down, picked up her flashlight, and turned it on Ravana as she stood.

Lips writhed in fast motion. No longer still, the arms reached and stiffened and swept up and down, back and forth; palms opened, fingers pointed, fists clenched and hammered air. She was watching a passionate but silent orator one didn't need to hear in order to know it was malignant.

And the voices were louder, clearer. All the same voice, but gibbering differently at the same time.

"We don't have much time," Buffy said. "Willow?"

Willow came to Buffy's side, unzipping her bag.

"You ready?" Buffy asked.

Willow nodded. "Sure, the sooner the better. 'Cause I think I'm gonna need to get to a bathroom soon."

Buffy turned to the others. "Spread out a little. Verrry slowly." She looked up.

The endless red eyes were still there. She couldn't tell if they were watching her . . . they were just there.

"Okay, let's go," she muttered as she turned and walked toward Ravana. Willow was right behind her.

They stopped at the opening of the path between the

candles. It was too narrow for them to walk it side by side, so Willow went first.

The instant Willow's foot moved forward to step on the path, there was a gut-churning shriek, like heavy metal being twisted and torn, crushed and ground together, a cacophany of high squeals with throaty growls behind them, coming down from overhead, making the air convulse, growing louder, closer . . .

Hell opened up on them from above.

The horrible screaming from above frightened Xander so much, he felt as if his bones were melting inside him. He didn't look up, because he didn't want one of those creatures to fall on his face. But as he bowed his head and hunched his shoulders, he had the presence of mind to raise his sword so the blade was pointing straight up. It suddenly became much heavier in his hand and Xander raised his head.

A Rakshasa was skewered on his blade, screaming and kicking, glaring at Xander with the promise of death in its red eyes. Xander quickly lowered the sword, and the creature slid off the blade and dropped to the floor.

"Good start," Xander said as he cut the creature into as many pieces as he could before the next came along, and the next and the next. Up ahead and to his right, another blade flashed in the darkness.

Oz hopped onto an old pinball machine lying broken and black on its side. It made him even taller than the small creatures that ran toward him, jagged mouths snapping. He swung the blade downward; it went through a neck and a horned, reptilian head tumbled through the air. Ran another through, severed an arm from a third. But there were too many of them coming too fast.

Angel became a part of the darkness. Instead of fighting the creatures off, he did what he did best . . . moved through shadows like a ghost and attacked them, leaving none remaining in his path.

The same thing was happening to Cordelia. Her back to a wet, dripping wall, she held the sword in both hands and swung it hard in wide half-circles from side to side. She did some damage with each swing, but not enough. They kept getting off the floor and coming back, with others rushing in behind them.

"Would at least some of you go away!" she screamed.

Something closed on her left leg and sharp points pierced her pants. Then her skin. Cordelia bent her knees so she could reach the creature and beat it with the heavy flashlight, while still holding off the incoming.

Buffy did the same thing in front of the candles, where the majority of the Rakshasa headed upon hitting the floor. More skilled with the sword, Buffy's movements were quick and economical, and very effective.

"Do it, Willow!" Buffy shouted over her shoulder. "Do it now!"

The soul-chilling cry from above had frozen Willow in place, but Buffy's shout snapped her out of it. Willow forced her legs to propel her forward along the candle path.

Two more fresh Rakshasa popped from the green blob and ran toward Willow. They darted around her as if she were merely an annoyance, eyes staring straight ahead, hurried to the walls, and started climbing toward the hole to go out for a night on the town.

Willow lifted her sword and brought it down on the

pulsating green blob again and again, until it was a thick, liquid puddle and connecting tentacles had collapsed.

No more newbies.

But Buffy couldn't hold off all of the Rakshasa so eager to stop Willow.

"Look out, Will!"

One of them slammed onto her back, clutched her shoulders, and snarled into her right ear. Its hot, moist breath washed over one side of her face and into her mouth and nose, as its snout opened wide to bite.

Willow screamed as she swung her left arm around and plunged the long, fat flashlight into the creature's mouth, down its throat. It made a belching, gagging sound and dropped off her back, taking the flashlight with it.

Willow turned around and chopped the creature a couple times with the deadly edge of her scimitar before kicking it aside. The thing was cut nearly in two diagonally, from shoulder to hip, but still in one piece as it tumbled into the mass of small flickering flames, knocking candles over, throwing angry shadows around the floor.

Realizing its body was virtually in two pieces, the creature pulled itself together with one arm and tried to get up. But it was already in flames. It released a high, guttural shriek before dissolving into a sizzling, smoking mess.

Another was on its way toward her, having shot between Buffy's legs.

Heart pounding rapidly, adrenaline flooding her body, Willow shouted, "The flame is quicker than the sword!" She swung the sword with both hands, sliced into the oncoming Rakshasa, and knocked him into the other blanket of flames.

"Good one, Will!" Buffy called back as she turned sharply to her left, swung the sword around, and threw the creature impaled on it into the candles. "Thanks!"

As the creatures screamed, Willow walked backward clumsily with one hand in her shoulder bag. She found the cold metal container, peeled the plastic lid off. She wrapped her fingers around the container and turned around.

The Ravana statuette was directly in front of her, not two feet away. She lifted the container from the bag, held it a moment in front of her as she looked at the gesticulating, chattering creature.

It stopped moving for a heartbeat. All the heads that could suddenly turned to Willow, their burning eyes locked onto her. Fingers pointed to her. The lips moved and the voices—closer now, louder—spoke furiously as one.

Willow stepped forward and poured the powder over the statuette. It clung to the damp surface, making the statuette look like some ghostly octopus.

Ravana's voice became sharply louder as it screamed at her, wailing like a thousand mad wolves.

She removed the plastic container of liquid from the bag.

A creature hit the back of her legs and buckled her knees. She dropped to a kneeling position until another hopped onto her back and knocked her to the floor. Her sword slipped from her hand and clattered over the floor as another of the beasts jumped on her.

"Buffy!" Willow shouted.

Upon hearing the hellish cry from their materializing lord and master, the majority of the remaining Rakshasa had stopped what they were doing and rushed toward the corner. Having removed the creature that was clamped onto her lower leg, Cordelia found herself free to strike at the oncoming creatures more effectively, because there were fewer of them. So did Oz, still standing atop the old fallen pinball machine. As did Giles and Xander, who were moving in slow circles, their backs to one another, to fend off the beasts.

Buffy backed up the path, swinging and plunging the sword, missing some, hitting quickly enough and often enough to make them drop. But another wave of them came.

Willow screamed, "Buffy! Bufffeeee!"

Turning her head as far as she could, Buffy looked over her shoulder and saw Willow fighting desperately beneath a mound of Rakshasa. Willow's left arm was raised, the plastic container in her hand.

Buffy spun around a couple times, slicing with the sword, kicking her feet, making solid contact again and again, redoubling her efforts as she moved backward. When her foot struck Willow's, Buffy spun around and attacked the Rakshasa on top of her friend. They scattered quickly, most into the candles, roaring and shrieking. A pile of rubbish had caught fire and the flames were rising. She snatched the container from Willow's hand.

"Pour it on the statuette!" Willow shouted as she rolled onto her back and sat up. Her nylon bag had been shredded to string-dangling strips and she pulled the strap off.

"You mean, just . . . pour it?" Buffy asked.

"Yes, and I'll say the words . . ."

Buffy quickly took the lid from the container and moved to step toward the statuette, listening for Willow to continue.

They were on her before Willow could say the next word. Three, maybe four, from behind and above.

The container left her hand.

Alcohol rushed from the container. It began as a single body of clear liquid, then broke up into smaller, glistening drops as it went down, scattering over the flames.

A tantrum of fire broke out over the candles and rose up, flames licking and whipping upward in ultra-fast motion before it disappeared in a small *whoosh*.

The alcohol was gone.

Chapter 22

Watching the alcohol spill, Willow felt as if her insides were running out of her body. Whether her potion would have worked or not was no longer a question. It was gone.

As Buffy fought off the Rakshasa that had jumped onto her like fleas on a dog, Willow tried to get to her feet. One of the creatures rushed toward her before she could get up, followed by another, and one after that.

Unarmed, helpless, Willow braced herself for their impact, the sounds and smells of them, for the tearing of her flesh.

The first one skidded to a stop as its eyes widened, lips pulled back, and mouth dropped open. The other two did the same behind it. Looking directly at Willow, they craned their heads forward and hissed. It was a sound that burned hotter than their red eyes, a gesture bubbling with the most livid hatred. And fear.

They took a few steps backward and, still hissing, the creatures turned and ran away.

What just happened? Willow thought. She looked down at her legs, her arms and hands. She was all wet, a mess, but nothing had changed. Except . . .

The carving of Rama was hanging on its chain outside her clothes, gently catching tiny shards of light from the fires growing on each side of her.

Willow pressed her hand over it and closed the tiny figure tightly in a fist.

A scream in an unfamiliar female voice pierced the darkness and shattered against the walls.

A male voice, not so unfamiliar, but not immediately identifiable, shouted in a foreign language loudly enough to give the words a whiplike reverberation in the building. Before the man's voice fell silent, it was swallowed up by a rumble of thunder within the building.

In a single wave, the Rakshasa had stopped what they were doing and hit the walls climbing. It sounded and felt as if the entire building were about to collapse on top of them. The clamor diminished rapidly and stopped.

Once again, the red eyes peered down on them from the upper darkness, and the sounds of waiting began again.

Buffy found it interesting, but didn't have time to give it any attention. She looked up at Ravana. The red funnel had spun its way up farther and had reached the top of the foreheads. The voices were richer, fuller. Almost complete.

"Will anything else work?" Buffy asked. "Besides alcohol?"

"No," Willow replied. Her feet slipped as she stood and she staggered a couple steps.

The top of the shimmering twister was moving up

the shiny bald scalp atop each of the ten heads. The voices were becoming louder much faster. Too loud.

To be heard over the foreign roaring, Willow raised her voice, nearly shouting, "Buffy, I should tell you—"

"S'cuse me, Will." Buffy walked toward the spinning swirl around Ravana. Held the sword between both hands. Spun around once for momentum and swung the edge of the blade into the wobbling funnel.

The spinning surface gave way just a bit, but the blade did not pierce it. Instead, the blade was thrown away from the funnel so hard, it nearly flew from Buffy's hand. It threw her off balance and she almost fell, but caught it back and moved in again, blade point straight at Ravana's belly. She drove the arrow-shaped tip of the blade straight into the funnel.

The same thing happened. Buffy stumbled backward and bumped into Willow.

"Buffy, this fire's getting real hot," Willow shouted, "but I should tell you—"

"There is nothing you could do to stop it." That voice again. Familiar. British.

"Ethan?" Buffy called into the dark. She looked around for her flashlight, any flashlight, found one, and picked it up. "Ethan Rayne?"

"At your service. Now please come here, both of you."

Buffy stalked toward the voice. She didn't know what was going on yet, but Rayne was there, he was part of it. She should have paid more attention to Giles's sighting of the troublemaker.

A woman's voice, thick from tears, cried, "Ethan? Ethan Rayne! You told me your name was Lloyd Kaufman! Why would you do that? Why would you lie to me! I would have—"

"Quiet!" Rayne bellowed, and Phyllis did as she was told.

Buffy turned on her flashlight, which she'd clipped to her belt after dispatching the policeman-Rakshasa. She could see them up ahead, their shapes, three she knew—*Where is Angel?* she wondered with a clench of panic—and two more, Phyllis and Rayne and . . . *No, there's another, someone standing very close to Rayne . . .*

Willow caught up with Buffy and clutched her arm. "The Rakshasa were afraid of Rama!" she shouted.

"What?" Buffy slowed her pace.

Willow held the small sculpture on a chain with her fingertips. "They were afraid of this. They ran away, didn't touch me. I-I-I'm not sure what that means, I—"

"We don't have time to figure out what it means. Give it to me."

Buffy let Willow drop the trinket into her hand. She stuffed it in a coat pocket and took the flashlight in hand. "It's just regular old stone, isn't it?" she asked.

"Carved into the figure of Ravana's enemy, by the hands of a devout believer!"

"That makes a difference?"

"I don't know!"

"Come here!" Rayne shouted. But even though Buffy was closer now, his voice was harder to hear because the unnatural voices coming from behind her were louder.

Buffy walked on, closer now, close enough to see that the figure beside Rayne was a woman, to see that she was—

"Mom?" Buffy cried as she broke into a run. Stopped when she got close enough to see the barrel of pistol pressed to the side of her mother's face.

Joyce was soaking wet, dirty, and there was terror in her eyes. Rayne had his left arm wrapped around her waist and held her in front of him. A shield.

"Mom, just don't move, don't do anything," Buffy shouted.

Joyce said nothing. Did nothing.

"Tell us what you want, Ethan!" Giles yelled.

"I want you to wait."

Buffy shouted, "We don't have time to wait!"

"Just wait . . . until the process is finished. After that, anything you choose to do will not matter."

"If it won't matter," Buffy said, "then let my mother go!"

Rayne grinned. "And let you do something I might regret?"

"Think what you're doing, Ethan!" Giles shouted angrily.

"I've thought it through, Ripper."

"Nothing is ever enough for you, is it, Ethan? Not only must you win, everyone else must die!"

"Not everyone, Giles. I'll need to enslave a staff."

Buffy's nerves burned. Emotions gushed through her: anger, fear, and horror at the sight of her mother at gunpoint. Ravana had to be near completion. It could happen any second.

"Let Joyce go," Giles demanded. "She has nothing to do with this!"

"It would be tragic if something were to happen to me just as the process is finished, don't you think?" Rayne asked with a laugh. "She is my insurance, Ripper. I'm not worried about that." He nodded his head toward the spinning funnel in the corner. "There's nothing you can do about Ravana."

The voices continued to grow. Cordelia put her hands over her ears and Xander and Oz winced at the sound.

"Rama stopped him!" Willow shouted.

"Rama had an arrow with a bladed point made by a god, by Vishnu. Those are hard to come by these days, young lady."

Buffy trembled, wanting to take him down with her sword. But not while her mother was there. She watched . . . and noticed something. Her mother was wearing . . . something dirty . . . something wet . . . something familiar but wrong.

She was wearing Buffy's long "South Park" nightshirt.

"Rakshasa," Buffy said with relieved realization, but it came out a croak and was buried by the skull-crushing cries coming from behind her. She pulled her right arm back, about to run the creature through with the arrow-tipped blade, but she couldn't. It was her mother to her eyes, even though her brain knew differently. Her arm was paralyzed.

A ghostly white face wearing reflective sunglasses oozed out of the darkness behind Ethan Rayne. A black-gloved hand cupped the Joyce-thing's chin and pulled her head back. Another held a shiny black metal cylinder above her head. A sliver spike snapped out from the end of the device with a sharp *ching,* and smaller curved spikes protruded from that. With an exquisite whir, the silver spike spun like a hellish drill bit and drove into the top of the Joyce-thing's head. A spray of gelatinous green fanned from the head, and the body collapsed into a heavy splash of it that scattered and disappeared when it hit the floor.

For an instant, after seeing her mother's double killed, Buffy's heart was maimed, crippled . . . but just a moment.

Rayne tried to turn the gun on the man behind him, the same man Buffy had seen in her house. The albino punched Rayne in the face and Rayne dropped like an empty suit.

Buffy rushed forward, swung the heavy metal flashlight and cracked it against the side of the albino's head. He staggered backward, fell.

Buffy let go of the flashlight and dropped to one knee beside Rayne. She grabbed the front of his shirt and pulled him a few inches off the floor. Pressing the tip of her sword to his throat, she asked, yelling to be heard over the clamor of voices, "How do we stop it?"

He was conscious, but cloudy. His eyes half-open, he managed a smile. "You can't stop it," he said. "No point in killing me . . . I'm the only one who will be able to communicate with him. And if you do kill me, the Rakshasa will eat you alive within seconds."

She would get nothing out of him. He was a waste of time. Buffy stood, took the chain from her jacket pocket. "But Vishnu's arrow worked, didn't it?" She began to loop the chain around the arrow-shaped tip of her sword. "I bet there was a lot of faith behind that arrow, too, y'think, Ethan?" She made sure it was snug and would stay on the blade. "The faith of a devout believer? Was Rama like that? He had strong belief in Vishnu, didn't he? And he was human, and the only thing Ravana didn't ask for protection from was humans, right?"

Buffy turned and ran toward the color. The fire was spreading out on each side as if it hadn't even noticed how wet it was all around, but there was still a narrowing path between the pools of fire.

Up ahead, the vortex spinning around Ravana stopped. The deafening cries stopped. For a moment, the loudest sound was that of Buffy's running feet.

The red shimmering glow remained around the still, silent Ravana, then began to spin its way downward. Fast.

The heads were revealed . . . the shoulders . . . flesh and bone . . . alive and ready to rule.

Ethan shouted in a strange foreign language.

Buffy didn't think her heart would stay in her chest. She pumped her legs harder.

The Rakshasa shrieked overhead as Buffy shot between the flames.

The twenty arms were revealed, the chest, abdomen . . .

An explosion of Rakshasa hitting the floor sounded behind her as she held the blade out, the tiny figure of Rama attached to the arrow tip. She threw herself into a storm of heat. Perspiration stung her skin immediately.

The eyes glared directly at her. The mouths grinned maliciously, lewdly, with anticipation. The red glow lowered past the thighs and knees, the calves, toward the ankles of the crossed feet.

Metal met flesh, hard muscle. The tip pierced them and Buffy twisted the blade as it went in, taking the innocent-looking trinket with it.

Ravana's body stiffened as the remainder of the red vortex surrounding it glowed brightly. Maybe he underestimated the power of humans. The movement and screaming of the Rakshasa behind Buffy ceased. The vortex slowed. Buffy struggled to keep the blade and trinket in Ravana as he tried to push her out in his effort to survive. The vortex stopped spinning and slowly sank down into Ravana's feet and deepened to a rich ruby color, which then turned a malignant black, and engulfed the Ravana statuette again.

Ravana's ten mouths yawned impossibly wide and black lips stretched back to reveal black-and-red gums equipped with fine, needle-like fangs. When Ravana cried out, the Rakshasa cried with him. New cracks opened in the walls and a front corner of the bus station collapsed; no one heard it.

There was an explosion, powerful but silent, that punched Buffy back so hard, her lungs stopped working. She heard nothing, saw nothing; she felt her brain shrink to the size of a scale on a minnow, enlarge again, shrink again . . . in and out of consciousness rapidly.

Her heart started beating again. Had it stopped? Or had she just awakened and heard it pounding in her ringing ears? She rolled slowly over, onto her back; her muscles told her how they despised her at that moment, how they'd all talked it over and decided she needed to be punished for a few days. Her vision was a bit blurry, but she looked around, slowly got to her feet. She heard the rustle of others doing the same.

Giles called, "Are you all right, Buffy?"

"Yeah. In one piece."

"Doubtless more than can be said for Ravana," he said with the quiet satisfaction that softened his clipped words when he was especially impressed with her work. Looking around he said, "Phyllis and Rayne seem to have gotten out of danger's way."

The corner where Ravana had materialized was black. The candles were gone, and there was no fire. Buffy went to the corner, looking over the floor. She turned her head up; no red eyes glowing in the darkness up there. There was no sign of Ravana or the Rakshasa. Even the Ravana statuette and its accompanying pieces had not been left behind.

Buffy walked toward the others as Xander asked, "Can we go now?"

"One of those things bit me," Cordelia said, sounding angry and still afraid. "Would somebody please, please tell me this isn't gonna make me turn into something! Because I probably don't get to pick what, do I?"

Giles straightened his glasses. "You'll be fine, Cordelia. We'll just need to treat the wound back at the library. There are, after all, bacterial concerns."

The albino man was gone. But another absence stabbed Buffy.

"Where's Angel?" she asked.

The rain had stopped, but the air was cloyingly moist.

Buffy was not surprised to see the white limousine outside, or the old man in the wheelchair beside it. Nor was she surprised to see Angel fighting with the tall albino guy with the sunglasses and the nasty lump on his head. What caught her off guard was the fact that Angel was really working the guy over . . . and he was coming back for more. With the others following, Buffy ran to the man in the wheelchair.

There was a square black pack attached to the back of the chair. From it extended four tubes that curled around to the front of the seat and disappeared into the man who could only be Benson Lovecraft. A tube provided oxygen for his nose and thick glasses sat on his nose, which was narrow, a little too long, and ended in a lumpy, fleshy bulb.

A shattered Phyllis and wounded Rayne slumped against the car.

"Is that man a vampire?" Buffy asked.

"Man? What man?" Benson looked around, his voice soft, low, and gravelly, wheezing.

"The albino guy! Is he a vampire?"

"Oh, no. He's my chauffeur. But apparently the other one is. A young one . . . preoccupied, it seems."

"Well, don't you think you should stop your chauffeur before he gets himself killed?"

"He's holding up well, I think. But . . . you're right. Otto!" When raised, his voice still held power, even at his extremely advanced age. But the shout seemed to drain him, make him shrink in his chair.

The ghost-faced man immediately turned away from Angel and hurried to Lovecraft's side.

"Put Phyllis in the car," Lovecraft said. "In the back with me."

Otto went to Phyllis's side, put a hand to the small of her back, and led her to the car.

"You lying bastard!" Phyllis spat at Rayne over her shoulder. "The things I did for you . . ." Then she was invisible inside the car, lost in the darkness, though her sobs could be heard, stifled and painful.

Angel moved to Buffy, put his hands on her shoulders and looked at her intensely. "Are you all right?"

She smiled up at him. "Dirty and wet, but fine."

"I came out here after"—he jerked his head toward Otto and Rayne—"them. To keep them from getting away. Guess I was wasting my time. What happened in there?"

"They destroyed my Ravana statuette, that's what happened," Lovecraft said with a particularly unattractive cough.

Heat flared in Buffy's throat and her knuckles whitened as she clutched the sword's handle. She turned to man in the wheelchair and said, "Well, I'm sorry if I broke your precious little statue, but if you wanna know the truth, it was uglier than you, and it was about to—"

"If all you did was break it, dear, then we're all up to our necks in raw sewage, if you get my meaning." Lovecraft smirked up at her as he reached over and patted her arm with genuine warmth. "It had to be done, and I'm glad you did it. But I wouldn't recommend interrupting a process like that before completion. You could potentially rip the fabric of time and space and next thing you know, you're an enzyme in the stomach of a warthog at the bottom of an ocean. And none of us wants that, do we? You have too much to contribute. Where is your Watcher?"

Buffy raised her eyebrows, blinked. How could he know?

Giles stepped forward. His face was thoughtful but alert, neither smiling nor frowning, but in his eyes, he was a little boy approaching Santa Claus on Christmas Eve at the mall.

"Rupert Giles," he said, offering his hand uncertainly. They shook, and Giles was surprised by the strength remaining in the man's grip.

"Benson Lovecraft. But you can call me Mr. Lovecraft."

"How . . . how did you know?" Buffy asked.

"At my age, everything is in shorthand. Even me . . . whatever that means." He smiled approvingly at Giles. He still had his own teeth, though they hadn't fared as well as he. "You've done a good job." He turned to Buffy again. "She's got a lot of life in her. Not the usual rigid look in the eyes, with all the individuality beaten out of her by the council's endless rules and edicts."

Giles's face registered surprise. "You know the council?"

Lovecraft's wrinkles deepened and his rubbery lips curled up in distaste. "Yes. But don't tell anyone. I seldom admit to it myself." He coughed again. "We're in different branches of the same business, Mr. Giles. My approach differs considerably."

"In what way would that be, Mr. Lovecraft?" Giles asked.

"They do it their way, I do it mine." He waved a hand. "Otto, kindly show Mr. Rayne to his seat in the front of our limousine."

Otto moved toward Rayne, who produced his gun.

"You'll do no such thing," Rayne snapped, aiming the gun at Otto.

The tall albino casually slapped the gun from Rayne's hand and twisted his arm behind his back in a single motion. Rayne cried out in pain.

Lovecraft said, "Mr. Rayne, I once had my head trapped in the mouth of an enormous Egyptian cat demon that was hungrier than a Texas cattle rancher after finishing a meal in a French restaurant, and I'm still here to tell about it. So you can imagine how little patience I have for the likes of you. Your way or mine, you're leaving in the limousine. We have some accounts to settle. I've found that most people prefer doing things their own way, especially considering how the opportunity seldom arises. So if I were you, I'd get my ass in the car before my fair friend here kicks it up and down the street like a crushed can."

When Otto escorted Rayne to the limousine, the

Englishman was clearly unhappy, but he did not resist. Otto closed the door after him with a sound of finality.

"I, uh . . . there, um . . . there are laws, Mr. Lovecraft, and as troublesome as Ethan is, perhaps it would be best if you left him—"

"Mr. Giles, your friend here—"

"He's hardly my friend!"

"My granddaughter is very special to me. She's a sensitive, delicate creature who . . . well, let's just say she's not really equipped to make some of life's more challenging decisions. That's why she lives with me. I take care of her because no one else in the family wanted to, which was fine with me, because I love her. But somehow"—he pointed at the front of the limousine—"that piece of work got over the back fence, took advantage of my granddaughter, seduced her, gained her trust, and used her to get to something else of mine, so he could steal it and use it for his own imbecilic purposes. Now, if you're concerned about that man's welfare, don't bother. After a brief stay on my lovely island, he will leave unblemished and pain-free, I promise. But I can also promise you that at some point during that stay"—his voice lowered—"he will beg me to kill him."

Lovecraft fingered a toggle on the armrest of his chair and wheeled over to the limousine. Otto accompanied him, detached the pack from the back of the chair, and gently lifted the old man out and into the backseat of the limousine.

As Otto folded up the wheelchair, Lovecraft said, "Don't forget to call ahead and have somebody waiting to wash off my wheels." Once his door was shut, the darkened window eased down with a vague hum, and Lovecraft smiled at them, turned his gaze to Buffy.

"Good job, young lady. Remember, be true to yourself and to those who are true to you and all the rest of life's junk pretty much takes care of itself, and don't let anyone tell you otherwise. But . . . I suspect you already know that."

Otto got behind the wheel and started the engine.

Turning to Giles, Lovecraft said, "Nice to meet you, Mr. Giles. Don't take any rubber pentagrams."

The window slid up as the limousine drove away, bright white in the night's darkness, glaring back at them with two large, red eyes.

"Is that what we'll be like in ninety years?" Willow asked nobody in particular.

"Not if we're lucky," Buffy replied, sheathing her sword.

Chapter 23

ONCE THEY RETURNED TO THE LIBRARY, THERE WAS A good deal of bandaging to do. Along with the contents of the first-aid kit, Giles kept some back shelves stocked with enough gauze, tape, disinfectants, and aspirin to keep a small clinic functioning for a week.

"So, it was magic," Buffy said. "Right?"

"I'm not sure," Willow replied. "Maybe. Sort of."

Xander said, "You've gotta stop being so specific, Will. It's gonna give you a tumor."

"Giles says magic isn't something we do, but something we harness," Willow went on. "Right, Giles?"

"Precisely."

"Well, what if magic isn't the only way to harness that . . . thing . . . that power? What if simple, perfect belief in something can harness a little of that power? I mean, you were right, Buffy, when you said Rama had to really believe that arrow was going to work when he fired it into Ravana, he had to have absolute and total faith in Vishnu about that arrowhead. Because if it didn't work, you know, like, he wasn't gonna take it back to Target and exchange it for one that works. Well, Mila's brother is a very devout Hindu, he has that kind of belief, and he carved that stone into the shape of something he believed in that strongly. Maybe ... maybe he left a little of that belief behind in his work."

Buffy said, "Or it was because we were human, and Ravana never thought enough of us to cover his butt from us in the first place."

Willow nodded. "Or that."

Angel came up behind Buffy's chair, got down on a knee, and put an arm around her. "I'm going to go," he said quietly. "You know ... keep an eye on things out there. You should go home, get some sleep."

"I don't think the jungle will be quite as wild from now on," she said, matching his volume and tone. She put a hand to his cheek. "Thank you."

They kissed briefly, with warmth, then Angel stood and went to the door.

"Thank you very much, Angel," Giles said. He turned to the others. "I'd like to thank you all. You were very brave tonight. You risked your lives and beautifully accomplished what we set out to do."

"But what if they come back? What if they aren't all dead? What if someone else ..." Xander looked a little nervous, as if he were being forced to consider eating brussels sprouts without catsup.

"That's always a possibility," Giles replied. "All we can know is what we saw. They seemed to be gone."

Angel left the library and Buffy gazed at his departing figure.

"This power you were talking about harnessing, Willow," Xander said. "Is it an energy field created by all living things? Does it surround us? Penetrate us? Does it bind the galaxy to—"

Cordelia groaned. Her injury had been dressed, but she looked miserable. "Come back to earth, guys! Can't you see I'm in pain here?"

Xander stepped over to her and asked, "How do you plan to explain that to your parents?"

"Explain that?" she croaked. "How am I going to explain my hair? And now I'll have to wait weeks for another appointment with Froi."

"Why don't you just go to someone else, Cordelia?" Buffy asked.

"Buffy, please. Life is filled with challenges . . . and then you find the perfect hairstylist. And you do not let go."

"Buffy," Willow said, and they looked at each other across the table. "Rama believed in Vishnu, and Mila's brother believed in Rama, Vishnu, and Ravana . . . what did you believe in when you shish-kebobed that thing?"

"Well, it was your idea. You told me the Rakshasa were afraid of the carving. I just sorta went with it. So . . . I guess . . . I believed in you." And they both smiled.

About the Author

Ray Garton is the author of thirty-seven books and numerous short stories. He and his wife, Dawn, live in northern California with their six cats and assorted outdoor wildlife. Garton is hard at work on his next novel.

Bullying.
Threats.
Bullets.

Locker searches? Metal detectors?

Fight back without fists.

fight for your rights:
take a stand against violence

. . . A GIRL BORN
WITHOUT THE FEAR GENE

FEARLESS™

A NEW SERIES BY
FRANCINE PASCAL

A TITLE AVAILABLE EVERY MONTH

From Pocket Pulse
Published by Pocket Books